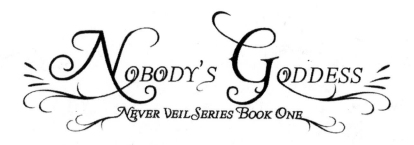

Nobody's Goddess

Never Veil Series Book One

Amy McNulty

Month9Books

Copyright © 2015 by Amy McNulty

NOBODY'S GODDESS by Amy McNulty
All rights reserved. Published in the United States of America by Month9Books, LLC.
No part of this book may be used or reproduced in any manner whatsoever without written permission of the publisher, except in the case of brief quotations embodied in critical articles and reviews.

Published by Month9Books
Cover designed by Kimberely Marsot
Cover Copyright © 2015 Month9Books

Month9Books

To Cameron, Melissa, Mom, and Sara: I write because you believe in me.

NOBODY'S GODDESS

NEVER VEIL SERIES BOOK ONE

Amy McNulty

≥ *Prologue* ≤

When I had real friends, I was the long-lost queen of the elves.

A warrior queen who hitched up her skirt and wielded a blade. Who held her retainers in thrall. Until they left me for their goddesses.

Love. A curse that snatches friends away.

One day, when only two of my retainers remained, the old crone who lived on the northern outskirts of the village was our prey. It was twenty points if you spotted her. Fifty points if you got her to look at you. A hundred points if she started screaming at you.

You won for life if you got close enough to touch her.

"Noll, please don't do this," whispered Jurij from behind the wooden kitten mask covering his face. Really, his mother still put him in kitten masks, even though eleven was too old for a boy to be wearing kittens and bunnies. Especially ones that looked likely to get eaten for breakfast by as much as a weasel.

"Shut up, I want to see this!" cried Darwyn. Never a kitten,

1

Darwyn always wore a wolf mask. Yet behind the nasty tooth-bearing wolf grin—one of my father's better masks—he was very much a fraidycat.

Darwyn shoved Jurij aside so he could crouch behind the bush that was our threadbare cover. Jurij nearly toppled over, but I caught him and set him gently upright. Sometimes I didn't know if Jurij realized who was supposed to be serving whom. Queens shouldn't have to keep retainers from falling.

"Quiet, both of you." I scanned the horizon. Nothing. All was still against the northern mountains save for the old crone's musty shack with its weakly smoking chimney. The edges of my skirt had grazed the dusty road behind us, and I hitched it up some more so my mother wouldn't notice later. If she didn't want me to get the blasted thing dirty, she should have let me wear Jurij's trousers, like I had been that morning. That got me a rap on the back of the head with a wooden spoon, a common occurrence when I was queen. It made me look too much like a boy, she scolded, and that would cause a panic.

"Are you going or not?" Darwyn was not one for patience.

"If you're so eager, why don't *you* go?" I snapped back.

Darwyn shook his wolf-head. "Oh, no, not me."

I grinned. "That's because you're scared."

Darwyn's muffled voice grew louder. He stood beside me and puffed out his chest. "I am not! *I've* been in the commune."

I poked toward his chest with Elgar, my trusty elf-blade. "Liar! You have not."

Darwyn jumped back, evading my blow. "I have too! My uncle lives there!" He swatted his hand at Elgar. "Get that stick away from me."

"It's not a stick!" Darwyn never believed me when I said that Elgar was the blade of a warrior. It just happened to resemble a tree branch.

Jurij's quiet voice entered the fray. "Your uncle lives there? That's awful." I was afraid he might cry and the tears would get caught up in the black material that covered his eyes. I didn't want him to drown behind the wooden kitty face. He'd vanish into thin air like everyone else did when they died, and then we'd be staring down at Jurij's clothes and the little kitten mask on the ground, and I was afraid I wouldn't be able to stop myself from giggling. Some death for a warrior.

Darwyn shrugged and ran a hand over his elbow. "He moved in there before I was born. I think a weaver lady was his goddess. It's not so strange. Didn't your aunt send her man there, Jurij?"

Jurij was sniffling. *Sniffling.* He tried to rub at his nose, but every time he moved the back of his hand up to his face, it just clunked against the button that represented the kitten's nose.

I sighed and patted Jurij on the back. "A queen's retainer must never cry, Jurij."

Darwyn laughed. "Are you still playing that? You're no queen, Noll!"

I stopped patting Jurij and balled my hands into fists. "Be quiet, Darwyn! You used to play it, too!"

Darwyn put two fingers over his wolf-mask mouth, a gesture we had long ago decided would stand for the boys sticking out their tongues. Although Darwyn was the only one who ever did it as of late. "Like I'd want to do what some *girl* tells me! Girls aren't even blessed by love!"

"Of course they are!" It was my turn to put the two fingers over my mouth. I had a tongue, but a traitorous retainer like Darwyn wasn't worthy of the effort it took to stick it out. "Just wait until you find your goddess, and then we'll see! If she turns out to be me, I'll make sure you rot away in the commune with the rest of the unloved men."

Darwyn lunged forward and tackled me. My head dragged against the bush before it hit the ground, but it still hurt; I could feel the swelling underneath the tangled knots in my hair. Elgar snapped as I tried to get a grip on my attacker. I kicked and shoved him, and for a moment, I won the upper hand and rolled on top of him, almost punching him in the face. Remembering the mask, I settled for giving him a good smack in the side, but then he kicked upward and caught me in the chest, sending me backward.

"Stop!" pleaded Jurij. He was standing between us now,

the little timid kitten watching first one friend and then the other, like we were a dangling string in motion.

"Stay out of this!" Darwyn jumped to his feet and pointed at me. "She thinks she's so high and mighty, and she's not even someone's goddess yet!"

"I'm only twelve, idiot! How many goddesses are younger than thirteen?" A few, but not many. I scrambled to my feet and sent my tongue out at him. It felt good knowing he couldn't do the same to me, after all. My head ached. I didn't want him to see the tears forming in my eyes, though, so I ground my teeth once I drew my tongue inward.

"Yeah, well, it'll be horrible for whoever finds the goddess in you!" Darwyn made to lunge at me again, but this time Jurij shoved both his hands at Darwyn's chest to stop him.

"Just stop," commanded Jurij. Finally. That was a good retainer.

My eyes wandered to the old crone's cottage. No sign of her. How could she fail to hear the epic struggle outside her door? Maybe she wasn't real. Maybe just seeing her was worth twenty points after all.

"Get out of my way, you baby!" shouted Darwyn. "So what happens if I pull off your mask when your *queen* is looking, huh? Will you die?"

His greedy fingers reached toward Jurij's wooden animal face. Even from behind, I could see the mask tip dangerously to one side, the strap holding it tightly against Jurij's dark curls shifting. The strap broke free, flying up over his head.

My mouth opened to scream. My hands reached up to cover my eyes. My eyelids strained to close, but it felt as if the moment had slowed and I could never save him in time. Such simple things. Close your eyes. Cover your eyes. Scream.

"Do not fool with such things, child!"

A dark, dirty shawl went flying onto the bush that we had ruined during our fight.

I came back to life. My head and Darwyn's wolf mask spun toward the source of the sound. As my head turned, I saw—even though I knew better than to look—Jurij crumple to the ground, clinging both arms across his face desperately because his life depended on it.

"Your eyes better be closed, girl!" The old crone bellowed. Her own eyes were squeezed together.

I jumped and shut my eyes tightly.

"Hold that shawl tightly over your face, boy, until you can wear your mask properly!" screamed the old crone. "Off with you both, boys! Now! Off with you!"

I heard Jurij and Darwyn scrambling, the rustle of the bush and the stomps of their boots as they fled, panting. I thought I heard a scream—not from Jurij, but from Darwyn. He was the real fraidycat. An old crone was no match for the elf queen's retainers. But the queen herself was far braver. So I told myself over and over in my head.

When the last of their footsteps faded away, and I was sure that Jurij was safe from my stare, I looked.

Eyes. Huge, bulbous, dark brown eyes. Staring directly into mine.

The crone's face was so close I could smell the shriveled decay from her mouth. She grabbed me by the shoulders, shaking me. "What were you thinking? You held that boy's life in your hands! Yet you stood there like a fool, just starin' as his mask came off."

My heart beat faster, and I gasped for more air, but I wanted to avoid inhaling her stench. "I'm sorry, Ingrith," I mumbled. I thought if I used her real name, if I let her lecture me like all the other adults, it would help me break free from her grasp. I twisted and pulled, but I couldn't bring myself to touch her. I had this notion that if I touched her, my fingers would decay.

"Sorry is just a word. Sorry changes nothing."

"Let me go." I could still feel her dirty nails on my skin.

"You watch yourself, girl."

"Let me go!"

The crone's lips grew tight and puckered. Her fingers relaxed ever so slightly. "You children don't realize. The lord is watching. Always watching—"

I knew what she was going to say, the words so familiar

to me that I knew them as well as if they were my own. "And he will not abide villagers who forget the first goddess's teachings." The sentence seemed to loosen the crone's fingers. She opened her mouth to speak, but I broke free and ran.

My eyes fell to the grass below my feet as I cut across the fields to get away from the monster. On the borders of the eastern woods was a lone cottage, home of Gideon the woodcarver, a warm and comfortable place so much fuller of life than the shack I left behind me. When I was near the woods, I could look up freely since the trees blocked the eastern mountains from view. But until I got closer …

"Noll! Wait up!"

My eyes snapped upward on instinct. I saw the upper boughs of the trees and almost screamed, my gaze falling back to the grass beneath my feet. I stopped running and let the gentle rustlings of footsteps behind me catch up.

"Jurij, please." I sighed and turned around to face him, my eyes still on the grass and the pair of small dark boots that covered his feet. Somehow he managed to step delicately through the grass, not disturbing a single one of the lilies that covered the hilltops. "Don't scare me like that. I almost looked at the castle."

The toe of Jurij's boot dug a little into the dirt. "Oh. Sorry."

"Is your mask on?"

The boot stopped moving, and the tip of a black shawl dropped into my view. "Oh. Yeah."

I shook my head and raised my eyes. There was no need to fear looking up to the west. In the distance, the mountains that encircled our village soared far beyond the western fields of crops. I liked the mountains. From the north, the south, and the west, they embraced our village with their jagged peaks. In the south, they watched over our fields of livestock. In the north, they towered above a quarry for copper and stone. And in the east, they led home and to the woods. But no girl or woman could ever look up when facing the east. Like the faces of men and boys before their Returnings, just a glance at the castle that lay beyond the woods against the eastern mountains spelled doom. The earth would shake and threaten to consume whoever broke the commandment not to look.

It made walking home a bit of a pain, to say the least.

"Tell me something important like that before you sneak up on me."

Jurij's kitten mask was once again tight against his face, if askew. The strap was a bit tangled in his dark curls and the pointed tip of one of his ears. "Right. Sorry."

He held out the broken pieces of Elgar wrapped in the dirty black shawl. He seemed very retainer-like. I liked that. "I went to give this back to the—the lady. She wasn't there, but you left Elgar."

I snatched the pieces from Jurij's hands. "You went back to the shack? What were you going to say? 'Sorry we were spying on you pretending you were a monster, thanks for the dirty old rag?'"

"No." Jurij crumpled up the shawl and tucked it under his belt. A long trail of black cloth tumbled out immediately, making Jurij look like he had on half a skirt.

I laughed. "Where's Darwyn?"

"Home."

Of course. I found out later that Darwyn had whined straight to his mother that "nasty old Noll" almost knocked *his* mask off. It was a great way to get noticed when you had countless brothers and a smitten mother and father standing between you and any form of attention. But it didn't have the intended effect on me. I was used to lectures, and besides, there was something more important bothering me by then.

I picked up my feet to carry me back home.

Jurij skipped forward to join me. One of his boots stumbled as we left the grasses behind and hit the dirt path. "What happened with you and the crone?"

I gripped the pieces of Elgar tighter in my fist. "Nothing." I stopped, relieved that we'd finally gotten close enough to the woods that I could face forward. I put an arm on Jurij's shoulder to stop him. "But I touched her." Or she touched me. "That means I win forever."

The kitten face cocked a little sideways. "You always win."

"Of course. I'm the queen." I tucked the broken pieces of Elgar into my apron sash. Elgar was more of a title, bestowed on an endless number of worthy sticks, but in those days I wouldn't have admitted that to Jurij. "Come on. I'll give you a head start. Race you to the cavern!"

"The cavern? But it's—"

"Too late! Your head start's over!" I kicked my feet up and ran as if that was all my legs knew how to do. The cool breeze slapping across my face felt lovely as it flew inside my nostrils and mouth. I rushed past my home, not bothering to look inside the open door.

"Stop! Stop! Noll, you stop this instant!"

The words were something that could easily come out of a mother's mouth, but Mother had a little more patience than that. And her voice didn't sound like a fragile little bird chirping at the sun's rising. "Noll!"

I was just an arm's length from the start of the trees, but I stopped, clutching the sharp pain that kicked me in the side.

"Oh dear!" Elfriede walked out of our house, the needle and thread she was no doubt using to embroider some useless pattern on one of the aprons still pinched between two fingers. My sister was a little less than a year older than me, but to my parents' delight (and disappointment with me), she was a hundred times more responsible.

"Boy, your mask!" Elfriede never did learn any of my friends' names. Not that I could tell her Roslyn from her Marden, either. One giggling, delicate bird was much like another.

She walked up to Jurij, who had just caught up behind me. She covered her eyes with her needle-less hand, but I could see her peeking between her fingers. I didn't think that would actually protect him if the situation were as dire as she seemed to think.

"It's crooked." Elfriede's voice was hoarse, almost trembling. I rolled my eyes.

Jurij patted his head with both hands until he found the bit of the strap stuck on one of his ears. He pulled it down and twisted the mask until it lined up evenly.

I could hear Elfriede's sigh of relief from where I was standing. She let her fingers fall from her face. "Thank the goddess." She considered Jurij for a moment. "There's a little tear in your strap."

Without asking, she closed the distance between them and began sewing the small tear even as the mask sat on his head. From how tall she stood above him, she might have been ten years older instead of only two.

I walked back toward them, letting my hands fall. "Don't you think that's a little stupid? What if the mask slips while you're doing that?"

Elfriede's cheeks darkened and she yanked the needle up, pulling her instrument free of the thread and tucking the extra bit into the mask strap. She stood back and glared at me. "Don't you talk to me about being stupid, Noll. All that running isn't safe when you're with boys. Look how his mask was moving."

His mask had moved for even more dangerous reasons than a little run, but I knew better than to tell tattletale Elfriede that. "How would *you* know what's safe when you're with boys? You're already thirteen, and no one has found the goddess in you!" Darwyn's taunt was worth reusing, especially since I knew my sister would be more upset about it than I ever was.

Elfriede bit her lip. "Go ahead and kill your friends, then, for all I care!" The bird wasn't so beautiful and fragile where I was concerned.

She retreated into the house and slammed the door behind her. I wrapped my hand around Jurij's arm, pulling him eastward. "Come on. Let's go. There're bound to be more monsters in the cavern."

Jurij didn't give beneath my pull. He wouldn't move. "Jurij?"

I knew right then, somewhere in my mind, what had happened. But I was twelve. And Jurij was my last real friend. I knew he'd leave me one day like the others, but on some level, I didn't really believe it yet.

Jurij stood stock still, even as I wrenched my arm harder and harder to get him to move.

"Oh for—*Jurij!*" I yelled, dropping my hands from his arm in frustration. "Ugh. I wish I was your goddess just so I could get you to obey me. Even if that means I'd have to put up with all that—*yuck*—smooching." I shivered at the thought.

At last Jurij moved, if only to lift his other arm, to run his fingers across the strap that Elfriede had mended. She was gone from my sight, but Jurij would never see another.

It struck them all. Sometime around Jurij's age, the boys' voices cracked, shifting from high to deep and back again in a matter of a few words. They went from little wooden-faced animals always shorter than you to young men on their way to towering over you. And one day, at one moment, at some age, earlier for some and later for others, they looked at a girl they'd probably seen thousands of times before and simply ceased to be. At least, they weren't who I knew them to be ever again.

And as with so many of my friends before Jurij, in that moment all other girls ceased to matter. I was nothing to him now, an afterthought, a shadow, a memory.

No.

Not him.

My dearest, my most special friend of all, now doomed to live or die by the choice of the fragile little bird who'd stopped to mend his strap.

Chapter One

L ike most of the village, we couldn't afford a mirror, but if you asked me, that was a good thing. By the time Mother was done trying to make me appear half a lady, I was ready to smash anything easily breakable within five yards of where I sat. "I don't care how long you spend running the comb through my hair, it's never going to be soft and supple."

It'll never be as beautiful as Elfriede's.

Mother dipped the wooden comb in the bowl of water she'd brought to the kitchen-table-turned-rack-of-torture. It wasn't working too well. I could tell from the constant battle between my scalp and the roots of my hair that so badly wished to tear free of the skin. But it was either that or bacon grease, and I wasn't having any pig fat slathered over my hair in attempt to tame it, not today.

She gripped a chunk of hair like the tail on a dead squirrel and ran the wooden comb upward. "Oh!" came the shout, followed quickly by the snap of the wooden comb Father had carved for her upon their Returning years ago. The comb that was only really a last resort, a gift meant for Mother to

11

treasure and run through her own silky, wavy golden hair. "We've broken the last of them," she sighed. "We can still use the grease."

"*No*." I could just imagine myself smelling of dead pig on the first day I'd look upon the face of the man I loved. Not that he'd care even if I showed up smeared in mud with a live pig under each arm and missing a few teeth. He only had eyes for his goddess.

"Mother," interrupted Elfriede, the goddess who'd have his love with or without the mud and the pigs. She stood by the sink, perhaps hoping to see her reflection in the musty water collected there. One hand held a wavy lock of golden hair that had escaped from the bun at the back of her neck. "This keeps falling out."

Mother crossed the room and ran the broken half of the comb through Elfriede's loose tendril. I yanked and jostled the tangle at the top of my head until the other half of the comb came loose. "Can't I just cut it short?"

"*No*," said Mother and Elfriede at once, in the same tone I'd used moments before.

Elfriede patted the sides of her head as Mother crossed back over toward the bed my sister and I shared. "*Really*, Noll," said Elfriede, without turning her head. "You act like a young boy enough already. What if someone glanced over and thought you *were* a boy—*unmasked*—running around? You'd scare the women in the village to death!"

I drummed my fingers across the table. "As if anyone could mistake me for a boy." At sixteen, I wasn't as oak-pale as Mother and Elfriede, but my chestnut skin was lighter than any man's.

Mother appeared behind me to tuck a small clump of hair behind my lobe. She pinched the top of my ear playfully. "Yes, your ears are round and smooth, but you can't expect a woman to check for the pointed ears of a man when she's worried she's going to kill you just by glancing at your uncovered face."

I tucked a strand behind my other ear as Mother glided across the room with a silky deep violet dress over her arm.

She grabbed Elfriede by the wrist and gently guided her into the shaft of sunlight spilling in from the open doorway. "Won't this look breathtaking on you?" said Mother, her face full of awe. She unfurled the dress and held it up before Elfriede. Its hem brushed the floor, kicking up a small flight of dust.

Elfriede beamed and stepped into the dress, sliding it over the slip she'd worn since Mother did her hair earlier. Mother grinned as she helped fasten the buttons at the back. "This was the dress I wore to my Returning," said Mother. She took Elfriede by the shoulders and spun her around. "And it's such a joy to see my dear girl wearing it for her own." She kissed Elfriede's temple and used a thumb to wipe a tear first from Elfriede's cheek and then her own. "What a fine color. It really brings out the blossom on your cheeks."

A dress the color of mud and vomit couldn't stop Elfriede's cheeks from blooming.

The goddess was stunning today, that was plain to see. I tried to imagine Jurij standing beside her, and the face I had never seen before. For some reason, the only male face I could picture for him was the one I'd seen every day of my life, a younger, leaner version of Father. Dark skin, the color of soil soaked in rain. Bold, sharp cheeks. Tall, pointed ears like daggers jumping out from his black, curly hair—hair that at least was familiar to me.

I longed to drink in Jurij's eyes, dark eyes that I knew carried flames within them, as did all men's, even when the only light for leagues was the smallest sliver of the moon. I'd known him for so long. But I could only see his face in my dreams.

I shook my head. "Have you ever seen a young boy's face?" I asked, more to Mother than to Elfriede. "I played with boys every day growing up, but I couldn't tell them from one another when I first saw them in the morning unless they said something." Jurij's tame masks an exception.

"Hmm? No. I didn't have any brothers or cousins my age, same as you, so how could I?" Mother left Elfriede and crossed the room to the chest at the edge of the bed once more, rummaging through the clothing inside. Elfriede stood patiently for what was no doubt something else to bring out the blossom in her cheeks. Her hands stayed clasped together, the corners of her mouth turned upward pleasantly.

"How do you know you're in love with Jurij, without ever seeing his face?" It was a silly question. I knew I loved him just the same. But it was different with me. Elfriede was always too dainty to battle with monsters; she hardly knew Jurij's name before he found the goddess in her.

Elfriede seemed a bit taken aback by the question. "What do you mean?"

"I knew you at thirteen. You and all of your girlfriends." I counted off the boys on my fingers. "There was the oldest baker's son. That one farmer boy. I think the candlemaker's son? You mooned over all of the handsome older boys in the village who had their love Returned and could take off their masks. Or that strong quarry worker. He takes his shirt off so much, it really doesn't matter what he looks like under his mask." I smiled as Elfriede blushed and wrung her hands together.

"All of you knew that none of those boys could ever love you, since they'd already found their goddesses, but surely they made for more entertaining daydreams than some scrawny eleven-year-old with dirt all over his kitten mask declaring his love for you."

Elfriede's face darkened. "I don't know what you mean."

"Oh come on, Friede! You cried when Jurij found the goddess in you! You were horrible to him for months, knowing he was the only one who'd ever love you—"

"Noll, stop teasing your sister." Mother plopped a neatly folded brown piece of clothing beside me on the table. "Jurij's a sweetheart. Elfriede was just scared and embarrassed, as most of us are when a man finds the goddess in us."

"I guess I'll have to take your word on that." I grabbed the folded clothing, and it tumbled over the table, the color of mud and vomit.

Mother didn't notice the frown that crossed my face as she

slid in behind Elfriede, now fussing with loose tendrils of hair that didn't even exist. "Your man will find you someday, Noll. You're not the first late bloomer. Why, there was a woman my age whose man wound up being a number of years younger—you know, Vena, the tavern mistress. She was at least fifteen before her husband Elweard found the goddess in her."

"I'm sixteen."

I think Elfriede legitimately thought she was helping when she chimed in with, "There've been stories of women even older than sixteen—thirty, even. Roslyn told me her grandmother knew a woman whose man was seventeen years younger."

I could have puked right then. It would've blended into the color of the dress I slid over my head. "Let's not go there. And let's not forget those are only stories, and there's no woman living over the age of thirteen who has yet to have her man find her. That is, no woman except me, and ... "

Her eyes. Huge, bulbous, dark brown eyes. Staring directly into mine.

"Hmm." Mother patted Elfriede's shoulders. "That reminds me. Ingrith is the only one who hasn't yet been invited to the Returning."

I rapped my fingers on the table. "Thanks, Mother. I love being compared to a crazy old woman who lives alone."

"I wasn't comparing you to anyone." Mother stepped over to the sink and picked up a dish from breakfast, wiping it with a cloth. Why she wasted her time washing dishes when she could just bat her eyes and Father would do anything for her was beyond me. "But someone has to invite her. The lord is always watching—"

"—And he will not abide villagers who forget the first goddess's teachings. I know." Although why the first goddess ever deemed that all should be invited to celebrate a Returning, I would never understand. "Why can't you or Father do it?"

Mother pushed aside a fallen bit of hair by rubbing the back of her forearm against her forehead. "The rest of us have been inviting people for weeks. We spoke to everyone else in the village. I think you could take the time to invite at least one person, Noll."

Nice of you to leave the crazy one for me.

Elfriede hugged her arms to her chest and tapped her elbow with her index finger. "You'd think my own sister could help with the invitations to the most important day of my life."

You'd think my own sister could have some sympathy for the fact that she was stealing my dearest friend from me.

"All right, all right." I stopped moving my restless fingers. "Goddess help us if the lord thinks we invited everyone but the old woman who would rather spit at people than talk to them." *Hope you like being wet on your Returning day.* "Anyway, it makes sense. Why not send one old loveless crone to fetch the other?"

"*Noll.*" Mother shook a bowl over the sink, spreading water droplets, and Elfriede jumped back to get out of the fray. Elfriede held an arm out to examine her dress, and her nose wrinkled. Mother didn't seem to notice. "I know your man will find you soon. It's just this feeling I have."

"I hope you're wrong." I sighed and stretched one arm above my head as far as it would go. The tight stitches in the shoulders of the dress made the movement uncomfortable. A seam ripped. *Great.* I plopped both hands on the table and dropped back into the chair. "Because if a man does ever find the goddess in me, I'm kicking him straight into the commune."

"How horrible!" came Elfriede's squeak from behind the delicate hand that covered her peach lips.

"Noll!" The bowl in Mother's hand dropped to the floor, clattering and echoing as it rocked back and forth. Luckily, it was made of wood. Another gift from Father, but this one for the wedding that occurred right after the Returning. At least Elfriede's and Jurij's wedding couldn't yet be held. It was Elfriede's seventeenth birthday, so she could perform a Returning, but Jurij was still only fifteen.

I sighed. "I'm not serious, Mother."

"I should hope so!" A look of rage spread across Elfriede's delicate features.

"Why?" I asked. "Because you never thought of doing the same to Jurij?"

"Oh!" Elfriede's hands clasped over her ears, her lips trembling. Tears started forming across her eyes.

Mother bent over to snatch the bowl off the ground. "Noll, hush now! Your father would be heartbroken to hear you talk like that!"

Speak of the man. A silhouette appeared in the open door, and Father stepped inside, closing the small gap between him and Mother with two huge strides and picking her up by the waist, wooden bowl and cloth and all. "What a beautiful day it is, my love!" said Father, oblivious to the tension in the room and the tears forming in his eldest daughter's eyes. He held Mother above him for a moment longer, craning his neck upwards to steal a kiss. "*Aubree* ... " He practically moaned her name.

Mother smiled and flung the cloth down at him. "Gideon, stop that. You're not young anymore. You'll throw your back out."

Father gently put Mother's feet back on the ground, but his hands remained firmly planted on her waist, his eyes locked intensely with hers. Mother was the first to look away. She searched Elfriede's face, but my sister bit her lip, unrelenting, not letting a single tear fall. "Elfriede, why don't you go visit Roslyn and Marden before the ceremony? You should be with your friends before the big day."

That's another thing I wouldn't be able to do even if I'd wanted.

Mother turned back to her sink full of dishes, sliding with difficulty even as Father still clung to her.

"What are you doing?" Father released Mother, only to scoop the bowl and cloth into his own hands. He scrubbed the bowl with fervor. "You should have the girls do that!"

I didn't think scrubbing dishes on your Returning day was a tradition, so that left me. I sighed and stood, but Mother waved me away. "The girls have other things to do today." She grabbed Father's hand in hers. "Honey, you're filthy. You were out there carving. Wash up first. Then you can do the dishes."

Father did as commanded, and Elfriede sent me a dejected look before stepping outside. "Bye, Mother. Bye, Father!" She left me out of her farewells.

"See you soon, dear!" called Mother. She faced me, her hands on her hips, her mouth poised to issue an order.

Watching Father wash up gave me an idea for how to deflect the next thing out of her mouth. "How come Father still obeys your orders?"

Father blushed and went back to pouring water over his hands in the sink and rubbing them together. "I don't." *Right.*

Mother raised a finger and walked over to the cupboard, removing a picnic basket. She rummaged through one of the clay pots and pulled out a roll. I heard it *clink* as she tossed it into the basket. She looked around at the counter next to the sink and plucked a wedge of cheese from a bowl. Someone— or maybe the mice—had started biting into it. Mother covered the top of the basket with a black cloth and dropped it on the table in front of me. "Why don't you bring these to Ingrith, and see if she wants to attend? We'll meet you at the Great Hall at dusk." She took my head and bent it gently forward to kiss the top. Good thing she hadn't smeared bacon grease into it.

I grabbed the handle of the basket gingerly with two fingers, almost feeling sorry for Ingrith if that was the extent of the gifts someone would offer her. It was little better than what the men in the commune got. Mother began to turn around but stopped suddenly, waving a hand at me. "And don't cut through the fields. Take the pathway. We don't want you getting your dress all dirty."

I think mud would blend right in with this monstrosity just fine. "Okay. Love you." I peered over her shoulder before I turned to leave. "Love you too, Father."

Elbow deep in water and plates, Father grunted.

≥ *Chapter Two* ≤

Swinging a basket around with two fingers was an excellent way to break those fingers, which was helpful if you were looking for an excuse to get out of working for a few days. But since the Returning had that covered for me, and my fingers were starting to stiffen in what looked a bit like a hook, I gave up and began to carry the thing properly. Having a hook hand was all I needed the next time someone made a comment about how no man would ever find the goddess in me.

Down and up and down and up again, among the violet lily-covered fields, I followed the dirt path that ran from the woods and the castle to the center of the village and out again in all directions. There were no houses between mine and the edge of the village, none but Jurij's, the Tailor Shop on the eastern outskirts.

Maybe if I hide my face behind the basket I could pretend I don't see it. Lifting the basket that high made my arms sore. But then again, it did house at least one rock-hard biscuit.

I stepped on the dog's paw before I even realized she'd run out of the Tailor Shop to greet me. We both yelped as I tumbled.

The basket went soaring out of my arms … and into the arms of a man with a male face carved from wood, complete with exaggerated pointy wooden ears that stuck out straight sideways. It was the mask a man only wore on the morning of his Returning.

"Whoa!" The muffled voice was all too familiar. He bent forward to pick up the partially bitten cheese wedge, which had landed on the back of Bow, his golden dog. "Cheese is generally a fine gift for a Returning, but … " He held up the wedge with one hand like it was the carcass of some dead squirrel Bow had brought him. "The fur-covered, half-eaten variety is not quite to my taste."

I grinned and snatched the cheese from him, blowing on it to get rid of all of the hairs. "I don't know. I hear furry cheese is an excellent cure for missing eyes."

"Amusing." Jurij's creepy wooden face tilted to one side. "My eyes are here and ordinary, just like every other man's."

There was no way his eyes were ordinary. Not if I could have them locked on to my own, even just once.

Bow opened her mouth and panted, watching her master eagerly, probably smelling that weeks-old biscuit and actually deeming it fit for dog consumption. Jurij bent to set the basket on the ground, cooing as he grabbed Bow's muzzle and rubbed the sides gently, preventing her from attacking the basket. Elfriede wasn't the only golden-haired mongrel that got his attention. "You're going to be a cute little mama, aren't you?"

I glanced at Bow's bulging belly as I snatched up the basket. "She's pregnant?"

"Yup. I think it was the butcher's dog. Because you love your sausages, don't you? So who's eating the disgusting old cheese?" Jurij asked, still simpering in his high-pitched baby voice.

I dropped the cheese into the basket and moved the old black cloth around until it covered the travesty of a gift I was tasked with presenting. It took me a moment to figure out Jurij was talking to me and not his dog. "Our favorite village crazy person: Ingrith. Apparently everyone conveniently forgot to invite her to the Returning, so guess who gets to do it? In case the lord decides to prove that he actually exists and comes down from the castle to say that your Returning is canceled because one old loon wasn't asked to give her blessing."

"No!" Jurij stood and twisted his wooden face to look over and behind me.

"I was joking, Jurij." I rubbed my temples. His every movement let me know just how much in the way I was of who he hoped to see. "She's not with me. She's primping with her girlfriends in the village." Apparently he'd just missed her. Strange. Jurij would certainly have visited his goddess had he walked past her home. Elfriede was clearly more concerned with the occasion than with the young man who was the entire reason she was the focus of the village's attention. At least until the next Returning.

I couldn't see his face, but the way Jurij's shoulders slumped forward was visual cue enough to express his disappointment. Bow sensed her master's distress and nudged his hand with her nose. Jurij pet it absently.

The Returning would be meaningless to me. We could hold the ceremony alone in the cavern for all I'd care. All I'd want is to be with you.

I clutched the handle of the basket with both hands, running the toe of one shoe over the dirt in the road. "I'd ask why you aren't doing the same and primping and chatting with a bunch of excited young men, but you have no friends. Must be wonderful to be a guy. Soon as your buddy finds his goddess, he practically forgets anyone else exists."

"You're my friend, Noll." He said it with such conviction and so quickly, I didn't know whether to be delighted or let down. "I don't miss the other guys."

"I do."

Jurij pet the back of Bow's head absently, rustling her floppy ear like he might a curl of Elfriede's hair. "It's hard to explain. They're not important anymore."

"They are—they *were* to me."

Jurij shrugged. "I don't mean anything by it. I know they

don't miss me, either."

I dug my heel sharply into the dirt. "Because your goddess is everything."

Jurij's wooden face bobbed up and down. "She is."

Unlike Mother, at least Jurij didn't try to soften the statement with assurance that some man would find the goddess in me one day. I was glad for it. "Nice face, by the way."

The smile carved onto the wooden face might have been genuine if it didn't look so freaky. "Looking forward to seeing what's under it?"

I forced myself to laugh. "Not as much as Elfriede, I'm sure." A lie.

The name of his goddess pulled Jurij into some dream state of mind. His wooden face looked off behind me again. I'd pretend to seek out what caught his attention, but if I chanced to look up and glance at the castle that lay flush against the eastern mountains, I'd have a bit of explaining to do to the village.

"Are you looking forward to today more or the wedding?" Sometimes it was easier to feed into his reverie than to try to snap him out of it entirely. Plus, today I was supposed to be happy for them.

Jurij tensed and rubbed Bow's head wildly. "I can't even think about the wedding yet."

"Why?"

He smacked Bow's back three times. She might have jumped, but her attention was focused on the basket in my hands. "It's just too much. Too much happiness to think about. I feel like I'm going to burst."

Hmph. I wonder if your father would agree if he had a mind of his own. "It's too bad you're not already over seventeen like my father was. He had his Returning and his wedding on the same day."

Jurij shrugged. "That doesn't matter. I can wait nineteen months and four days." Of course he had the exact days counted. "But today ... "

Today he could finally kiss Elfriede.

Not that some clever couplings hadn't managed to before their Returnings by blindfolding the woman or making sure she kept her eyes shut tight when the man took his mask off. But Elfriede and Jurij were both too naive to try such things. "Today you get to walk around without a mask once and for all, never again fearing the eyes of women."

Jurij didn't respond. His mind was on the kisses, I feared, not the fact that he could finally let the skin on his face get acquainted with the sun.

"Well," I said, not wanting to keep the woman who would spit on me waiting. "I guess I should get going. I'll see you later. Congratulations."

"Thank you." Jurij stopped. "Do you want me to come with you?"

I felt the heat rush to my face. Of course, the only person in the entire village who could at all sense my discomfort was the one who was about to be lost to me forever. To a primping girl who had never fought a single monster with him.

"Sure. Thank you. I mean—" I shut my mouth, took a breath, and opened it again. "If you're not too busy. Today being what it is."

Jurij shrugged and made his way to the Tailor Shop door. "What more do I have to do? Swapped my mask, wore my cleanest clothing. I could use the distraction, actually. Every moment is proving to last forever." He opened the door and Bow bolted past him to get inside. "Luuk! Watch Bow, will you?"

A young boy poked his wooden face out of the door and nodded. As ever, Luuk wore his timidity on his face, his features obscured by a darling wooden puppy. Rather like a certain boy forever in a kitten or bunny mask who used to tag along with me.

"Where are you going?" asked Luuk. At least I think that's what he said. Thanks to his murmuring voice and the muffling veil over the puppy's mouth hole, he might have asked, "When is dew snowing?"

Jurij understood his brother better than I did. He patted

his head. "Old lady Ingrith's." He leaned in to the house and reached for something that must have hung near the door.

Luuk pulled back shyly to allow Jurij more room. He tapped his two index fingers together, like he was waiting for a turn to speak. But no one else was speaking.

Jurij pulled a red apple out from the doorway and lifted it to his mouth hole. Laughing, he tossed the apple, unscathed, onto the top of the cloth covering the rest of the food in the basket. "Can't snack just now, I guess. I always forget you're not a guy, Noll."

Thanks so much for that.

"Mama ... " Luuk coughed. "Mama says you and her are not to be bothered today."

Jurij scoffed. "Mother says not to bother her most every day."

That's especially true for her husband, I imagine.

Jurij grabbed the basket from me. He bobbed his wooden face toward the grassy fields. "Should we take the shortcut?"

I grinned, hitching up the bottom of my skirt. Dirt was sure to blend in. Who would notice a few grass stains? "I'll race you there!"

***

My legs weren't made for running anymore. About halfway between the Tailor Shop and Ingrith's, I gave up and started walking because there was no way I could run with the pain in my side. "Okay, you win, you win."

Jurij had managed to get several paces in front of me, even with the basket in tow. He strode confidently through the grasses like he didn't know the meaning of fatigue. But his body seemed to have noticed the exertion. By the time I caught up to him, I could hear his stomach rumbling.

"Do you need to eat?" I asked, thinking of the apple.

Jurij shook his wooden head. "No. Don't worry about it.

Besides, we ought to present Ingrith with *something* edible."
He stuck his hand into the basket and rummaged around.
"What did you put in here? A stone?"
I tore the basket away from him and cradled it in my arms
like a child. "I didn't pack it. Mother did."
Jurij nodded. "I suppose the gesture is all that's important.
It's ill luck to have a Returning with the threat of the lord
refusing to give the first goddess's blessing."
*It's ill luck to hold a Returning when your "goddess" forced
herself to love you.* If Elfriede didn't love Jurij, he wouldn't
live through the end of the day. Not if he still removed his
mask. How could he be so confident that she loved him? After
how she treated him?
I didn't know what to say. I didn't know how to even begin.
But if his life was in danger ... "Are you sure Elfriede loves
you?" That was subtle.
From behind that contemptible mask, I heard what had to
be a laugh. "Wow, Noll. Elfriede is lucky to have you as a
sister."
My chest tightened. "I just meant ... " What did I mean?
I didn't think she'd kill him on purpose. She wasn't a bad
person, really. But how did she know she wasn't just fooling
herself into accepting the only man who'd ever love her? I
couldn't see Elfriede taking up a trade and sending a man to
the commune. To her, there was no other choice.
Jurij stopped walking, and I stopped too. "I know, I know.
You're scared about today. But, Noll, I'm not going to die.
Elfriede loves me." He squeezed my shoulder. "Have a little
more faith in your sister. Sometimes I worry you don't realize
how wonderful she is."
Jurij's faith in her stung. "She can be nice. I'm happy for
you. Really." There was a sharp burning taste in my mouth.
"But we're talking your life here."
The earth shook beneath us. I stumbled and Jurij, the fool,
reached out to catch me. Even as the ground kept shaking, I
wanted to fling his hands off my arm and shoulder. The touch
was so intoxicating, my hands were trembling. From the quake

or the contact, I couldn't tell. The basket I held, like everything about this awful village, kept the distance between us.

The shaking stopped. I looked up into the black holes in Jurij's mask, and he let me go, his face poring over the horizon. "That started nearby." Jurij rubbed his wooden chin. I'd have stopped to think about the ridiculousness of the gesture were it not for the seriousness of the situation.

I shook my head to clear it of the chaos under my feet and in my heart. "We should hurry."

Jurij nodded, and he sprinted. With the basket and my heavy heart weighing me down, I had no chance of catching up to him. My legs felt like they were caked in mud, and they were pulling me down, keeping me from him.

When at last I caught up to him in front of Ingrith's shack, Jurij was reaching out to the shriveled-up old woman, and the crone was batting his arms away, even as she stood on unsteady feet. The dirty black cloth she wore over her head tied her thick hair down and made her a bit less menacing than she'd seemed when I'd last seen her close up. When she was digging her claws into my shoulders.

Ingrith placed a hand on Jurij's chest and pushed him backward. "You just leave me alone. I've got no need for masked men 'round here."

"But Ma'am—"

"No buts. Get outta here." Ingrith tore her eyes from him and let her glare fall over me as I approached them. "Wonderful. Now there's a fine face I won't soon forget. Come to bother an old woman again with your fancy games, girl?"

Better to pretend I had no idea what she was talking about. "Did you cause the quake?"

Bad idea. Ingrith's face grew even more sour and puckered, and I wouldn't have thought that was even possible. "Yes, I did. And never you mind."

I glanced beyond the old woman to the rest of the northern dirt path. "But won't the quarry workers notice? They're close enough to have felt—"

Ingrith scoffed. "You let me worry about them workers."

There was no sign of movement from the quarry, but still. "It's got to be dangerous to look at the castle so near where there are men working." She couldn't have meant to kill the poor men, could she? "Dangerous nothing, girl, I just made a mistake. A bird startled me. Can't blame an old woman for lookin' when something starts screeching at her." Ingrith's mouth clamped shut, and I could see the muscles tense in her jaw. She bent over to reach the walking stick she'd dropped.

Jurij tried to grab the stick for her. "Let me—"

"Oh, no." Ingrith slapped his arm, and Jurij pulled back, cradling his forearm and staring at the woman with his blank-eyed face. Ingrith snatched her stick and stood back up. "Didn't need no man's help then, don't need no man's help now."

Jurij turned his wooden mask toward me. The opened-mouth grin probably didn't match his real expression underneath as the ungrateful old woman smacked him. But that was the Returning mask, and that was the countenance he was stuck with for the day. Until dusk, anyway. *I hope I really do see his face. Surely Elfriede forcing herself to love him is enough. Surely ...*

"Let me guess. Ol' Ingrith is the last to know. Ol' Ingrith just has to be invited, though there's no one who actually wants her to come, but goddess help us if the lord don' give his blessing. I take it you two are having a Returning today?" Her eyes rolled up and down, as she examined Jurij from head to toe. "You look too young to get married."

I didn't often ask the first goddess for anything, but I prayed that no one would notice the flush that I could feel spreading across my face.

"She's not my goddess." He said it in the same manner one might say, "Please pass the potatoes."

"Huh. If you say so." The way Ingrith stared at me, I had a feeling the first goddess had failed me. Again.

Jurij didn't seem to notice. "But I'm having my Returning today. This is my goddess's sister."

Ingrith's eyes narrowed as she looked up at the wooden

face beaming down at her. "And let me guess. The goddess is too busy primpin' to bother with the likes of someone like me." Her gaze fell on the basket in my arms. "What's that? A collection for your blessed day? I haven't got no gifts left to give all these young'uns Returning every other week."

"No gift is necessary." Jurij uncovered the offerings within the basket. They looked even more pitiful strewn haphazardly among the old cloth, with plenty of empty space beside them. "We just brought you some food. We thought you might like something. And yes, we'd like to invite you to my Returning."

Ingrith stuck her head over the basket so fast I jumped backward, thinking she might be intending to ram her head into my chest. She leered up at me. "There's not a thing here worth havin', but for that apple." She snatched it out of the basket and took a bite. I might have heard her teeth crack. "You go take the rest of that garbage back where you came from." Bits of apple and spittle escaped from her mouth with each bite. "You invited me. The lord is satisfied. I'm not goin'. Now get out." She tossed the half-eaten apple on the ground, snatched the basket from me, and shoved it at Jurij so quickly he had no choice but to catch it before it fell to the ground. She started hobbling back to what she called a home.

Jurij sighed. It took a lot to make him sigh. Especially when you considered the mother he had. "Come on, Noll. We invited her."

Ingrith turned around as fast as someone a tenth her age. "No, *you* go, boy. Girl, you come in here and help me. Time you make up for that foolin' around you did years ago."

Jurij's head tilted slightly. It was possible the only thing he remembered about that day four years prior were the parts with his golden-haired goddess.

Well, why not? What else was I going to do for the rest of the day? Find Elfriede and tuck that golden strand into her bun for the fiftieth time? I squeezed Jurij's shoulder. "It's all right, Jurij. Your mother might have noticed you went missing by now. I'll see you later."

I let his shoulder go and stepped forward. Ingrith nodded

and went back to hobbling. In a few short hours, Jurij would be gone. He would vanish, or he would be hers. Either way, he was gone forever from me.

Goddess, if you hear my prayer, you'll make time stand still, just for a little while. Or take me back. Back before love could hurt me.

Chapter Three

We'd barely stepped inside when there was a pounding on the door. My chest squeezed in fright, but it didn't bother Ingrith. She hobbled over to the corner of her small shack, where a chest lay at the foot of the rotted wooden frame and the mildew-covered slab of hay she counted as a bed and mattress.

"Ingrith! Ingrith, you in there?"

The pounding wasn't stopping. Something thudded behind me. I pointed at the door. "Should I—"

Ingrith's dark, bulbous eyes were right in front of me. She was shorter than I remembered—or I was taller, I supposed—but she was no less frightening when viewed so close. "Should you nothing, girl. This is my house." She seemed to have lost a front tooth since the last time we'd had the pleasure of talking face to face. Or, rather, face *in* face.

"Ingrith! Why can't you open this door when I ask nicely?"

"I don't have to open my door for nobody but the lord's men." Ingrith leaned around me and cupped her free hand around her mouth. "You one of the lord's men? I suspect not, since I can hear you speak."

"Ingrith, we're coming in."

Ingrith pushed me aside and hobbled to the door, ripping it open with that one-tenth-her-age speed once again. A man stumbled inside, grabbing the door to steady himself. "You almost killed me, you crazy old—"

Ingrith shook her walking stick a little off the ground. "If I'd wanted to kill you, I'd've popped this under your mask and knocked it off. You're not welcome here."

She was right. He was still wearing a mask. And he didn't seem like one of the skinny, gangly teenagers running around the village. His face was that of a wooden fish, complete with a puckering set of lips over the black hole covering his mouth.

Behind him was a man whose face was uncovered. He had no reason to fear my eyes or Ingrith's. His love had been Returned.

Fish Face shook his vacant mask. "Did you cause that earthquake?"

Ingrith poked at his abdomen with her walking stick. "I did. What of it?"

Fish Face swatted the walking stick away with one hand and held his mask tighter with the other. "You keep that away from me, you old biddy!"

"Tayton, please." The unmasked man stepped inside and put a hand on Fish Face's chest. He turned to Ingrith. "There are men working in the quarry most days, Ingrith."

She sniffled and clasped both hands on top of her walking stick, which she lowered back to the ground. "I know. I can hear their racket. Makes my head ache and my ears ring."

Fish Face tapped his foot. "And crazy old crones looking up at the castle makes rocks fall on our heads."

She snorted. "Good. Then maybe I'll get a day of peace."

Fish Face nearly choked. "You senile, unloved woman—"

The unmasked man spoke as if he hadn't been interrupted. "I'm sure it was an accident."

"It wasn't," said Ingrith, as I said, "It was. She told me so."

Fish Face threw both hands into the air. "Who's this?"

"My guest." Ingrith poked at the floor near his feet. "Which *you* are not."

Fish Face scoffed. The unmasked man looked me up and down. I had to let my gaze fall. They were all so handsome when they were unmasked. And it was rare to have any take notice of me. And Jurij, he would be the same. Handsome, blind to me.

"Woodcarver's daughter," he said at last. So he actually knew of a woman besides his goddess?

Fish Face seemed as perplexed as his masked expression. "The one with a Returning today?"

"No," I admitted. "I'm her sister."

Fish Face started laughing. At least I thought it was a laugh. It sounded coincidentally like a fish flopping and gasping without water. "The only other unloved woman in the village. Figures."

My blood boiled. "Oh, like you have room to speak!"

"I'm married!" protested Fish Face.

I shook my head and gestured to his fishy face. "But your wife obviously doesn't love you, or you wouldn't still be wearing that ugly mask! Unless what's beneath is really much worse."

Ingrith cackled at that. I think she was actually happy.

Fish Face pointed at me. "Can you believe these women? If I had—goddess's blessings, whose mask is that?" I turned around to look at the chipped and cracked table behind me. There was a wooden mask there, all right. A snake. As chipped and cracked as the table on which it sat.

Fish Face might have been frothing at the mouth if he'd had one. As it was, his puckering fish lips looked oddly out of tune with the tone of his voice. "You murderer!"

The unmasked man put his hand on Fish Face's shoulder. "Enough, Tayton. That mask looks too old to be someone she might have killed recently."

"So you're saying it's all right; she must have killed that man years ago." Fish Face's expression perfectly matched his flabbergasted tone.

The unmasked man put his fingers to his temple. "No, Tayton. I'm just saying she's unlikely to have killed a man since we set out to work this morning. I think we would have heard if she'd killed anyone years ago."

Ingrith laughed and pounded her walking stick on the ground. "Shows what you know!"

"I need to get out of here," said Fish Face. "I can't stand to be around these crones one second longer."

These crones? As in the both of us?

Sighing, the unmasked man shook his head. "We're leaving. Ladies." He nodded first at me, then at Ingrith. I ignored him.

"Take care not to let it happen again, Ingrith," said the unmasked man as the two workers left. "It's dangerous for there to be earthquakes near the quarry."

Ingrith started muttering to herself and hobbled past me toward the table. I caught something like "useless, oblivious men" as she stepped past, leaving behind her scent of decay. With a groaning, scratching sound, she pulled a chair out from the table and plopped herself into it. She stared back at me. "Well? You goin' to stand there all day, like your mind has gone numb? Sit down!"

It was as if I were a man, and she were my goddess. A cloud of dust flew out from under my mud-colored skirt as I sat. The chair I was in was dustier than Ingrith's, but it seemed to be in much finer shape than the rest of the furniture. It was as if the chair had been sleeping, waiting for someone who never came to use it.

Ingrith pounded the walking stick, still in her hand even though it soared above her head while she was seated, making me sit taller in my chair. She pointed to the chipped and cracked snake mask on the table between us. "You know what that is?"

I raised an eyebrow. "A ... mask?"

"*A ... mask?*" Ingrith echoed my words as if they left a vile taste in her mouth. "Yes, we both have eyes, girl! I'm askin' if you know what that is!"

Okay, maybe hanging out with the crazy old crone to pass the time before I lost the only man I'd ever love was a bad idea after all. Then again, it did get me out of extra primping. "A snake?"

Ingrith pounded her stick on the floor again. "Oh, for the love of ... " She grunted and reached across the table to snatch up the snake mask. She held it next to her face. "This was a man's face, girl! How do you reckon I got it and got no man for it to be wearin', eh?"

"I don't know. Your brother's or something?"

Ingrith sighed as if she needed to clear her lungs of all that dusty air in her house. She tossed the mask back onto the table, where it landed with a *thud*. "I never had no brothers, girl." She held up a finger. "Tut, tut. And before you go guessin' it was my father's, he was a loved man since the day my mama turned seventeen, so no, he had no need for another face when I knew him."

What did men do with their masks if they had their love Returned and could be rid of them? Smash them, break them, as I might do if I were them? No, they had other things on their mind. Like happiness and goddesses.

Ingrith sighed and shook her head. A white tendril broke free from the cloth covering her scalp, and I was reminded, with a jolt, of Elfriede. "You ever heard of a man called Haelan?"

I shook my head.

Ingrith heaved that weary sigh again. "Of course you haven't." She narrowed her eyes. "Your parents ever wonder how come there's no healer?"

What is she talking about? "Someone who ... fixes boot heels?"

Ingrith pounded her walking stick not once, but three times. "No, I'm talkin' 'bout a *healer*, you damn fool! Someone who makes people who are sick or injured feel better."

"No." Wonderful. I was going to spend the rest of the day talking nonsense with this woman. "Mother tends to us when we're sick. I suppose women make their loved ones feel better."

"Some broth-and-huggin' home remedies aren't the same as sewing up a man to stop him from bleeding or blowing air into a girl's lungs if she stops breathin'." Ingrith let out a breath, and I could smell the sour scent across the table. "What do your parents think of me, then?"

That you're a crazy old crone, like the rest of us do. "They don't speak much of you."

"They think I never had a man to love me?"

"Yeah ... " *They think that their daughter is probably going to do no better.*

Ingrith scoffed. "Bunkum! Every woman gets her man."

I cradled one arm against my chest and squeezed my elbow tightly. "I don't have one, either."

"Oh, sweet goddess. Can't be more than sixteen and she thinks no man will ever find her. Well, isn't that convenient?" Ingrith cupped her chin, pinching her lips together as she looked me over. "You in love with that boy you came here with?"

I bit my lip. "Why would you ask that?"

Ingrith shook her walking stick in the air. "'Cause you're a fool, girl, if you go lovin' where love is not needed! That boy's your sister's, he says? You get your *own* man. Love 'im or send him to the commune, don't matter to me. But if you get your heart so set on another, and your man come callin', don't you dare go pretendin' you're in love with that poor soul of his, you hear me?"

Don't pretend you're in love with him. Elfriede. "But ... what happens if a girl convinces herself she's in love with her man? When she's really just—I don't know—in love with having her Returning? Or afraid to be alone?"

"Then she ought to delay the Returning until she's sure. No need to rush the day you turn seventeen. Don't know what's wrong with all these young fool girls, thinkin' they can't possibly wait any longer." Ingrith pointed the top of the walking stick in my direction. "I had my Returning when I was seventeen."

Something felt sour in my stomach. "But you have no man!"

Ingrith pounded her walking stick and her free palm on the

table. "*Every* woman gets her man! You never heard that lord's blessing garbage at a Returning?"

I had, but—

Ingrith's large, round eyes grew even larger, even wider. "We invited them all, you see, we ought to have had the lord's blessing! *He* even came, that boy I truly fancied!" She laughed, but the laugh stuck in her throat like a fly caught in a spider's webbing. "Bernhard. Bernhold. Something. I don't even remember his name anymore! What a fool I was! He wasn't worth none of my love, no! He had *her*!"

My palms rested against the table. I pushed back, letting the chair move slowly away.

Ingrith leaped up, summoning that secret speed of hers. "But I *had* to have a Returning, you see! My man was good enough. Nice fellow. Did whatever I wanted, though that'd be no surprise, seeing as all men follow their goddess's orders when they're still wearin' those masks of theirs." Ingrith hobbled closer to me, and my palms pushed forward, my legs tensed, ready to jump as soon as she got too near.

She leaned forward and stuck those bulbous eyes in my face before I even had a chance to jump. "*Haelan*. Village healer. Yes, we had one of those back then. Lived right here. He had no family by then, so no one else could do what he did." She leaned back slightly and grinned, but it was a strange smile, a smile out of place on her sour, wrinkled face. "I promised to give him sons and daughters. Told 'im he could teach me and we'd all keep up the trade. Never seen a happier wood-faced man." The smile vanished. "Though I suppose I could have told 'im we'd be living in the quarry under rocks and mud spending our days eating insects and he'd've been just as happy."

Ingrith straightened as best she could, but she still looked hunched and twisted. "What made me happy is she'd once told me she liked Haelan." Ingrith nodded and stared off above my head, not even looking at me. "But after that, her man found the goddess in her, and just like that, she was so in love with him. With *him*. She was my dearest friend, and she knew how much he meant to me. She knew how much I loved Bernie."

Ingrith hobbled over to her door and pulled it open. She stood, staring out into the open, both hands clutching the top of her walking stick. Slowly, I moved as close to her as I dared, keeping her well in front of me.

A small gust of breeze blew in through the open door, rustling that free tendril of hair that covered the old crone's forehead. "But she loved Bernie. She proved it at her Returning. He took off his mask and clear as day, her love for him was made plain. He was still living, and they kissed each other as if their kisses were as necessary for them to breathe as air."

The wind blew a bit stronger. I shivered. We were too close to the mountains. It was cold.

Ingrith took a few small steps out into the open. "So I thought, why not hurt her as much as she hurt me? Why not share those kisses with her first love as she watched, watched as her soul wrapped 'round her heart and wouldn't stop squeezin'?" She paused, squeezing her fist as tight as it would go. Then she hobbled around the home and out of view, toward the east.

She'd forgotten I was even there. I could run, forget any of this nonsense ever happened. But I thought of Elfriede, and of Jurij. I hitched my skirt up and ran out the door.

Ingrith walked eastward a few paces in front of me, shouting to no one at all. "I was a fool to think I could hurt her! I was a fool to think that the love of little children meant anything to anyone but me!"

Or me.

Ingrith stepped into the lily-covered fields and tossed her walking stick aside. It vanished into the knee-high grasses. "The goddesses are all that matter! There's no room for love where love's not wanted! There's no room for hurt, for jealousy, for a love intended if not fully felt!"

I had no idea where she was going. Into the woods? Could she make such a long walk? Ingrith stopped and snapped around to face me, suddenly realizing I was still there. "I looked before I loved, girl! I looked at the Returning!"

Her eyes seemed about ready to roll out of her head. "He vanished, leavin' nothin' but his clothes and mask behind him!"

I stopped, and Ingrith closed the distance between us. She smiled. "And no one remembers. No one but me." She closed her eyes and started laughing. "They didn't even know what we'd all gathered for!" She put one hand on my shoulder to steady herself as she cradled her belly with the other hand. "I tried to hurt her by Returning with her first love, and she couldn't even remember he ever existed!"

I stepped back, trying to let Ingrith's hand fall, but she clutched harder, digging her yellowing nails into my dress. "Look!" She pointed behind her, upward—above the woods where I dared not look. I slapped a hand in front of my eyes.

"Look, girl!" She let my shoulder go, and her decaying old fingers pried at the hand I held tightly over my eyelids. "Look! There lives the heartless monster! The lord who gives the first goddess's blessing! Have you ever seen him? Does he even exist? Who eats the bread, who wears the clothes? What becomes of the things the men deliver there?"

I swatted at her with my free hand. "Stop! Let me go!"

"Who are the servants bathed in white? Where are their goddesses? Do none speak? Did they punish me? Why is some *man* ruling over this village and giving the blessings of the first goddess, a woman?"

I jumped back, my eyes clamped shut, but she was still gripping my arm, pulling it downward with a force not even a man could muster. "Let go, you crazy old—"

"Oh, *now* she remembers to shut her eyes! When it's not a life at stake, but a measly old earthquake. Well, I'm not afraid."

The ground began to shake. Ingrith laughed, and the ground beneath my feet shifted until I had no choice but to fall into the grasses. My eyes flew open, as wide as Ingrith's.

There it stood, dizzyingly high and regal, dark and dominant against the pale eastern mountains, ringed in verdant green trees from the woods before it. It was taller than I imagined, almost half the height of the mountain behind it. Its wide berth supported two great, jagged spires, so thin as to be impractical, but as menacing to me then as if they were actual swords, great daggers the building needed to defend itself against monsters. The castle. Forbidden to the eyes of all women.

The earthquake grew stronger, and my palms, scuffed and scratched already, clutched for the safety of the broken blades of grass and the fallen lilies, but the earth wouldn't stop moving. The old crone danced, somehow staying upright even as the ground shook around her.

"I'm not afraid, you heartless monster! Live forever, you will never die, but you'll never know love neither!" She grabbed her skirt and kicked her feet up high. "Punish me, lord! Strike me down and punish me!"

I didn't know what to do. "Ingrith!"

Her feet stopped moving, and a gasping, scratching sound came from her throat, as if she'd forgotten how to breathe.

Her clothing fell beside me, her body already gone. The ground stopped shaking. But my heart kept beating, strong and fast, as if the ground would never again be stable.

~ Chapter Four ~

I touched the dirty, dark shawl that had once covered her white head. It lay between a lily and an indentation in the grass, where Ingrith had once stood. Her clothing was now all that remained.

Had the lord actually killed her? But why? And how? He'd never executed anyone before.

No woman has ever looked at the castle for that long, either.

And no one ever really complained about him before. No one said what would happen if we went against the first goddess's teachings. They just asked his blessing, like he was some ever-watching shepherd spirit, like we were his mindless flock. *Someone has to eat the food, wear the clothes. Unless it's all the specters.*

The lord's servants. Less reverently and more often called "the specters" in my mind. To a child they were too-real monsters, appearing without fanfare and dissipating into the mist once they were done with their errand. They showed up any time anyone had so much as a disagreement in Vena's tavern, not that there was much room for anything resembling an actual fight like those in the tales of queens and kings in the village of simpering men and goddesses. They also did the lord's shopping for him, silently handing merchants notes with the lord's orders. Clothed from head to toe entirely in white, the specters would have been hard not to spot even from leagues away. But their hair—each one had hair to his shoulders—was white. Their skin was white, as white as snow. It was as if they were men who'd had every bit of life, every bit of color drained out of them. They were like a walking death, if anything of our bodies was left behind once we died.

Only once had I gotten close enough to look at one's face. It was there that I saw the only hint of color: blood red eyes.

I shook my head clear of the image. In any case, at least we had an image to put to the specters—unlike the lord, whom no one had ever seen.

The heartless monster. She called him that. Was it all just Ingrith's delusion?

"Damn you, you crazy ol' crone! Ingrith!"

There was no mistaking that voice, muffled and angry and distant though it might have been. *Fish Face.* I wondered if this time someone in the quarry had gotten hurt—or worse. And they would come with their anger, itching to find Ingrith, and they would find me. Just me.

I released the shawl from my fingers and stood up, ignoring the soreness in my muscles. Before I could even stop to think, my feet kicked up the dress and flew farther into the fields. If I could just get out of sight before they came. If I could just pretend I'd been long gone before the second earthquake.

They knew you were with her beforehand. They'll see you running through the fields. There's no reason for them to keep their eyes down.

I ran, though, as if there were no other choice. I couldn't deal with all of the questions. I couldn't deal with the stares, the hatred. Not on this day.

Thanks to the hills, I might have gotten out of sight before they found her clothing. I made for the eastern dirt path as soon as I could, ready to insist I'd just been walking homeward.

Home was so close. I was running at a speed I'd thought I'd lost, staring at the ground all the while, fighting through my body's struggle to breathe. Ready to pretend I'd never even cut through the fields.

My dress! There were tears and grass stains all over the skirt.

Home was right there. Mother and Father might still be inside; there had to be a little time before dusk yet. I could cover the skirt up with an apron. I could grab another dress when Mother wasn't looking. *They'd notice. We don't have any other nice dresses.*

I kept running, straight past the house and into the woods. The trees kept the castle from view, so I looked up at last. I found the well-worn foliage to the side of the path and burst through the trees. I didn't care that stray branches scratched my arms and ripped at already-torn seams. I was going somewhere where I could rest and think, where I could quiet the insanity running through my head, where I could figure out what choices were left to me, if any at all.

A shriek, or more like a giggling squeal, tore through the air as something fast and hard slammed against my abdomen. I felt a sharp poke in my leg and heard a snap.

"Noll!" The little girl whose bushy, twig-filled head had just rammed into my abdomen stepped back and looked up, rubbing her forehead with one hand. In her other hand, she held a branch. The top of it dangled by a thread.

My pulse was still racing, and I shut my mouth, worried my heart might escape through my throat. I ran a palm over the pain in my side, swallowed my heart back inside me, and spoke, breathless. "Nissa." A farmer's daughter. A friend of Luuk's. We'd all played together before. "What are you doing here?"

It was a dumb question. I was the one who'd shown her the cavern in the first place.

Nissa tilted her head, pointing the branch at the cavern's dark mouth behind her. "Slaying monsters." Her mouth pinched. "It broke." She tossed the branch onto a nearby pile of moss and rocks.

I smiled, even despite everything. "Elgar's always broken. It'll mend next time you pick it up." *Pick it up somewhere else entirely.* My smile faded. "Were you in there alone?"

Nissa shrugged and clutched both hands behind her back. "Everyone else is getting ready for the Returning." Her gaze fell on my dress. "Aren't you going to get ready?"

I was ready. But maybe I'll never be ready, not really. "I will." I stood beside her and nudged her gently onward. "You go get ready, too."

Nissa walked a few paces, then stopped and turned around. She stared at me quizzically with her large, brown eyes. "Aren't you coming?"

I shooed her onward. "Not just yet. I'll be there soon. Go on."

Nissa shrugged and skipped forward through the foliage, humming a tune as she went. I watched her until she blended into the trees and vanished from sight.

Vanished. Right in front of me.

I walked over to the broken branch Nissa had discarded and picked it up, turning the wood in my fingers. It'd been so long since I'd been the one to clutch Elgar. But there were monsters ahead; there were monsters behind.

***

When the queen and her retainers were brave enough, they'd chase monsters into the blackest pits. The cavern off the main path in the woods held countless monsters and endless secrets, and the queen, who lost her retainers one by one, had never explored all its vast depths.

She'd tried to crown another generation of queen and retainers after her, to keep up the adventures, but good retainers were hard to find when they kept falling in love with goddesses one after the other. Nissa, in any case, just wanted to be her friends' equal, and although they battled monsters, she'd never called herself queen.

The queen was gone. It wasn't the same anymore. I swished the stick in front of me, not even bothering to pretend it was a blade, and certainly not screaming a battle cry.

This is stupid. I got bored and tossed the stick to the side. Because I'd had the wonderful idea of taking the stick instead of one of the candles the kids left by the entrance to light their way, I was marching forward in total darkness. But my eyes adjusted, and after all those years of playing as a child, and then watching after Nissa and Luuk and their friends, by now I knew the path well enough to navigate it in the dark.

If only there was somewhere I could go. But what was there, beyond the mountains, beyond the thick air that covered the edges of the land in mist? Nothing. There was no place for me to run and hide.

Nowhere but the "secret" cavern. The cold, dark, neglected cavern. Perfect for me.

***

I found a stalagmite on which to lean my back and sat down on the floor of the cavern, hugging my knees against my chest. My mind was blissfully blank for a time, for how long, I didn't know. I shut my eyes and listened to the drip, drip, drop of some distant source of water that fell from the cavern ceiling and the dangling stalactites. I laughed quietly. We could never say those words as kids. We just called them "ground spears" and "ceiling spears."

"Hey."

I nearly tipped over. My palms shot out to steady me as my eyes flew open.

Jurij stood over me, his man-mask on, a lit candlestick in one hand. He slipped down beside me, carefully resting the candle atop a rock.

"Hey," came my brilliant reply. No "How did you find me?" "Why did you bother looking for me?" "Am I wanted for killing some quarry workers?" or "Don't you have a Returning to get to?" or "Tell me you won't die today!"

I went back to hugging my knees.

"It's beautiful, isn't it?" Jurij hugged his knees and looked up, where traces of his flickering candle caused shadows to dance on the ceiling. "I'd forgotten. I haven't been here in a while." Jurij stretched his arms and then his legs. "Luuk tells me you take him and his friends here on occasion, though."

The corner of my mouth twitched. "Probably not the safest thing to do, considering they could get hurt in here." I thought of Nissa, playing alone.

Jurij shrugged. "You and me had a lot of fun here."

I smiled, despite myself. "If by 'a lot of fun,' you mean I let you hold the candle while I did all of the sword-swinging, then yeah."

Jurij laughed. "Hey, the *queen* once told me that carrying a candle is an important job on any quest to the secret cavern. What was it? The candlelight keeps the monsters at bay?"

I pointed at the flickering shadows on the cavern ceiling. "That's what I told you, but the candle actually made the monsters come out in the first place."

"I wasn't stupid, Noll. I knew that. I just let you believe otherwise."

I always thought I was ever so clever. "Sorry."

"Don't be." Jurij let his man-mask scan the dancing shadows on the ceiling. "I liked being told what to do."

"It got you ready for life with a goddess, I guess." That was low.

Jurij didn't seem hurt so much as amused by my statement. "Always so much hatred for goddesses. You won't feel the same when your man finds you." He laid a hand on my knee.

I tore my leg out of reach. "Oh, *please*, not you, too."

Jurij's arm was left awkwardly reaching toward me without anything to touch. He pulled it back and ran it through the top of his dark curls. "Sorry. What happened with Ingrith?"

So that was why he was here. Everyone thought I'd killed her, and Jurij knew right where to find me. "She's dead."

Jurij's man-mask bobbed up and down. "I know. She vanished after causing another earthquake. Luckily the men in the quarry were just leaving to get ready for my Returning and no one else was hurt, but they had no reason to believe Ingrith knew that. They ran to her cottage, but all they found were her clothes in the field. They figured she might have had a heart attack from the shock."

Or an always-watching lord punished her as she'd asked. At least no one else was hurt. Maybe they'd let me off with a lecture, after all. "What about me?"

Jurij's mask cocked slightly. "What do you mean? Nissa stopped by to talk to Luuk, and she told me you were headed into the cavern, which I found odd. So that's what I was asking. Did Ingrith tell you she was going to cause an earthquake again before you left her? I'm not too sure I believe her about the bird now that she went and caused such a tremor. We felt it halfway into the village this time."

No one saw me leave. "No. I … " I bit my lip. It wasn't like I'd killed her. And I'd barely looked. That crazy old crone did it to herself. "She was rambling about something awfully weird, so I left." *What if Ingrith wasn't completely crazy? What if a goddess who just thinks she's in love can still kill her man when he takes off his mask? Jurij's life could really be in danger.*

Jurij put his palms back on the cavern floor and leaned back. "You look worried."

I blushed. I'd gotten so used to never being able to see his expressions that I'd forgotten my face was as legible as an open book. "I'm worried about your Returning."

Jurij's mask bobbed slightly. I could almost picture his eyes rolling behind those soulless black eye holes. "Noll, I don't know how many times I have to tell you, I'll be fine." He sighed that rare and frustrated sigh. "Can we try focusing on how this is the greatest day of my life for once? Please?"

I bit the inside of my cheek as the heat rose to my face. "Of course you think it's the greatest day of your life. But you could die, Jurij! You just don't realize that because you don't have a mind of your own!"

Jurij sat up straighter. "You're some friend, Noll. You don't know anything about what it's like to have a goddess. So why don't you keep your opinion to yourself for once?"

I jumped up. Jurij wasn't like this. He wasn't bratty like the other boys had been. But he was blind, so blind. Blind to all of my suffering. "I'm only trying to make you think for once because I care about you!"

Jurij shook his mask-face and leaned on a stalagmite to stand up. "Do you think I don't realize that my life is in danger from the moment I open my eyes in the morning to the moment I shut them at night? Do you think I've never worried that some girl or woman not related to us will burst in one morning and kill me, my brother, and my father while we're eating together? Do you think I've never worried that Father's mask might fall off while he's sleeping, and Mother might look over and kill him where he lays?" He clenched his fist. "I know when love exists between a coupling, Noll, and when it doesn't. We men adjust. We're careful. We know what we're doing."

I grit my teeth. "You all spend so much time worshipping your goddesses, I doubt you know much of anything."

Jurij threw his hands into the air. "When has a man ever died at his Returning? When has a man ever died from a woman looking at his face at all?"

An excellent point. How did we even know men had to cover their faces? Maybe this was all some twisted game of the always-watching, never-present lord and his imaginary "first goddess."

Haelan. "Ingrith. She told me she killed her man at their Returning. And no one but her remembers the man ever existed."

Jurij tapped his fingers impatiently against his thigh. "You're using the ramblings of a crazy woman to try to delay the greatest day of my life?" He pointed at me. "With your own sister, I might add. Why do you hate Elfriede so much?"

Because she took the only thing that ever truly mattered to me. And she doesn't even realize what a treasure she stole. "I don't hate her!" *I don't. I don't.*

"Then why are you always talking as if she's lying about loving me and is going to kill me?"

"I don't think she's *lying*." My throat felt parched, but there was no hope for the dryness to ever be quenched. "I just think she doesn't even know herself. She never knew you before you found the goddess in her."

Jurij waved a hand. "That's not important."

"*Yes*, it is! You were nothing to her! She only convinced herself she loved you because it was you or no one."

Jurij shrugged. "So? It's the same for me. It's her or no one. Her or the commune. Her or death."

"But you have no choice but to love her! You don't realize what it's like for a woman. We have the choice to love or not, to not even know if what we think we feel is real or just some crazy mixture of desire and filial affection." Tears formed at the edges of my eyes, and I bit my lip to keep it from trembling. "Jurij, I love you!"

Jurij sighed and shook his head. "I love you, too, but—"

"Not like that!" I dug my fingers as deeply into my arms as they would go. "I love you, like you love Elfriede."

Jurij ran a hand up and down his forearm. Before he spoke, there was nothing but the drip, drip, drop of the distant source of water. There was no horrible past, no terrible future. Time was standing still, and in my mind, an impossible future was still a possibility. *I love you, too. Say it.*

"Noll, I'm sorry. I don't know what to say. I don't know what you hoped to accomplish by telling me that. It's weird enough that I still feel like being your friend after finding my goddess. Isn't that enough for you?"

The tears were rolling down my cheeks now, and I didn't know what made me angrier, him just standing there with that stupid wooden expression or the fact that he could see the tears streaming down my face. "Is that just to make Elfriede happy? What, did she command you to stay friends with me just because she didn't want me to lose all of my friends? Did you think—"

Jurij's hand stopped moving. "Yes."

My mouth snapped shut. "I'm sorry?"

"Elfriede commanded me to remain your friend, back when I first told her I loved her and she was overwhelmed by my confession. 'Go with Noll,' she told me. 'Keep being her friend. This is all so sudden. Please go.' She might have forgotten about it. Or not realized she was issuing a command when she stated it. But she hasn't told me to stop or said to forget that command, so I'm still bound by it."

Something bubbled up from my stomach and forced its way out of my mouth, like the simper of a dying wounded animal. It was quiet, but in the echo of the cavern, it grew louder and repeated, reflecting my pain back at me over and over again. I clenched my teeth as hard as possible, not caring about the pain in my jaw, doing everything I could to stop myself from making that sound again.

Jurij snapped up straighter and held his arms outward as if ready to embrace me. "Let me comfort you, Noll."

I could barely see through the torrent of tears building. "No! You're just saying that because the command is making you!"

Jurij shook his head and lowered his arms. "Look, Noll, after the Returning, a goddess's command isn't really so absolute."

Tears were spilling out. I thought of stupid Father and the stupid dishes. "What does that matter? You'll still do everything you can to make her happy."

"Yes, but … " He moved closer. "I'm just saying, I'll show you, I'll still be your friend. It won't be because Elfriede commanded it of me."

I jumped backward out of his reach. "Leave me alone!"

"Noll, I'm sorry!"

I stepped around the stalagmite and farther into the cavern, to the very edge of the candle's glow. "Go away! You have a Returning to get to, don't you? Hope you live through it!"

Jurij lunged toward me, desperately grabbing for my arm, but I jumped back, back into the darkness. "Noll, I really do think of you as a friend. I didn't mean to hurt you. Please—"

I turned and ran, not caring that I stumbled over rocks and dips in the ground and whatever else was thrown out there to trip me. I ran as fast as I could, deep into the darkness, farther than I had ever been before. We'd been too afraid to go this far as children. But there was nothing in this cavern more terrifying than the future that lay outside of it.

"Noll!" His voice echoed and faded into the distance behind me.

I ran and ran. There was only darkness for yards. But then, there was a violet glow. It grew closer with each footstep. At last I neared it, putting my hand on the last stalagmite blocking my view as if I could tear it down with my fingers.

A pool, awash with bright violet. A light source, like a roaring, searing fire that burned underneath the depths of the waters. And something else. The laughter of children, the sound of Jurij calling my name. Only his voice was high-pitched, shy, and inviting. Like he'd not yet been corrupted by his goddess.

My feet flew forward across hard, slippery rock, at last puncturing the water's edge. I wasn't thinking. But there was no more reason to think. Just to find that laughter.

Though I'd never swum before, I dove. I started kicking and splashing as the water crushed me on all sides. But I was going forward. By all that I had in me, I would find some way to reach that happy sound. I bobbed up and down. Water streamed down my face, from the tips of that frizzy, wild bush of black hair I'd always despised, from the tears welling in my eyes.

The violet light grew blinding, positively blinding, shooting upward from beneath the water's surface. I closed my eyes to block it.

As I took one last breath of air, my nostrils filled with a

scent so strong, my stomach turned wild with waves of nausea. A soaked animal, sopping from the sudden rain. An uncooked fish lying lifeless on a pond's grassy shore. Wet leather. I'd once spilled a mug at the Tailors' as they worked the material into clothing.

"Noll!" The sound of Jurij's voice—his deeper voice, his lost-to-me voice—was the last thing I heard as I tumbled below the water's surface.

But at the same time, almost an echo of Jurij's scream, another voice called me, a voice cold and far-flung, even though the emotion entrenched in it more than matched the intensity of Jurij's terror. "Olivière!"

There were none who truly knew me who would say my actual, feminine name aloud.

My eyes shot open, but the world was a blur around me. The violet light grew dull. The water threatened to fade to darkness, and I knew if I fell down there, I would never, ever get back to the surface.

Is that what you want? Part of me wasn't sure. I kicked and opened my mouth to scream, but I shut my mouth quickly when instead of sound escaping my lips, water started pouring inside, determined to consume me.

I heard a muffled sound beside me, but I couldn't make out the words. An arm wrapped around my chest, and I kicked once or twice more before I discovered that kicking wasn't going to do any good. I went limp in Jurij's arms, and with his more powerful, focused kicks, we shot upward and broke the surface.

Only it wasn't Jurij.

There was a black leather glove resting on my shoulder, a bare and ghastly arm wrapped across my chest. In the violet light, I could see the pallor of the skin, an odd, creamy, soft rose, washed pale with white. *One of the specters? The lord's servants? No, not that pale.*

We'd come to the surface, but I couldn't breathe. My eyes drifted closed, and open again, my vision blurry. The black glove, the pale arm became a dark hand, a tan sleeve. *Jurij.*

Jurij kicked us toward the shore. My eyes closed, and opened. The black glove, the pale arm.

A hard smack against my back. "Do not fight the reflex," said an unfamiliar voice. Water spilled out of my guts. "You must purge yourself of the water."

My eyes shut again as the water spilled out once more. As I struggled to keep them open, I tried to focus on the shoreline, and the tiny yellow flicker of candlelight I saw there. But the violet water stained my eyelashes and blurred my vision. Then I noticed the dark hand, the tan sleeve. My head twisted slightly to search for the wooden face.

"Close your eyes!" screamed Jurij.

Jurij grabbed the back of my head by the hair and shoved my head under water with a strength I didn't know his thin arms possessed.

"*Close. Your. Eyes!*" I struggled to breathe and started kicking and thrashing. For a moment, I thought Jurij meant to kill me, perhaps for another excuse to comfort my sister.

And then I knew what had happened. I nodded as hard as I could under the water, shut my eyes tight, and I felt Jurij's grip on my hair relax. He gently pulled me up, and I felt us reach the shore. He rolled me over onto my back. Perhaps not willing to trust me when it came to his life, I felt one of his hands clamp firmly over my eyelids.

"Are you all right?" he asked.

"*Olivière. You could have died.*" The other voice was faded now, the strange glove and arm no longer in sight.

"Yes." I almost choked on another mouthful of water. *But I'll never really be all right again.*

"Keep them closed," said Jurij.

I nodded. I would never—not on purpose. Not even after we'd fought. I loved him.

Jurij decided to trust me. He lifted his hand from my face and helped me sit up, pounding on my back until I coughed up the last of the water that had tried to swallow me from the inside out. *The scent of wet leather. So sickening.*

I wiped my arm over my mouth to clean up the last of the

spittle. My eyes were clamped so tightly shut I was afraid I would never be able to open them again.

"I'm going to go get my mask," said Jurij quietly. "It's floating on the pool's surface a few paces from here. Keep your eyes closed." Jurij's voice seemed wary.

I wouldn't risk your life, Jurij. Not like Elfriede would.

I heard him enter the water. Jurij was a natural swimmer, which I knew well from the times he and the other boys went swimming in the pond near the livestock fields, and this pool was even smaller in size. It was only complete idiots like me who could turn the thing into a death trap.

"You can open your eyes now."

I tentatively opened first one eye and then the other. Jurij stood above me in his man mask, looking wet, otherworldly, and beautiful in the deep purple glow. I embraced him, squeezing him more tightly than I thought possible, and he wrapped me in his arms, tapping my back lightly before pulling away.

I let the moment go.

I faced the source of candlelight. The candlestick was perched on a rock, with no one at all around it. "Where's the other man?"

"What other man?" asked Jurij.

"The other man." I turned my head this way and that, searching desperately for the stranger. "The pale one. Wearing leather."

Jurij squeezed my shoulder. "It's just you and me here."

"But—"

Jurij heaved a weary sigh. I supposed he'd had enough of dealing with me and my delusions, on what was the *greatest day of his life.* "Noll. We're both wet. It's cold. We need to get ready. It was already late when I came in here." He stood and walked over to the candlestick, picking it up and starting back down the way we came.

I stood, but I hesitated. The candlelight was shrinking before me. I looked once more at the pool. The violet glow still illuminated the surface of the water, although it was subdued and fading. Amongst the stalactites, the ceiling seemed to sparkle, like violet stars in the blue moonlight.

"Noll?" Jurij's voice echoed off the ceiling, almost like he was stuck there somewhere above me. "Are you coming?"

I shook my head to clear it of all its fantasies. There were no stars masquerading as violet lights in the ceiling. There were no laughing children deep in the cavern. No pale man calling me by my full name.

And no true love at all in the heart of the man I loved most.

≥ Chapter Five ≤

In the Great Hall, all was quiet.
The two figures that drew everyone's attention held hands and stared into each other's eyes—or in Jurij's case, the black holes in his mask. Over his features was the Returning mask, only it wasn't wet and sopping, so I guessed perhaps he borrowed his father's. Not that his father had yet had a chance to use it himself, but he kept it on hand "just in case" the impossible suddenly happened. Jurij's new attire, red and bright and stunning, was a tad too large for him, so I guessed that was borrowed, too.

I could feel Mistress Tailor's gaze boring into me from the seat on the other side of Luuk. Father might have done the same from my other side—I was, after all, barely dried and still wearing a damp, torn, and grass-stained mud-and-vomit dress—but his eyes were forward, locked on the woman at the center of the stage behind the coupling, as if she were the only thing that mattered.

Mother stood behind Jurij and Elfriede, a black leather book in her hands. It was the book of the lord's blessing, the one kept at the Great Hall in a dark corner, layers of dust upon its sour pages, only touched when it was time for a woman to show to all that she was truly in love. *So come on, Elfriede. Prove that you're in love.* How was it possible to want and not want something all at once?

Mother smiled and stared out at the gathered crowd, waiting for the right moment.

Although there was a pit of worry buried deep in my stomach, I was almost falling asleep out of sheer exhaustion. It felt nice, having that land of dreams almost within reach. I hoped I would wake up and forget the day had ever happened.

Mother cleared her throat and held the book open, a bit of dust escaping from its crinkling yellow pages. The mother of the goddess didn't officiate her daughter's wedding. That occasion was less momentous and could be handled by some figurehead in the village. But at her daughter's Returning, the mother stood in ceremony, ready to do as her mother did for her and her mother's mother before her.

"*In a dismal time, long ago, in our village enshrined in endless mountains gray and white, love was sparse, love was rare.*" Mother licked her fingertip and turned the page. What she saw there made her smile and glance at Elfriede, who looked away from Jurij in order to grin back at her. "*A mother's devotion to her child, a sister's loyalty to her siblings, might have been all one knew of love, of warmth and passion.*"

I swallowed at the mention of a sister's loyalty, my mind lost in a mixture of guilt and revulsion. Without realizing, I'd clutched the skirt of my dress until my knuckles grew pale.

After a moment more of droning, Mother's voice grew louder, snapping me back to attention. "*But then the first goddess came down to touch the ground, from peaks unreachable, from nothingness beyond the endless mountains.*

"*My children, I have heard your screams, seen your tears. You stirred my heart at the first cry, and so I leaped from the mountains and fell for ages, watching you suffer for years on end. At last my feet have touched the ground. You are no longer alone.*"

No longer alone. How wrong those words were. I couldn't focus on what other drivel Mother spouted from the lord's "blessing." The pain in my chest was too great.

Luckily, I was distracted by Mistress Tailor's sudden loud breathing, so deep I thought she must be snoring. Beside her, Master Tailor reached out a hand to touch her shoulder, and she shrugged it away.

Mother's voice grew stern. *"The goddess's words gave the women more than hope. She spoke and the women became goddesses themselves, goddesses with power to lock out the darkness. To keep it where it was deserved: across the faces of men."* I looked to Jurij, keeper of the darkness, but whatever he thought of this part of the story, his mask kept it from me.

Mother looked up from the book, the words seeming to come from her instead of the old and dusty pages. *"We mask our boys and men. Deserving of the love of mothers and sisters and aunts and cousins they may be, and to them they may show their faces. But to prove themselves truly worthy of love and of the first goddess's blessing, they must find the goddess in a woman of no blood relation when they grow from boy to man. They must treat her kindly, regard her with reverence, and win her affection. Should the goddess in turn love the man when she is at least seventeen years of age, she may Return her feelings to him and reveal his face to the light. From that day forward, he is free to walk unmasked, having proved himself worthy of love, never again to fear the power of a woman's gaze, no matter what the years may bring."*

Mother's eyes wandered back to the book, and she turned a page gently. *"Every goddess shall have her due. Every woman shall get her man. So spoke the goddess, and so it shall always be."*

With that, Mother shut the book. *Every woman?* That was proof enough that the first goddess wasn't as all-powerful as they claimed. *But Ingrith mentioned that line …*

My thoughts were racing, foolishly distracting me from the danger. Jurij let go of Elfriede's hand and ripped off his ceremonial Returning mask.

He's going to die!

And Elfriede's smile grew wider. She closed her eyes, leaned forward, and the two shared their first kiss, forever sealing their union.

She loves him. That can't be true! It can't be!

My mind was screaming at me. I wanted to run up and fling him back from her, guarding his face from her eyes, from the eyes of all of the women around me.

Mother put the book down on the table behind her and grasped both Elfriede's and Jurij's hands in her own, raising them high above her head. "The goddess has judged Jurij, her man, worthy of love!"

The crowd exploded. Shrieks and cries echoed throughout the space, hurting my ears.

Unmasked men and women melted into each other's embrace. Father jumped up and ran toward Mother, his arms outstretched. "Aubree!" called Father, devotion pouring into both syllables of Mother's name, over and over between kisses. I looked away. I bit my lip, willing myself not to cry.

As Luuk stood from the chair next to me to join the celebration, I squeezed his hand tightly. His puppy face met mine and he sat back down beside his owl-masked father and his sour-faced mother. But only a moment had passed when he stiffened. Summoning strength I didn't know he had, he ripped his hand free from mine, walked across to the room to the end of the row, and hugged a girl seated between her parents. *Nissa.* She was grinning as she hugged him back.

Mother unhooked herself from Father's embrace and laughed, pointing at Luuk and Nissa. "Look, everyone!" she shouted. "The Returned's brother has found his goddess!"

Laughter. Clapping. My hands clasped feebly together. *Another one. Another coupling. All because of the first goddess. All because of a woman who appeared out of nowhere, barking out orders and vanishing from sight. All because of the lord and his goddess's blessing.* My awful attempt at clapping ceased, my body flushed with rage.

There were two others who didn't bother to laugh with joy

at the little boy who'd found his goddess. At last, I saw that stunning face I'd never seen before as it pulled away from Elfriede with great effort, its flame-filled eyes still mesmerized by her features.

Chapter Six

"Half the village is here," observed Master Tailor. "How wonderful." Everything was "wonderful, wonderful" with that man. Must be great to live in a rosy, wonderful version of your awful life. *If only I could. But I'm a woman, with a woman's mind.*

After the Returning, everyone had filed up to the Returned to smile and pretend like they cared for the happiness of a man and goddess not their own. That left the families of the goddess and her man off to the side, waiting for the ceremony to be over. I stood as far away from Jurij and Elfriede as I could without leaving the area. But next to Master Tailor stood Luuk and Nissa, their hands clasped, and every so often, I heard them giggling. There was no escaping it.

"Do you remember Elweard and Vena's Returning? What, fifteen, twenty years ago?" asked Mother. She cradled a cup of wine in her hand. She'd offered me some, but I said no thanks. Wine, like the terrible laws of the village, made me nauseous. "The whole village was there."

Father had one arm around Mother's shoulder and the

other stuck firmly across the front of her waist. "That one was a long time coming."

Master Tailor had neither food nor drink nor a wife who loved him to occupy his hands. No surprise. He couldn't eat with the mask on with all of the unrelated women about. But he could talk. "Didn't they marry before the Returning?" Mistress Tailor looked up between bites of the roll she was stuffing into her mouth.

"I believe they got wed *seven years* before the Returning." Alvilda, Master Tailor's sister, gulped down most of the contents in her cup, which I suspected to have some pretty strong liquor. She sloshed the little remaining. "Vena was nine-and-twenty when she Returned Elweard's love."

Luuk's puppy face actually tore away from Nissa, and he made a little choking noise. I wondered if he was gasping behind his mask. "So it's not too late for you, Papa!"

Master Tailor laughed. "Your mother's a bit older than nine-and-twenty, sweetheart."

Mistress Tailor, her jaw clenched, knocked against him as she made her way back to the buffet table.

My gaze followed her, even as Mother jumped to pick up the conversation with Master Tailor with some unimportant comment about the Great Hall's decorations. Mistress Tailor grabbed another roll and watched the crowd, her gaze resting on first one coupling, then the next. Although she was the mother of the Returned, although her other son had just found his goddess, no one spoke to her.

Alvilda was also watching. She nudged me with her elbow and lifted a finger off of her cup in Mistress Tailor's direction. "They shame her. Even more than they shame me."

"Is it really so bad not to Return love to your husband?" *At least* she *didn't risk killing him before she was sure.*

"Of course." Alvilda still hadn't finished the drink. She seemed fixated on creating little waves of turmoil within her cup. "It's expected for you to Return love to your husband. If you can't, you're supposed to be honest about it and refuse him."

"Dooming him to the commune? Isn't it worse for a man to live like he's dea—" I realized who I was talking to and clamped my mouth shut.

Alvilda laughed, and not out of mirth. There was something a little awkward about the way she spoke, and I wondered if she'd drunk too much. She wasn't normally the type who did. "I know, I know. I sent a man there." I noticed she didn't refer to him as *her* man. She sloshed her cup again. "Better that than being constantly reminded of my failure to love him."

"Then why do some women marry their men, if they don't love them?"

"Who knows?" Alvilda leaned her head back and poured the last of the drink down her throat. She looked around for a place to toss the cup and dropped it on the edge of a nearby pillar. "Maybe they just want children? No other man but theirs will help them with that. Maybe they feel guilty about dooming a man to the commune?" She squinted at Mistress Tailor picking up a cup and filling it from a flask of wine. "Or maybe … maybe they truly hope they'll love them someday, even though deep down they know it's just a lie they tell themselves?" She patted me on the back. "Well, take care, Noll." She gave one last pat on my shoulder. "I think I'm done celebrating for the day."

I glimpsed Jurij with his arm around Elfriede as they hugged yet another couple of almost strangers from the village who had come for the free wine and food. I was done celebrating for a lifetime.

As Alvilda hugged her brother goodbye and rubbed a hand in Luuk's mop of dark curls, Mother whispered something in Father's ear and the two broke apart, Father's face clearly full of the reluctance in his heart. He moved across the room to Jurij and Elfriede, and Mother came to visit me, sticking an arm through mine. She fanned a hand over her chest. "It's hot in here. I thought we might take a walk."

You mean perhaps I should explain to you in private what I'm doing here in a damp, torn, dirty dress. We made our way through the crowd, Mother smiling and nodding at the few who looked away from their beloveds long enough to offer congratulations. When we broke free of the Great Hall door, I saw that night had already fallen. It was quiet in the village center. For once.

"Is there anything you want to tell me?" asked Mother.

Do you want to know why I'm a mess on the outside or on the inside? I clenched my jaw, looking forward. We walked westward, a wise move for a pair of women who might want to scan the horizon from time to time.

"You know, your father wasn't the first man I loved."

That made me look at her. "I doubt that!" I wondered if I should point out that their mouths were practically sewn together most of the waking day. And the sleeping night.

Mother grinned. "No, it's true." The edges of her mouth drooped somewhat. "Of course, it was a doomed love. One man for every woman."

"Or no men for one woman."

Mother rubbed her shoulder into mine and tilted her head. "Come now, Noll, you know what I think about that."

I shrugged. "It's all right. I don't mind, I was just ... " *Being angry.* "So. Tell me about this man of yours."

"He wasn't *my* man." She, of course, took what I said literally. "He was Alvilda's."

Oh. "But that means—"

Mother tipped her head forward a bit. Her fingers dug into my skin. "He's there."

By *there*, she didn't mean any of the rows of houses along the path we were walking, nor the fields of crops that went on for leagues until stopped by the western mountains. Certainly not Alvilda's home at the western edge of the village, where she peddled her woodcarvings as Father's only competitor.

No, between the fields and Alvilda's lay a small outcropping of dilapidated shacks. Their roofs had holes in them. Their flooring, I was told, was just dirt and rocks and filth. Each shack looked likely to topple over. It was lucky for the men who lived there that no woman bothered spending much time nearby because if one happened to look up to the castle in the east, surely the entire commune would fall over.

"That's sad. Still, if Alvilda didn't love him … " I knew I'd feel guilty in her place, but there was no avoiding it. "I mean, it doesn't seem fair that we can't love who we want to."

Mother kept the slow pace toward the west, silent for a while. Then she opened her mouth, her lips almost trembling. "Women are not forced by nature to love. When we love, we do so of our own will. Men have no choice. But we have three: love at once, learn to love, or never love at all."

"You forgot one. Love a man who will never love you."

Mother squeezed my arm closer to her bosom. "That's so poor a choice I wouldn't wish it on anyone."

We didn't speak for a moment more. At last, I moved my tongue. "But if it does happen?"

Mother stopped. "Then you do the best you can to forget him."

You don't know how I feel. You couldn't have loved that man like I love Jurij. I strained to read her light-brown eyes. In the dying light, I thought I saw the glisten of a forgotten choice. "Do you still love him?"

Mother let go of my arms and fanned a hand at me. "Don't be ridiculous. I was a child. That was long ago. Before your father found the goddess in me."

I sighed. Of course. There couldn't be anything to tarnish the sweet love between my parents. "So what was it about Father? The way he was bound to follow your every order?" *Useful for commanding a man to be a lonely loveless girl's friend, that.*

"*Noll.*" Mother shook her head, but there was a smile on her face. "To tell the truth, that part is sort of … disconcerting. Especially if you forget that anything you say that could possibly be construed as your direct command he does immediately. Even if you were joking."

"Do the commands and obeying really die down after the Returning like they say?" I snorted, thinking of this morning with Father. "It doesn't seem that way." *Great. Jurij is going to keep pretending to be my friend, even though I could never live down what happened in the cavern.*

"That takes a bit of the pressure off. If it doesn't appear that way to you, well, that's just the man acting out of love. But don't confuse it with pre-Returning commands. Those are absolute."

I thought of the little scene in the Great Hall. "I'm sure women like Mistress Tailor find that a benefit of not yet Returning their husbands' affections."

Mother rolled her eyes. "Yes, well, women like Siofra take advantage of it if you ask me. Maybe some little revenge for the poor men who had no choice but to love them in the first place."

"Is that why women whose husbands are still masked seem to get more scorn than the women who send their men to the commune?"

"Well, at the very least, those women are honest with themselves. And by choosing to devote themselves to a profession or hobby, they have value in the community. Still, I wouldn't wish any woman to be in either position."

I forced myself to smile. "How lucky for you that it all worked out."

Mother paused before speaking. "Yes."

We stopped. We'd reached the western edge of the village. If we were going to go for a walk in the fields, we'd have to pass through the commune first. The stench was off-putting.

A man in a faded, cracked mask stumbled from one edge of the commune to the other. I couldn't tell what animal his face had once resembled. I figured he wouldn't remember, either.

He stopped and slumped over next to a basket. Dirt went flying as his rear hit the ground. The basket was full of bread and veggies, all of which were rotting. What didn't make it for mulch for the fields got dumped to feed the men in the commune. *At least the lord doesn't seem to care if these unloved men are not invited. Not that they'd go.*

The man's hand fumbled into the basket. He stuck the bread up beneath his mask, and I saw the mask bobbing. Between slow, slow bites of bread, he mumbled something, over and over and over.

"What's he saying?"

"The name of his goddess." Mother's lips puckered. I wondered if the name was Alvilda, or if seeing any man in this state would give her the same reaction. "Let's go." She pulled us away in the opposite direction. Her gaze immediately sank to the dirt path and the footsteps we'd left behind. Mine did the same.

"So what happens if a woman stops loving her man? I mean after she's already Returned to him?" *What happens if Elfriede wakes up tomorrow, her wonderful Returning day behind her, and gets bored with Jurij?*

Mother shook her head. The smile on her face seemed strained. "You ask every possible question, Noll."

"I just wondered if it's ever happened before."

Mother tilted her head one way and then the next. "He's safe once the Returning takes place. No woman's eyes can ever hurt him." She pressed her shoulder into mine. "Didn't you hear the lord's blessing? He proves his worthiness to his goddess, and his reward is a safe life thereafter, no matter how the goddess's feelings change."

It seemed strange to me. "But how do we know for sure? A man has no choice but to love, but a woman's heart … " *A woman's heart could love one day and hate the next. Couldn't it? Could I hate Jurij? Even after what he told me …*

"*I* know." Mother chewed the inside of her cheek. "That is, we know. We know the men stay safe after a Returning. It's happened before." She patted the back of my hand. "Not that there's anything for that woman to do, but to accept the man she's deemed worthy by then. No one else will ever love her anyway."

Something seemed off about what she said. Maybe I was supposed to be worrying about her and Father. *As if I didn't have enough to worry about.*

We stopped to let a cart pass onto the dirt road in front of us. I lifted my head up as much as I dared and saw the door to the bakery shut, a cart full of heaping hot loaves and sweet buns, and a man in a mask in front of us. "Darwyn?" I ventured a guess. The baker had many sons, but this one was of a height with Jurij.

He stopped pulling and turned. I couldn't look up at his mask, though; he was too tall, and the castle was off in the distance behind him. "Miss, Ma'am," he said, lifting up his cart handles and pulling his cart forward.

"Miss?" I muttered. "We were friends for twelve years, you—"

Mother stopped me. "You know they forget things like that once they find goddesses. What you and Jurij have is quite unusual."

What Jurij and I have was only at the command of his goddess. I wondered if in a few months we'd all be attending Darwyn's wonderful Returning. Roslyn would soon be old enough, and they seemed as in love as every other coupling in the village. In fact, I overheard one of Elfriede's sappy friends whisper that the two of them had even experimented a bit in the darkness. Guess the lips of one he used to find so girly and repulsive just couldn't be waited for.

"Where's he going?" I asked. The Returning ceremony was surely almost over, and I knew we hadn't ordered *that* much bread. There was enough to feed a hundred more guests at least.

"To the castle," replied Mother.

A cart or two passed by our house on the way to the path through the woods almost every day. Goods the lord ordered to feed him and his servants. The deliveries would keep the lord appeased, so he'd never have to venture out to see us himself. They'd continually make sure this village had the first goddess's blessing.

"Have you ever seen him?"

Mother laughed. "No woman is allowed to look at the castle, much less set foot in it. Why would I have seen him?" We didn't say anything for a moment more, listening to the wheels turning on the cart a short distance in front of us. "I heard you were with Ingrith right before she died today."

That was rather blunt. I stopped walking, pulling on

Mother's arm to make her stop as well. "She was acting crazy, Mother. Even worse than usual." Did she suspect I'd witnessed it? "She … she scared me."

"I'm sorry I sent you alone." Mother took both of my hands in hers. "We were just all so busy." She looked up and down at my wreck of a dress. "I figured there might be some explanation for how your dress got to be so tattered. Did you fall into one of the ponds during the earthquake?"

Close enough. "Yeah. I didn't have time to change." Best to shift the focus elsewhere. "Mother, Ingrith called the lord a heartless monster."

Mother's lips puckered. "That's a rather rude way to address our benefactor, but I've heard the term before." She put her arm back through mine and gently tugged me forward.

"Who calls him that? And what does it mean?"

Mother shook her head. "No one who's properly grateful calls him that. And it doesn't mean anything. Not what you're expecting. Do you remember me telling you about kings and queens?"

The little elf queen. That's what I called myself. But kings and queens were just mythical figures in stories Mother used to tell Elfriede and me. "Yes."

"They make for wild tales." She pinched my shoulder playfully. "The type that keep little girls lost in their own little fantasies. But they're not real. They're just what some person thought of, to fantasize about a world where women and men might have once been equal."

I wasn't sure where she was heading with this. "So the lord isn't real?"

Mother snorted. "Of course he's real. He watches over us, and he pays us well for our wares."

I nodded. "The men leave the supplies in the castle foyer and pick up the copper pieces left there." Jurij had even gone once when he was smaller, to leave a few new sets of jerkins and trousers entirely in black. Odd, since the servants wore only white. "So even the men haven't seen him before?"

"No, they haven't." Mother heaved a deep sigh. "And

when you don't lay your eyes upon something yourself, it's easy to make up stories, to fantasize about a man who doesn't die."

"What?" Forgetting myself, my gaze was a little higher up than it ought to have been. Darwyn and his cart were still ahead of us, heading through the eastern part of the village, but we'd arrived back at the center. I stopped and faced Mother. "The lord doesn't die?"

"Don't be silly." Mother smiled and started tugging me back toward the Great Hall, though it was hard for me to tear my eyes from the cart, even if it was off in the eastern direction. "The lord watches over the village from the shadows, but he must pass the job to his son when he's older, or maybe a child of one of the lord's servants. They're a secretive lot, never speaking, always just showing us the lord's requests on parchments—that's why we all learn to read. I refuse to believe that never finding your goddess makes you immortal. Every woman gets her man."

I couldn't believe what I was hearing. Did Mother even know of any women who'd been a lord's goddess? Who'd been a goddess of a specter? I never thought about it before. How were they going to have children without goddesses? Yet they were unmasked, so they must have had them at one point. When? "But does every man get his goddess?"

Mother stood in front of me, sliding her hands onto both of my shoulders. "I'm not sure I'm comfortable with all of these questions. The lord is good to us. He watches over us on behalf of the first goddess. His secrets are his own. There is but one thing we all know for certain: If a woman lays eyes upon the lord of the castle, the penalty is death."

Chapter Seven

I shivered. The night was young, but it was promising to be cold. And I was in a damp and tattered dress with no time to stop at home and change.

If Darwyn was making a late-night delivery, surely the lord would be awake and expecting his order. But would he be expecting me? Was he watching? Did he know? I'd fled the Great Hall almost as soon as Mother and I had arrived back, letting Father know I wanted to go home to change in case anyone missed me. He waved a hand and took his place at Mother's side without saying anything. I watched him go briefly, but my gaze soon fell on the face I ought to have known for ages, the face I'd never before seen. Jurij had the widest eyes that I had ever seen, almost perfectly spaced below the softest eyebrows and the longest eyelashes. His lips were curled into a smile that set off dimples in each of his cheeks. The cleft in his chin cried out for a finger's caress.

His beauty was more than I imagined, his face impossible to forget. But it was because of Elfriede's love that I was able to see him, and for that, the sight of his face made it so much harder. I tore my eyes from his beautiful features and turned to leave, quietly and unnoticed.

She needed only love him for today, and he's safe forever. That means he's free.

I shook my head to clear it. I'd been wrong about the Returning. But what would Jurij feel if he were actually free? I had a feeling that was something that only the goddess might be able to tell me. And since she was nowhere to be found, the lord was my only option. I trembled with expectation, with fear. *This is it. I have nowhere else to turn. I can't just go to bed and wake up, day after day, pretending my heart is still whole. I refuse to. The elf queen wouldn't.*

I was on the road home, out past the eastern edge of the village. I jogged a few steps and then walked briskly, jogging and brisk walking, whatever it took to get down the road quickly without drawing too much attention. Looking at the ground as I went made jogging decidedly more difficult.

I hesitated in front of the door to my house, then flung it open to check inside. I didn't have time to change, and I didn't care if the lord saw me in the ripped damp dress I was still wearing. It was my battle dress, a garment to show how hard I'd fought to make things right. Because if I was wrong and I wasn't able to free Jurij from this mess, it might be all I left behind.

I swallowed, but I was still determined. I couldn't yet face Jurij again after what had happened, after he sealed a pact with my sister. Not unless I had something to give him. Not unless his heart was finally set free. I grabbed a dirty apron Mother had hung off the back of one of the chairs and wrapped it around my shoulders, using one fist like a broach at my neck to hold it in place. Better than wasting time searching for a proper cloak.

I dashed off outside, not caring to properly close the door behind me. I jogged into the woods and heaved a great sigh of relief once I could look up safely again. It was then that I heard the turn of the cart, and I dived into the foliage. My heart just about jumped out of my throat when I glimpsed the wooden fox-face heading down the pathway in the western direction, the empty cart behind him. *So the delivery is done. It's time.* I waited for Darwyn to pass, not daring to move a muscle. Possibly not even breathing.

Once I heard the turn of the wheel fade away, I exhaled and jumped back onto the path. By then, the moon was so full that silver light poured from the sky and lit the way before me. Eventually the trees encroached upon the path so fully that I could no longer see the moon at all, but its silver light speckled through the leaves so softly I felt no reason to be afraid. I ventured on, pushing the occasional stray bough out of my way to go farther. And then the trees parted completely.

There were walls of dark stone as far as I could see. It took me a moment to realize that one layer of wall acted as a fence. Its gate swung open.

I braced myself. The ground shook.

Ancient, monstrously huge wooden doors beyond the outer wall parted slightly like I had seen Father's lips part when he longed for Mother's kiss. I stepped through, lifting one foot and then the other, willing myself to stay upright. A thin sliver of moonlight came with me and lit some of the way.

But even so, it was dark, darker than the cavern and the cloudiest of nights. I traced the shaking slit of moonlight with my feet as I continued to walk into the darkness, my gentle steps echoing like thunder in the empty space.

And then the shaking stopped. The door shut behind me.

"I've come to see the lord," I whispered, as loudly as I dared. Now that I was here, my courage faltered. There was no answer. My heart was racing. *What am I doing here? This is foolish, I still have time, I should go back—*

I thought I heard a trickle of water and paused. There was nothing but the stone floor and a pile of bread and buns at the door, and the more I stared at the moss-covered stones, the more apprehensive I felt. I closed my eyes, shutting out the only sliver of light, and listened for the noise. My hands out before me, I walked toward the soothing sound of the trickling water. I moved unheeded for some time until my hand brushed against a hard surface. Opening my eyes, I found another slit of moonlight pouring through another set of wooden doors.

Tentatively, I put one eye against the slit and saw a fountain surrounded by an empty space and then a circle of white rose bushes. The fountain resembled a little boy, his face unmasked, his arms and head raised towards the sky. In place of the eyes were two spouts of water that poured out and downward, sparkling deep blue in the moonlight.

I want to see his face. It was a stupid thought, considering what danger I had put myself in. But I was overcome by it. I tried to pull open the doors, but they moved only a hair's breadth even with all of my might. I threw my hands wildly over the doors to search for a better grip but found nothing amongst the rough surface of wood. Then I found the handle, but before I could grip it properly, my finger caressed a jagged sliver.

"Ow!" I sucked on my sore index finger and cursed a few times. It stung so much, I was tempted to rip it out with my teeth.

"Who goes there?"

The voice was haunting. Almost familiar.

I thrashed around to face it, but I couldn't see anything. The echo of gentle footsteps came toward me.

"A woman?" the voice remarked as it drew nearer. I could feel the air part to allow that smooth, tenor tone to reach me, and I shivered. *This was insane, he's going to report me, I'm going to die—*

The echoes paused, and the toe of a black boot settled on the edge of the arrow-shaped trail of silver light.

"What have we here?" It wasn't a threat, more like the indifferent curiosity I'd heard from Father when I was child, while he was tinkering with his latest woodcarving and I walked into the room carrying a slimy baby frog. It was a man, I knew, although the voice was nothing like Father's. It seemed younger, but older at the same time. Sweeter, but teetering on the edge of iciness.

"I … " The nipping air hurt my throat as I tried desperately to suck it in and clear out my mouth. The apron around my shoulders fell lightly from my fingers—a small breeze slid through the crack in the door behind me, and the cloth glided through the air. It settled in the trail of moonlight in front of me, just brushing the man's boot as it landed. "I'm looking for the lord."

The man laughed, whether joyfully or angrily, I wasn't sure. "You're shivering."

A black leather-gloved hand reached out into the silver arrow of light where I stood and grabbed my apron from the floor. I caught a glimpse of a lock of dark hair as he bent to retrieve it, but he retreated quickly into the shadows before I could make out more. Another gloved hand emerged beside the one clutching my apron and motioned for me to draw nearer.

"Come here," he said. "Do not be afraid."

My mind froze. A man in the castle. A man not all in white. Who could it be, but the lord? But if it were him, I'd be dead if the rumors were true. And yet here I was, and he didn't chastise me for my trespass.

"I, uh—" I started. Did the laws of the first goddess apply to the one who watched over the village for her? I looked away. "Do you need me to close my eyes?"

"Oh," he exclaimed. He pulled his hands back into the darkness with a start.

"Yes," he said. And, as an afterthought, "Thank you." I thought I heard him swallow uncomfortably in the silence that followed.

Good. Maybe he'll think favorably of me. Maybe he won't— I shut my eyes tightly. My quest seemed suddenly immensely stupid. *The penalty is death.*

Unlike with Jurij after the swim in the cave, there was no hesitation on this man's part. The moment my eyelids clamped shut, his boots echoed as he drew closer. I felt his presence overhead as he wrapped the apron back around my shoulders.

"Hmm," he said, perhaps lost in thought. "An apron for a cloak."

His breath glanced across the top of my head as he spoke.

It ought to have been warm, but it was cool and refreshing somehow, even though I shivered from head to foot. I heard rustling and then felt a gust of cold air. I jumped a little as a heavy leather jacket came down atop the apron over my shoulders. Although the material was cold to the touch, warmth instantly flooded my body. "Do you feel warmer?"

"Yes, thank you."

The man began tying what I assumed was a cord of some kind around my right shoulder. I shifted uncomfortably from one foot to the next, as I had often seen Jurij do when he was around Elfriede and her attention was drawn elsewhere. I could feel the jacket slip a little as he let go, but it held in place, leaving only the area near my neck uncovered. "I need to speak with the lord of the village. It's … it's urgent."

The man scoffed. "I can tell. You seem to have rolled out of a muddy pond and caught your dress on a hundred branches. Perhaps you also bumped into a fair maiden, making off with her apron."

I forced myself to smile. "Not far off. But the mud is just the color of the dress."

"Of course. It suits you."

"Thanks." It might not have been a compliment, but I couldn't possibly care less what his opinions were of my appearance at that moment, not when he held my life in his hands. My fingers poked around inside the too long arms of the jacket and gripped the soft seams nervously. "I have a request. Of the first goddess."

"Does not everyone? If only she could hear the voices calling her." He paused, his voice wavering. "Some more desperate than others." I jumped as leather brushed against my hand. He pulled on my sleeves and rolled them up so that my hands were free. He grabbed my palm and turned it over to separate my splintered finger from the rest. In my nervousness, I'd forgotten the slight pain that ebbed now from the tip of my finger.

"Can't you speak with her then?"

"You are injured," he said as if I hadn't spoken. My heart

sank. What was I doing? I had a sinking feeling I was chasing a mythological woman, no more real than my queen and monsters.

The tips of a glove ran smoothly across my finger and reminded me of the delicate softness of bird down. When I'd played with my friends by the livestock, we'd often tickled one another with the down left behind by farmers' chickens, but this elicited so much more aching and none of the giggles. And there was something more, a warmth mixed in with the chill of the leather. *Leather*. Leather, like in the cavern pool.

I tried to pull my hand away, but his grip tightened and my palm was locked firmly in his grasp.

"It's fine, thank you," I said, a little more sternly than I'd intended.

He let my hand free. I stumbled, a bit off balance, and he steadied me at the shoulders.

"Let me get a needle," he said, "and I can remove the splinter for you."

"You needn't trouble yourself."

"It is no trouble at all, I assure you."

"I'm sure I can get it myself later, thank you." I cradled the finger protectively against my shoulder, lest he try to wrest it from me again.

"But you would not forbid me from treating it?" His voice seemed odd. Tentative.

"Uh, no," I mumbled. I didn't know whether or not giving in would end the embarrassment sooner.

"Wait here a moment."

The echoes of his footsteps reached my ears, and he was gone. I stood, wondering if it would be more foolish to stay or to go. *You came here for a reason. But you're risking your life! What is life without Jurij?* The dilemma was meaningless, as I hadn't made even a blind step forward when I heard his echoing footsteps again. A bottle clanged against the floor in front of me.

"I brought some ale to numb the area and bandages with which to wrap it."

I laughed before I could stop myself. "It's just a splinter."

He made a sound that I thought to be laughter as well, although it echoed throughout the chamber in a tone both sweet and melancholy. "Yes, well, I will do all I can to help you." The leather feathers cradled my injured hand that still rested atop my shoulder. "May I?" he asked. His speech was warmer and more confident.

"All right." It was my turn to speak tentatively.

He took my hand in his and pulled on it a little as he bent down to retrieve the bottle of ale. The cool liquid didn't sting as it should have and reminded me of nothing more than water. A rustle of leather and the hand touching mine became as cold as ice, as smooth as marble. He'd removed one of his gloves and now the icy fingertips grew warm. Somehow, I felt both comforted and violated. The pain from the splinter vanished.

"What is your request?" he asked as he began poking my fingertip with the needle. My heart soared a little at the idea that he might be able to ask the goddess to help me after all, that she might actually be out there somewhere, watching. My finger throbbed, but I felt that it should have hurt more than it did, that he was taking great pains to minimize my soreness. The needle pricked just a little harder than previously. I squeaked a little in shock.

"Did I hurt you?" The man's hand stiffened.

"Uh, no," I responded. *Better to finish this sooner rather than later.* Heat rose on my cheeks. "No more than anyone could help."

The man's grip loosened slightly. "But I should do better than anyone else."

My muscles weakened from being held aloft for so long, but I gritted my teeth and refused to let my limb waver. *Speak your mind, Noll. Tell him why you've come.* Now that the opportunity had presented itself, I couldn't make myself voice the foolish thoughts inside of me. The man went back to work, prodding the needle into my skin even more gently than before. At rare moments, the needle or the splinter made my finger ache considerably more, but I bit the inside of my bottom lip and made no more sudden movements.

"You must need something very important," said the man after a bit of silence. "You are aware of the penalty for a woman setting foot in the castle?" The man gave one final thrust with the needle. "I have it!"

This is it. I flinched. The splinter gone, I hoped I'd be free to pull my hand back, but the man gripped harder. "Wait a moment," he said. Then he added, "Please."

What choice did I have? I wasn't about to win a bout of strength against him. I relaxed my pull. "I ... " I straightened my shoulders, doing my best to act the queen. "I was willing to risk death."

"Were you?" The trickle of the stingless ale fell over my fingertip again, and what followed was a gentle patting with what felt like cloth. Then the iciness of his fingers burned warmly again, and I felt no trace of pain. "That seems foolish. To risk such a treasure."

My face flushed, and I was almost glad that my eyes were closed so I could imagine he didn't notice. I felt exposed and vulnerable.

"I came to free my friend from the curse that binds him to a woman."

He laughed. The sound made me go cold. "Who has the power to do that?"

I bit my lip, but I couldn't give up now. "Who else would, but the first goddess?"

"And why would she ever break her own law?"

My lip trembled. My voice, when I could finally speak, was nothing but a hoarse whisper. "Is there nothing to be done?"

"Nothing." His voice was sharp, and I couldn't tell if it was my question or the answer to that question that had offended him. He sighed and let the sternness pass. "How strange of you to have a friend bound to a woman."

"He ... " The admission caught in my throat. "She commanded him to remain my friend. Accidentally."

"In women there lies a careless sort of power." He patted my hand gently. "Why do you fear for him? Does she intend to send him to the commune?"

"No, it's not that. In fact, he's—" I stopped. I felt coddled and spoken down to, and my fear of punishment was overriding my desire for the impossible. "Never mind. I was foolish to think—" I wanted my hand free, with every bit of my desire. I felt strange, locked in this man's grasp, blind to what was going on before me. His fingers loosened, and I was finally able to pull my hand back.

His voice grew quiet. "You love this ... friend?" He took such a sharp intake of breath I thought something must have hurt him. My blood went cold.

"Yes." I had said the words in haste and anger to Jurij in the cavern and spoken them in my heart a multitude of times before. But never had I admitted it to anyone else, and none but my mother knew to ask. And she at least had the pity not to.

My hand was enclosed in the gentle leather grip once more, and I let him take it, my muscles growing limp. Marble, as chilled as snow and as smooth and plush as satin, pushed gently against the back of my hand. I heard a light smacking noise upon its release, not unlike the noises Mother and Father made every time they met. *A kiss?*

"So you know," whispered the hollow voice. "Perhaps you understand now. Men have no choice but to love, for that is their curse. Women are free to love, for what good it does. You need not fear death here." He pulled me close to him, his body pressed against mine. I felt strange, revolted, but at the same time, an unbidden sense of exhilaration spread from my head to my toes. His hand stroked the back of my head, and I felt patches of his cold, thin arms sweep across my cheek. My other cheek brushed against the silken fabric covering his shoulder.

"That decree was my own doing, and I am delighted to at last be free from the order. For what would become of me had you not ventured here, against all counsel? What is your name?" he asked.

"Noll," I whispered. My lips froze as they brushed against

the icy surface of his ear.

His hand stopped stroking my head and balled into a fist around some of my hair. It hurt a bit, but I couldn't express my alarm. My voice choked at the realization of what was happening.

"Olivière," his voice croaked through the darkness. Somehow he knew my full name, the girly name I couldn't stand to hear spoken. *Like the vision in the cavern.*

"Oh, Olivière," he spoke again, his voice trembling. He let go of my hair and wrapped both arms so tightly around me, I thought he must have worried that I would float away.

And then I knew he would never again let me go.

Chapter Eight

He let me go home that night, but I could never truly be my own again, never truly be out of his embrace. Four months had passed since the lord of the village had found the goddess in me. I was only half a year away from turning seventeen.

And Mother was dying.

Before my thoughts were consumed with Mother's illness, I found myself bitterly thinking like Ingrith said she once did, hoping at the very least that the news of my foolish trespass might spark some jealousy in Elfriede—what was a scrawny, puppy-face boy compared to the lord of the village?—or some kind of regret in Jurij that I, too, had someone else to love me.

But I was lying to myself. A scrawny, puppy-face boy was everything. And Elfriede and Jurij were so dreadfully excited for me. It was the only time they bothered to spare me any thought as of late.

"Wasn't Mother right? We all knew your man would find you. And soon you can have your Returning and be as happy as me."

"Now you know the joys that exist between a man and his

goddess! Now you know real *love.*"

Their happiness was like the fangs of a monster, tearing into the defenseless flesh of the queen who'd foolishly set out to slay the beast, only to meet her own doom. I couldn't get used to the idea that I was somebody's goddess. Not just anybody's goddess, either. But it was so far from what I'd wanted I didn't know what to do. Not only was Jurij's curse unbroken, but I left the castle that night knowing my future. Knowing I had someone to Return to.

Because no one seemed to consider that I might not want to Return to him.

My only refuge was Alvilda's workshop, as far west from the castle as one could get, short of living in the commune.

Alvilda's trade had once been secondary to Father's, considering she took it up only after refusing her Returning. However, since my mother's illness, Father was less inclined to work than ever and only did so when Mother was conscious enough to remind him. Alvilda stepped right up to fill in the void, and she got most of the real work these days. At least Father was too far gone to care. In fact, he helped her from time to time. Or just gave her a tool he no longer felt he needed. Mostly because he no longer felt like working.

I knocked and let myself in at the usual call of "No masked men here, come in!" Master Tailor sometimes visited his sister, and he could take his mask off in front of her.

But she failed to warn me that an unmasked man was there.

"Noll! What brings you here?" Alvilda looked up from her work—an ornate bed headboard, I believed. The smile that flashed over her features was genuine, although she couldn't be torn from her work for long.

Jurij and Elfriede were seated at the small dining table, eating. The table was covered with a thin layer of sawdust that belied how often Alvilda really used the table for its intended purpose.

Elfriede laid the rest of her crispel on the table and wrinkled her nose. "Good day, Noll." At least I think that was what she said. Elfriede's gentle voice and Alvilda's tools running across the wood made for a bad combination. *If I care to hear what she has to say, anyway.* I shook my head. I was being awful. It wasn't so bad when we were home without Jurij and she could tell me how *happy* she was that "my man" had found the goddess in me. But whenever Jurij showed up, I felt like there was nothing but frost in the air between us.

I'd spent the morning in the garden, trying not to think about anything, to little avail. I saw Elfriede leaving with a basket, and I figured she was off to fetch her man. I didn't figure on encountering them here.

It's almost like she knows what you told Jurij. She probably did.

"Good day," I said at last. "Didn't know you were here."

"Gideon sent us on a quest," said Jurij as he shoved the rest of the cheese in his mouth.

Alvilda laughed as she ran her file back and forth against the large rough edge that remained on the future headboard. "Not one of those monster-hunting quests, is it?"

It was my turn to smile. "No, we haven't been on one of those in a while."

Elfriede spoke at the same time, and rather loudly. "I always thought those games were rather stupid."

I opened my mouth to point out that her "beloved" enjoyed those games she found rather stupid, but I thought better.

Jurij looked first at Elfriede and then at me. I was surprised he was able to tear his eyes off her for someone as unimportant as me. He stretched and stood from the table, strolling over to examine some of the pieces of wooden art that lined Alvilda's walls from one side to the next. Jurij pointed to one of the pieces. "Have you ever seen this one, Noll?"

He's talking to me. I watched Elfriede out of the corner of my eye as I came up behind him. She seemed bored, more concerned with straightening imagined wrinkles in her skirt. But then I stood on my toes and put a hand on his shoulder in order to get a closer look. Elfriede got up at once and made her way to stand beside me.

I pulled my hand back immediately. *He's just your friend.*

He's her *man. I thought you'd gotten used to that.* I focused on the carving. It showed a little girl smiling with a triumphant look on her face. She held a long tree branch—Elgar—high above her like it was the mightiest blade in the land. Beside her—but a little behind her, I took note—was a heroic-looking diminutive retainer wearing a kitten mask. I spun to face the artist. "Alvilda! Is that Jurij and me?"

She grinned. "It is indeed." She paused to wipe her brow with the back of her arm.

I laughed and exchanged a smile with Jurij, forgetting for just one moment that there was anyone else with us, that there was anything but happy feelings between us.

The chirping bird cleared her throat. "I've asked Auntie to do one of our Returning." *"Auntie."* Of course. *She'll be one of the family soon.*

My smile faded and I stepped back. Elfriede stepped in immediately to intertwine her arm with his. Jurij smiled peacefully and tilted his head so that Elfriede's golden curls caressed his cheek.

Alvilda appeared behind us, wiping sawdust from her hands with a rag that she carelessly tossed over the fireplace mantle once she finished. "I'm definitely looking forward to carving that." She focused her dark brown eyes on me, and I saw something in them that made me wonder just how much she meant her words. "But first, I'm a little busy with a special gift here."

She got between the coupling so she could grab Jurij by the shoulder and shake him playfully. The blush that covered Jurij's entire face said it all.

A bed headboard. An upcoming wedding. But Jurij wouldn't turn seventeen for a year. I forced myself to smile. "Are we thinking about wedding gifts already?"

Elfriede studied me a moment. She didn't seem to like what she found. "Headboards take a while, and Alvilda's too busy to spend all of her time on it." She smiled sweetly at me. "Of course, I know your Returning comes first, Noll. Just let me know what you'd like. I'm quite excited."

My Returning. A woman had the choice to send her man to the commune, but …

No one's ever been the goddess of the lord, not in my lifetime or my parents' lifetimes, either. It seemed to go without saying that I'd accept him.

Alvilda wiped her brow and slipped an arm around both Elfriede's and Jurij's shoulders as she stuck her head between them. She had a bit of sawdust in her hair. "Which tools did Gideon want now?"

I cocked my head. "Father wants to borrow tools?"

Alvilda nodded and stepped back. "More like he wants the tools I've borrowed back." She made her way to her toolbox and started picking through its contents.

"It's Mother, really." Elfriede hugged Jurij tighter. "She was doing a bit better this morning. She got mad that he'd given away so many of his tools when she was in and out over the past few days, and she asked that we get them back, so Father could start working again." Elfriede pinched her nose. "It'll make her happy."

But it won't make him work, she seemed poised to say. Alvilda laid out a number of tools on her workbench. "That seems a bit much to carry like that. You can borrow some baskets."

Elfriede walked to the cupboard and pulled out a basket like it was her home and she knew were everything was. She took out three and Jurij started filling them.

Alvilda crossed over to where Elfriede was standing. She smiled as she put one of the baskets back into the cupboard. "I think two baskets should be enough." Jurij finished loading the second basket as she spoke as if to prove her words true. "And I'd like to elicit Noll's opinion on that special gift I'm working on."

Beautiful. Now I'd be helping plan the décor resting over their wedding bed.

Elfriede's shoulders relaxed, and I suspected she was relieved not to have to fight for her man's attention on the trek back home. She stepped to the door without picking up either basket. "Thank you again for lunch, Auntie."

Alvilda nodded. "Sure thing. You're always welcome!"

Jurij slipped his arms around both baskets. I wondered if Elfriede knew that if she offered to carry one, he'd refuse, or if she didn't even bother to worry about him carrying all of that without assistance. Either way, he seemed delighted. "See you later!" he called, and then both were gone, Elfriede shutting the door behind them.

I turned back to the carving and sighed.

Alvilda left me to my thoughts for a few moments. I could hear her pick up the file and continue working. "I didn't really want to ask you about the headboard."

I jumped. Alvilda rested her file back on her workbench and grinned. "Come, now. Even I'm not that heartless."

Heartless. Ingrith had called the man who had found the goddess in me the heartless monster. I didn't know what it meant. I didn't understand anything about him, and I was so scared to find out more. So frightened to acknowledge that I had a big decision to make.

I snapped out of my daze just long enough to pull out one of the sawdust-covered chairs at the eating table. Alvilda followed suit.

"It's all right," I said, breaking a few tense moments of silence. I wanted to talk about everything. I wanted to ask her if there was a way to act as if I'd never gone to the castle. I wanted to ask her if it would be okay to delay the lord's courtship as much as possible, to pretend to be preparing my heart for the Returning day after day, year after year as I continued living as if nothing had changed.

But why is it different for me? Why do I have to Return at all? I'd rather live the rest of my own days in the commune.

Alvilda of all people should have been able to understand my feelings, but even she thought it a bad idea to reject the lord. "He's good to us. He pays the villagers well for their wares." But what did I care? If even Alvilda thought that I should sacrifice myself so the rest of the village could pocket a few more coppers, I couldn't betray any of my plan to delay the Returning. "Plus, he's—" Alvilda had dropped what she was going to say then, choosing to bite her lip instead. It was probably "always watching." The people in the village were worried he'd punish them for forgetting to invite someone to a Returning, so what would he do to them if his goddess refused to love him?

He's not always watching, though. He can't be. He's just a man.

So I couldn't ask any questions. Not questions that mattered anyway. Still, I figured it would be rude to pass up a rare invitation to get to know Alvilda better. She wasn't one for musings. "A waste of time, effort, and the brain our foremothers blessed you with," she often said.

"Why did you choose woodworking?" I asked. Maybe she'd mistake my intentions and tell me about the beauty of the craft; I could let it wash over me and retreat back to the emptiness in my heart.

"Well," said Alvilda softly. "Women have the right to choose what their hearts tell them. It's a gift from the first goddess."

My eyes welled again. "That's a lie! It's not a gift—and it's not even true!"

So much for sidestepping the issue.

Alvilda coughed. "It's not an easy gift, I know." She tapped her fingers over the table and looked thoughtful, a rarity on her features. "I know."

She let me cry a bit without saying anything more. I almost grabbed a rag with which to wipe my face, but I remembered the sawdust and spread my tears all over my sleeve instead. I no longer could stand to wear aprons.

Finally, I managed to compose myself. "Whatever it is, it's different for me." *I can't send the lord to the commune. I just can't. No one would let me.*

"I know, dear. I'm sorry."

What else was there to say?

Alvilda broke into the silence. "You know, I tried to love Jaron." So that was his name. Mother's first love. "I really did.

I certainly didn't dislike him."

I scoffed. I hadn't intended to be rude to Alvilda, especially as she opened herself up to me. But even though I felt Alvilda was the closest person I had to someone who might understand, it wasn't the same.

Alvilda didn't notice or at least didn't comment. "Whenever I let my thoughts wander, I feel so ill at the idea of what my choice has done to him I want to retch."

I met Alvilda's eyes. They were strong, dark brown like mine, but I detected a glisten in them. Unlike me, though, she held it in, her throat making a gurgling noise as she steeled herself to speak further.

"I thought about marrying him even without the Returning. So many had done it before." She looked upward at the art carvings behind me. "But I couldn't decide if his muted happiness at being near me would be worth the torment of my own soul in his stead."

I nodded. "And people didn't urge you to marry him anyway? Tell you how sometimes the Returning is delayed years and that there could be a chance you would both one day be happy?" The words were not my own, but the echoes of voice after voice and lecture after lecture.

Alvilda bit her lip and didn't look away from the wall behind me. "Yes, they did. But no, I would never, ever be happy."

My gaze followed Alvilda's. She saw me looking and tore away, but I saw the carving in which she had been engrossed. Her family. Luuk as a toddler in his bunny rabbit mask, his mother holding him in her arms with a sour look carved deep and permanently into her features. Master Tailor stood next to Mistress Tailor, one hand on Jurij the puppy dog who stood in front of him, his other arm tightly around Mistress Tailor's shoulder, his demeanor projecting a sense of joviality that his face could not. Because Master Tailor still wore a mask, his face obscured by that of an owl's.

Of course. Alvilda had witnessed her brother marry without the Returning. As his blood relation, she knew his face, but she chose to carve him with his missing features. Perhaps to guard his secret from the wandering female eye. Or perhaps to remind herself of what could have been, had she chosen to marry Jaron against her heart's desire.

"In any case," Alvilda said, her tone calm but still trembling, "I'm sorry for my foolish ramblings. I know that your circumstances simply don't compare to mine. The lord is—well, in any case, you don't want to go through what I did." Alvilda walked across the room, rummaged through her toolbox, and came back to the eating table.

"Here," she said, tossing a small chunk of wood and a chisel on the table. "It's the most I can do for you. You're going to learn woodcarving."

Chapter Nine

Woodcarving was the only thing I had, the only thing that
quieted my thoughts. When I worked, I was able to forget.
I first took a tool in my hand and turned a rough piece of wood
into a sphere. It wasn't much, but I controlled what the wood
would be. And no one told me I didn't really get to choose.

I'd grown better in the past few weeks. Elfriede thought
woodcarving was a wonderful idea—as a *hobby*, she
emphasized. And then on further introspection, as a hobby *for
now*, she would add. As if I could forget that I had so little
time before I was expected to perform a miracle. I already had
a miniature sculpture of Elfriede's new golden puppy, Arrow,
to present to her as a gift. It was only after I had finished that
my numbed mind remembered that Arrow himself had been an
early wedding gift from Jurij, and I probably shouldn't have
spent so much time carving his image into my mind before the
happy coupling and I went our separate ways.

Father had little to say about my talent, or the tools I
borrowed from him without asking. But I forgave him. I felt as
numb as he did these days.

Mother was only sometimes with us.

Father was behind the house on a tree stump, whittling what looked to be a bowl or a cup. Mother sat beneath the shade of a tree on the edge of the woods, her hand clasping a small piece of wood. Mother should have known that if she was near Father when he worked, she'd wind up distracting him. But lately she was loath to part from him at all.

"How are you feeling today?" I nestled into the grass and leaned against the tree beside her. I clutched little wooden Arrow in my hands to work on the finishing touches, although my model was off somewhere with Elfriede and Jurij.

It took a moment for Mother to acknowledge me. She turned her head slowly. There were dark circles beneath her eyes, a sallow tinge to the once-beautiful oaken shade of her skin. "Better," she lied.

I looked up to watch Father's reaction. He held the bowl and chisel in his hands as if he were still carving, but his hands were frozen.

"Your father's working," Mother said. "He's making beautiful things."

Father's hands moved again, slowly.

I took a closer look at the wooden figure in Mother's grasp. "What's that?"

Mother turned it over and lifted her arms weakly to bring it closer to me. "It's a lily. Isn't it beautiful?"

Seeing the hint of a smile on Mother's face made me genuinely happy. I gestured to the fields behind Father. "It's lovelier than all the ones around us." It was getting colder, and those blooms were dying.

Mother leaned her head against the tree bark and shut her eyes. A moment passed and she began to breathe deeply.

I shifted the wooden flower that was slipping from her grasp to the center of her lap. I laid her hands across it. She didn't stir.

"She's getting worse every day." Father continued to carve his bowl. His interest in me was usually so decidedly little it took me a moment to realize he was speaking to me.

"The others in the village are still sick." I pulled my legs to my chest and wrapped my arms around my knees. A merchant's wife. The butcher's daughter. Even little Nissa's mother. All struck ill, the same day as Mother. The day after I visited the castle.

But Father had little interest in the rest of those ill in the village. He threw the bowl and chisel down into the grass, cradling his forehead. "I don't know what to do."

I swallowed. I didn't know what to say.

Father looked up from his hands. "Will you ask the lord if he can help us?"

"The lord?" I'd tried my best not to think about that night. Even though I always failed. "What could he do?" My voice faltered.

As if in response to my question, I heard the sound of a wooden wheel and the clip-clop, clip-clop of horses' hooves on the dirt path. It could have been perfectly timed, but the same thing had happened every evening since the specters brought me home the night I met the lord.

The black horses and the carriage burst through the trees and halted in front of our home. A specter sat atop the carriage, his back stiff, his hands clutching the reins. Two specters stepped out of the carriage and stood in front of it, their hands clasped behind their backs, as still as if there was no breath within them.

Now, as always since that first night, I was drawn to their eyes, all of them red like blood on ice. As a child, the eyes had scared me a little. But then I noticed that there was no trace of flame there, and that too set them apart from other unmasked men. Somehow, this made the specters more sad than horrifying.

Father clasped his hands together and leaned his arms over his thighs. He tilted his head toward them. "Go with them. Ask."

I stood, quickly. "I can't." I couldn't. Going there in the first place had been a terrible mistake. But I couldn't possibly explain it to Father.

Mother's eyes fluttered open. She brushed a hand against the hem of my skirt. "Noll … "

"They're here again." I swallowed the sour taste in my throat. "The specters. His servants."

Father appeared beside Mother, kneeling beside her. "How are you feeling, darling?" He placed the back of his hand against her cheek. "Warm."

Mother laid a hand on Father's knee gently. "Gideon, I'm fine." She turned her head to look up at me. "Does he want you to visit him?"

"I … I think so." The specters appeared day after day at twilight. If I walked near the carriage, they gestured inside. I'd never once stepped foot in it since that first night it had brought me home.

"She should go visit him," said Father. "It's rude of her not to. He ought to be able to see her."

"Gideon, no." Mother cupped Father's cheek in her hand. "How many times have I told you? You can't rush these things. Let her be."

It was odd how I'd finally gotten a man of my own as she wanted, and here she was, the only one to counsel patience. I ran the chisel over Arrow's wooden rump too hard, nicking it. Tossing the figure and the chisel down on the ground in frustration, I sighed and cradled my knees against my chest.

"Aubree—"

Mother put her finger over Father's mouth to stop him. "Go tell them she's not coming today."

He may not have been compelled to follow her orders, but he did anyway. I poked my head out from my knees. "Thank you."

Mother pulled one of my hands away from my knees to squeeze it. She cradled her wooden lily with her other fingers. "I just want you to be happy. I need to know you're happy."

Would I ever be happy again? "Don't." I squeezed her back and did my best to smile. "Don't talk like that."

Mother pulled her hand out of mine and placed it over her wooden flower. We sat quietly for a moment. The specters crawled back into the carriage, never once opening their mouths to respond to Father. The driver flicked his wrists, and the horses turned around by crossing the grass. They'd done that so often over the past few months, the lilies were crushed and broken in that small patch of grass in front of our home.

"Noll," said Mother, her voice quiet. She coughed a few times. "Let love find you."

"It did." I clutched my knees even tighter. "And I don't want it." *Not from anyone but Jurij.*

Mother patted the flower in her lap. "I won't rush you. It's not fair that it took so long for love to find you. You haven't had enough of a chance to get used to it."

"You mean like Elfriede got used to Jurij?" *Until she tires of him. If she hasn't already.*

Mother nodded weakly. "You were right, you know. She used to be so cold to him. One day, she stood inside the house, helping me wipe the dishes. She looked out the window in the kitchen, at you two running off to play beyond the hills. When she saw you whap him across the side with your tree branch—"

"Elgar."

Mother smiled. "Right. She asked me, 'What if I never Return Jurij's love? What if he's doomed to walk around with his face hidden forever? What if I send him to the commune?'"

So I was right. She only forced herself to fall in love so she wouldn't feel guilty.

With a grunt, Mother placed her wooden flower in my lap. "I told her that love, even when you didn't expect to find it, can prove a beautiful thing."

And what of the love that never came from where you hoped to find it?

Father kneeled down beside Mother, sliding his arm around her back. I carefully set the wooden lily beside my attempt at a dog and did the same, reaching across her shoulders to support her other side. Father grimaced as I did; he probably hoped to support his goddess all on his own. I wasn't sorry to disappoint him.

The three of us walked across the knoll and back into the house, a distance that might have taken either Father or I a tenth of the time on our own. Neither of us minded the pace, though, and for once, it was peaceful, with the tepid breeze that rustled the lilies all around us.

I tucked a strand of golden hair behind Mother's ear just as we reached the door. Father nodded toward it. "Open that, will you?"

As I did so, I got a fairly good view of the figure seated at our table, lit by the small lantern on the table before him. His hand, still clutching the lantern, trembled.

"Luuk? Jurij isn't here. He and Elfriede—"

"It's Nissa." Luuk's muffled voice was shakier than ever. "Her mother's dead."

***

Mother was the last one living. The illness had claimed the lives of three women in the village, one by one.

And because life without a goddess is apparently too much for men to handle, three men died shortly thereafter. Vanished, out of grief. Poor Nissa had no one left but Luuk, and because she was his goddess, Mistress Tailor decided to let her live with them.

Because she was his goddess. *I need to see him. I need to ask him to save Mother.* It was ridiculous. What would I do, command the lord to save her? Why would he be able to save her? *But you have to try.*

I let it go four more days after Luuk came looking for Jurij. Four more days of women and men dying. Four more days Mother moved closer to death.

Four days I'd clung to my woodcarving and felt sick to my stomach and let my stubbornness stop me from acting. *Ask him. And then you can tell Father how ridiculous it was to hope for anything.*

When the carriage came down the path as the fourth day shifted to evening, I was ready. When the specters opened the door and one extended a hand, I took it.

I clutched my shawl and felt the sweat pour off my palm in waves. The black leather seat beneath me felt hot. The air was stifling. But I had to try. I had to breathe.

Halfway through the woods I felt queasy—my mind playing tricks, that whisper of my full name in my ears—but it soon passed. I straightened my shoulders. *What am I so afraid of? He's my man. He'll be happy to see me.* But that was just it. By going, I was acknowledging he was my man.

You can't run away from this forever. I'd spent long enough trying.

The carriage ground to a halt too soon, the short trip made even shorter with the horses' assistance. The door opened and I took a specter's outstretched palm with my own trembling hand. It was cold, so cold, and I wondered not for the first time how these men could seem so lifeless and still be among the living.

The gates and then the castle doors opened as the specters approached, and I stumbled inside the thunderously shaking castle. Only once I was indoors did the earth settle. The castle wasn't dark this time. Torches lit the entryway, revealing an empty room, the scene of our first meeting. Even with the slight warmth of the air outside, it felt cold in the castle, like a gust of frigid wind encircled it forever.

I jumped as I felt a hand on my shoulder. Shivering, I turned, expecting to come face to mask with the lord at last, but it was one of the specters. He stepped back and gestured up the nearby staircase. Other specters lined the stairway, each gesturing upward. I cringed at the strange, inviting yet somehow unappealing sight. But I straightened my shoulders, clutched my shawl tighter around my throat, and ascended the stairs.

The line of specters continued onto the second floor and up another stairway to a third. I lost count of how many specters there were, perhaps a hundred, red eyes bearing down on me, red eyes watching from the edge of the light, each with one foot in the darkness. By the time I reached the top of the second flight of stairs, I exhaled, relieved there were no more steps awaiting me. Instead, a line of specters gestured down a hallway, their red eyes watching. I followed the path set out for me, stopping halfway when a line of specters blocked my way. "I'm here to see the lord." *Who are these men?*

The four specters before me nodded and gestured to an open doorway. I let go of my shawl, rubbed my palms against my skirt to dry them, and stepped in.

The room was huge—far greater even than the cavernous entryway two floors below. But it was practically empty. I followed a long, thin, and threadbare black carpet thrown down over cobblestone flooring. At the edge of the carpet against the wall was a large black chair—a throne, no doubt, like something out of the myths about rulers called kings and queens, only they would have kept their throne rooms on the lower floors of their castles. Above the throne was a sword that glowed violet. A *sword.* Something I'd only seen in drawings for made-up tales about the kings and queens who wielded them. Something there was no use for in everyday life, so there simply was no need for our blacksmith to forge. Axes were for chopping wood. Knives were for butchering and cooking. But a sword? The kings and queens of tales used them to battle, and once men found their goddesses, they simply lost all interest in swordfights and adventure. And most women never had such interests to begin with.

Most women besides me.

This sword glowed brighter than the flames of the torches lighting the way. I'd never heard anyone mention that swords glowed in stories. There were no windows, so the glowing could hardly be a trick of the light. The only other thing in the room was a bookstand with a single, large tome closed atop it. *The book of Returning, perhaps? Always conveniently in the Great Hall on a Returning Day.*

"Well, Olivière. Welcome. I am glad to see you chose to make yourself so comfortable."

I dropped my hand immediately, not even realizing I was

leaning against the throne, reaching up toward the sword. I didn't even remember walking those last few paces.

"Please. Do turn around. I assure you I am now prepared for your visits."

I turned, the sword somehow forgotten. His presence drew my eyes with such force I couldn't bear to look at anything else until I'd absorbed all of him.

He was cloaked entirely in black. Not only was his embossed leather jacket darker than a shadow, his folded hands were covered with what appeared to be smooth, black leather gloves. Instead of a mask or a beautiful face, a gauze veil dark as ink covered his head, the corners of the material tied closed with a somber broach on his left shoulder. Were it not for the wide-brimmed hat he wore atop the veil—which was just as dark as the rest of his attire, if perhaps a little more resplendent—he might have very well sucked all of the light from the room. As it was, the hat—a sort of metal, pointed hat—was glossy enough that it reflected the flicker of the torches' firelight in small, spectacular movements.

He walked past me before I could speak, his close stride rustling my skirt. I moved back to give him room, and he sank into the black throne, crossing one black boot over and resting it on his knee. He brought the tips of his gloves together, his elbows resting comfortably on the armrests. "I had hoped to see you again much sooner."

I swallowed and ran a shaky hand through my hair, tucking a chunk of it behind my ear. "I figured. I—I saw the carriages. I just needed some time."

"Time? Time for what?"

I clutched my shawl again, as if that would somehow save me from the chill that hung over every room of the castle. I formed my words carefully. "I'm not yet old enough for a Returning." It was true, and I wasn't saying there was going to *be* a Returning. Not the moment I turned seventeen, anyway.

The lord dropped his fingers and gestured around him to the empty room. "Since when does that stop a man from seeing his goddess?"

"It doesn't. Usually. But you didn't come to see me, either."
The lord scoffed. I could hear the sound clearly even through his veil. "You expect *me* to visit *you*?"

I blinked. This wasn't going at all how I expected. "No, I ... " *I was quite happy not to have to think about you*, I wanted to say. But there was no need to tell him that. A man could crumble at even the slightest hint of harshness from his goddess. "It's just that ... that's the way it's normally done. Men visiting their goddesses."

The lord tossed his head and cradled what must have been his chin with his thumb and forefinger. His face seemed turned a bit sideways, like he wasn't going to look at me, although I couldn't be sure. "I cannot leave the castle." His voice broke a little, and I was almost unsure I'd heard him right.

I didn't know what to say. It wasn't like I'd wanted him to come anyway. And arranging courtship was hardly the first thing on my mind. "Um, sir, Lordship ... " The lord dropped his hand back to his lap. "My mother is unwell. Women have been ill these past four months, and they started dying this week. I thought ... we all thought they'd get better, but now that doesn't seem to be the case, and ... " I didn't know what else to say.

The lord tossed his hand in the air with a flourish, gesturing for me to go on. "And?"

I felt something snap in my chest, like the one word from him, the callous tone of his voice, was enough to stomp all hope I'd managed to muster. The hope that had gotten me to accept that carriage ride at last and face the fact that I was somebody's goddess, and that somebody wasn't who I wanted.

"And you're our lord. Isn't there something you can do?"
The lord drummed his fingers on one of the throne's armrests. "You have tried all the herbs?"

"Yes!" I regretted the tone of my voice the moment I said it. But it was obvious we'd tried that much, wasn't it? I tried to soften my voice. "I mean, of course. It seems to help with the pain a bit, but they're still—that is, my mother now, just her, she still has no strength."

The lord's fingers stopped tapping at once. "You say women have died?"

"Yes!" I squeezed my shawl tighter. Wasn't he listening? Wasn't he paying attention at all to the people he ruled over? *Why, then, do people say he's always watching?*

"There is no typical sign of illness? No rash? No sores?"

"No ... " I bit my lip, thinking about Ingrith and her "healer" man. "I knew a woman, who ... well." I swallowed, struggling to summon my courage to face this man. "She said there was once a family of healers in the village."

The lord's head snapped forward slightly. "Healers? I thought they had all been forgotten."

"They have. That is, if they existed at all in the first place."

"No matter. They are gone. They cannot help." The lord held a hand out to silence me before I could inquire further. He leaned his veiled face into his other palm. Neither of us spoke. Then he straightened in his throne. "Four months they have been ill?"

"About that, yes." I dropped my hand from my shawl and let my arms hang limply at my sides. Even without seeing his eyes, I felt them boring into me. I didn't know how very much I'd hate the attention. "They got ill the day after I first came here."

The lord jumped out of his throne so quickly I almost fell backward to the ground as my feet scrambled to give him ample room to pace. He walked to his bookstand and flung the heavy tome open, flipping through pages as if his life depended on it. Maybe my mother's actually did.

Can he read through his veil?

As if hearing my thoughts, the lord sighed and slammed the book shut with a grunt of frustration, sending dust into the air. "You will have to leave!"

I took a step back before I could even think. "Pardon?"

"Leave. Now." He gestured toward the door and flicked his fingers, summoning four specters from behind me. They held their arms out, leading me toward the door.

My head spun from one specter to the next, to the pacing

lord before the throne. "What about my mother?"

The lord slowed his pace, but he didn't stop moving. He waved a hand absently at me. "I will do what I can, of course. She will live to perform our Returning."

If his first statement offered me a bit of comfort, his second was a kick to the stomach. "What do you mean? Is she going to die of this after that?"

The lord stopped and sighed, quite audibly. He positioned both hands on his hips. "I cannot tell you. I do not know."

"But you know *something*, obviously."

The lord took a few steps forward, closing the distance between us. "Olivière," he said, grabbing one of my hands. He squeezed it and brought it up between our chests. "I will do what I can. Please worry instead about preparing yourself for my Returning."

I ripped my hand out from his grip. "Your Returning? How can you speak to me about a Returning when my mother might be dead tomorrow?"

The lord leaned forward, trying to reach for me. I took a step back. "Olivière, the timing of your mother's illness is unfortunate, but—"

"The *timing*?"

"If you knew how long I waited. If you knew how hard this is for me, to accept your love."

"Accept *my* love?" I crossed my arms tight against my chest, all timidity forgotten. "What love? I don't even *know* you."

"A fact that could be remedied if only you would accept my invitation more often."

"And what do you mean, how hard it is for *you*? Do you think I want to be the lord's goddess?" I threw my hands in the air at him. "That I have any interest in this black void of a man who stays locked up inside this monstrosity of a castle, ignoring the needs of his people, a heartless monster who doesn't care if they're dying?"

The lord straightened his shoulders and clenched his hands into fists. "A *heartless monster*?"

"I was wondering what it meant. But now I know. You think nothing of your people."

"And whose fault is that?" His tone was so accusatory, I flinched. He started pacing again before his throne, back and forth, back and forth. "I cannot leave this castle, Olivière! I do not know one person in this village from the next. I blink and they die. I die and they would not know—they could not *imagine* the depth of the pain I feel."

I sighed heavily. He was making no sense. Leave it to me to wind up with the recluse with little grip on his sanity. "Don't talk to me about a Returning until my mother's health improves."

The lord stiffened, and I realized, far more clearly than I had the first time we'd met, that my words had power over him.

I decided to test it. I pointed above the throne. "And give me that sword."

Chapter Ten

I'd had to ask for the scabbard, too. And he gave them to me. Without a word. Thrusting them at me like he couldn't wait to be rid of them. Or of me.

The scabbard rested now around my waist. I hoped I wore it right; we'd used our sashes to hold our stick blades. I held the sword out in front of me like a violet torch that lit my way down the path that ran between the castle and my home.

I was stupid to think he could do anything. I bit the inside of my cheek. *That he would be helpful at all.*

I wouldn't have been comfortable with a simpering sycophant, true. That was part of the reason why I couldn't bear to see him again at first. The idea of a man weak at the knees and lost without me made me almost as ill as seeing Jurij acting just that way with Elfriede. Even if it might have been different if Jurij acted that way with me.

But this man wasn't at all sane. He was, impossibly, rude to his own goddess. He babbled on about things that made no sense. Cared about things that weren't anywhere near as important as my mother's illness.

But since when did a man care about anyone other than his goddess?

I shook my head. It may just have been because Mother's illness worried Elfriede, but Jurij was as worried about her as the rest of us. If the lord truly loved me, he would have been worried sick.

If he loved me. He'd said it was hard to accept my love. For *him* to accept *me.*

I stopped my manic pacing halfway down the path and let out a roar of impatience.

The blade glowed even brighter. It seemed to pull at me, like if I let it go it would fly right out of my hands. But that was crazy.

"Olivière ..."

That voice again.

I headed through the foliage, where the blade seemed keen to take me.

***

The glowing light.

I stood before the violet pool in the cavern, Elgar's hilt clutched in both hands. Yes, Elgar. It seemed a fitting name for the blade. Elgar had taken me there, to the pool. And the pool still called to me.

Elgar drooped in my grasp, perhaps because of my faltering arms, weak from holding it aloft so long.

"Olivière," called the pool. *"Olivière!"*

It was a chorus of voices, a hundred women and men, both familiar and unknown. What would I find if I finally went all the way down to the violet light?

The pool gave me its reply. *"Olivière."*

I stood straight, snapping Elgar back upward in my grip. *This is stupid. Ridiculous. I should go home. I need to check on Mother.*

Elgar shot downward, yanking my arms more forcefully than anyone ever had before, pulling my body aloft briefly before we punctured the water and dived into the depths below. I hadn't had a chance to catch my breath. The toes of my boots had scraped against sediment for a moment, and then I felt nothing. It was as if I were floating, only I was flying downward, deeper and deeper into the light.

And then I stopped so suddenly it was as if my body had forgotten all movement. In my panic, the need for air ceased. There was nothing. There was no one. Nothing but me and the blade in my hand, the blade that spun and twirled round and round gently, slowly.

With every blink of my eye, I saw what I'd once seen. What I wanted to be again.

Jurij and Elfriede's Returning in reverse, coming undone. Little Jurij and me, battling unseen foes before we ventured outside, leaving the cavern behind. The old crone and Darwyn still with us. With every moment that passed, more friends came back to me.

But then friends became Mother, her face alight, bending down to the floor to pick me up and cradle me against her shoulders.

Then what I saw became unfamiliar. *Was that Mother as a child?* The images passed by faster and faster, and I spun so I could hardly bear to look. I squeezed my eyes shut and tried to shield my lids from the light.

I stopped turning with my arms tightly above my head.

No more vertigo. I opened my eyes. Nothing. Only violet light.

Is that what was to become of me, then? Would I float aloft in the light forever?

"*Olivière!*"

There was life outside the light, if I chose to seek it.

I clenched my jaw and nodded. Anywhere but home. Anywhere but that life. Somewhere I wasn't that man's goddess, if just for a little while.

Elgar shot upward, pulling me with it. This time, my arms

didn't ache. This time, as we broke through the light and back into the waters, I felt as if I were swimming. As if I were in control.

I emerged from the cavern pool more skillfully than I had entered it. I had somewhere to go. So I went, following the familiar path through the woods and to the dirt road, trotting toward the village.

And I felt immediately disappointed. Even stupid. I was home. Of course I was. The lilies still dotted the hilltops. And my house was right there beside the—

No, my house wasn't there.

The hair on the back of my neck stood up. A chill swept the air, and a breeze rustled the tresses I could never tame. I turned.

My gaze fell on the castle, which towered over the land and threatened to make me cower.

You idiot. I squeezed my eyes shut. My knees buckled in anticipation of the fall.

But the ground didn't shake. I slowly opened one eye and then the next and openly stared at the castle, dumbfounded.

"Who goes there?"

That voice. So familiar, so scornful. But not entirely unwelcome. I could picture the voice now, asking me to wash dishes for Mother. To grab a chair for Mother.

My gaze darted from the castle to the dirt path through the woods behind me. A group of unmasked men covered in crisscrossing chainmail exited the woods behind me. They laid their hands lazily over the sheathed blades at their sides.

"You, boy," said one. What was that voice again? Fish Face? Had his wife unmasked him with a Returning?

Another slapped him across the chest. "That's no boy!" I didn't recognize him, either. But I guess I didn't know everyone in the village.

The men shook to life, some pulling their swords out and pointing them toward me, others jolting awake and staring at me with a look of utter confusion. Their faces, varying in their beauty, all had a degree of allure that stirred my heart. Yet I knew none of the faces. And none were masked. True, most men of that age were unmasked, but to find so many together at once? *And they have swords. Like out of made-up tales. This is clearly not real!*

"What are you doing here, woman?" demanded the one who had first spoken, the one whose voice I had mistaken for Father's. There actually was a bit of a resemblance, but the man had just a few different features, a bend to his nose, a sneer to his lips that Father didn't. The man hadn't drawn his blade.

There was something off about these men. Before I even realized I wasn't playing games with a stick blade, I'd pulled Elgar out of its sheath and fixed it readily in their direction. Both of my hands gripped the hilt. They'd come from the direction of the castle. "Who sent you?"

Some of the men burst out laughing, letting their blades fall. A few stuck them into the ground and leaned on them like walking sticks.

The leader took a few paces forward. I backed up uneasily, poking Elgar out in front of me.

The man dodged my awkward thrusts easily and knocked Elgar from my grip with the back of his hand. I cradled the sore spot without thinking, and the man slapped me across the cheek just as he had my wrist, with the back of his hand.

I cried out in shock. It was as if my own father had hit me. But he wouldn't have. No man would have. I mean, unless their goddesses asked them to, but then why would a woman ever do that?

The rest of the men laughed, and the leader gestured to where Elgar had fallen.

"Pick it up!" he ordered.

One of the men scrambled forward to do as instructed. He handed the blade with two hands to the leader, who picked it up and turned it around in the air, staring at the violet glow. The leader's brow furrowed and at last he lowered it.

"Take this back to His Lordship." He thrust it at the man, who nodded and turned back to the pack waiting behind him before disappearing into the woods.

His Lordship? Since when does the lord have a set of speaking servants?

The leader slapped me with the back of his other hand across my other cheek.

I jumped.

"Thief!" he cried. "How dare you walk around with a sword from His Lordship's castle?"

My tongue caught in my throat. "It's mine! He gave it to me!" Had he sent these men to get it back? Where had they come from?

But your house is missing, Noll. This can't be real. I rubbed my sore jaw. *But it sure feels real.*

The leader laughed, but his smile faded quickly. He grabbed me by the chin, and I winced from the pain of the pressure he exerted, a pain especially sharp in the cheeks that bore his blows. He turned my head back and forth, observing me like Mother often observed a piece of meat in the market.

He gasped. "Your ears! You mutilated your ears!" Despite the strangeness of the situation and the force exerted tightly over my face, my fingers instinctively brushed the tips of my ears. They were the same familiar, unwounded smooth edges as they were always.

I felt more lost now than I had before I entered the secret cavern.

The other men walked forward to join their leader in glaring at me.

"You're right!" said one, his voice cocky and assured.

"Whatever possessed this one?" said another.

They were puzzled and introspective. A flash of light burned in their eyes and then faded. But it was not the flame I expected to see, just a trick of the moonlight, an echo of a shadow. These men didn't carry flames in their eyes—and yet here they stood living before me.

The leader was confused, and he was angry. There was something about the way he looked at me, the way Father had always looked so longingly at Mother. Or Jurij at Elfriede. He let my face free and grabbed me tightly by the arm, yanking me forward down the dirt road and toward the village.

"Stop!" I screamed. The leader paused, looking over my head to address his compatriots.

"Let's go!" he said. "It's time we show those women exactly what happens when they disobey."

He pulled me forward. I started struggling, but another of the men appeared at my side and grabbed my free arm, yanking me forward just as forcefully. A third man appeared behind me, and a black cloth flew in front of my face, wrapping tightly across my mouth and digging hard into my teeth and tongue as it was knotted behind me.

The men dragged me down the path, away from the castle. Even the Tailors' home at the edge of the village was altered. My heartbeat echoed in my ears. Home, but not home. The village was much the same, but not entirely. *I'm drowning. I stupidly leaped into the pool again and this is my dying dream.*

The one place that seemed hardly changed was the commune, where the men stopped dragging me at last. A fire was burning in the center, and a few dark figures stood in front of it. The men in the commune could never bring themselves to bother building a fire.

"Come out!" screamed the leader of the pack. "All of you women, come out now and look at what we bring with us!"

The commune was changed after all. Women and girls stepped out from shacks. One after another, they surrounded the small roaring fire that was lit in the center. They huddled together in packs of threes and fours. Only occasionally did a woman stand apart—mostly the women who had been standing before the fire—her eyes narrowed.

And again, as with the men, I thought I saw women I knew, only to discover something that made their faces not quite familiar. I wasn't home, I knew that much. But I had no explanation for where I was. And why now, why when I had so much else to worry about, I found myself in this place.

"This *woman*," spat the leader, "dared to take a treasure from your lord! She violated her ears!"

Gasps and whispers broke out from the crowd before us. There were so many terrified faces and murmuring lips amongst the rare angry expression and the jaw clenched tightly. The women were thin and frail and looked defeated. Even the few who were with child looked malnourished. Though there were some lighter in skin tone and even a few as oak-tone fair as Elfriede with the same blond curls, quite a few were the same dark earth tone of the men.

And their ears. Every last one of them had the pointed ears of men. If this was a dream, I needed desperately to wake up. But I wasn't waking.

The leader let go of my arm, and the other man did the same. I barely had a moment to register my newfound freedom when a sharp kick on my back sent me hurtling forward.

"I don't know how many times we have to make this clear," said the leader. "You follow our orders! You never go against them! And don't you *ever* disrespect our Lord Elric!"

Elric? I couldn't remember if I'd ever heard someone say the lord's name.

The man grabbed at the small of his back and produced a whip. I raised my arms to defend myself, but two other men appeared at my side and flipped me back over.

The whip cracked fast, the snap echoing in my ears only after I felt the sting of pain shoot through my back. I tried to scream, but my tongue was bound. I tried to flinch, but the hands on me gripped tighter.

"This is what becomes of a disobedient woman!" He cracked the whip again.

My eyes rolled to the back of my head, a flash of light offering to let me flee with it into unconsciousness.

"Goncalo! Whatever is the ruckus here?"

A third crackle echoed and the whip lowered, hitting what I thought to be the ground behind me instead of my back.

"Lord Elric," said the leader, the man named Goncalo. "Only just punishment."

The men holding my arms let go and kneeled. The women before me crouched, their faces pushed tightly into the ground, while the men beside me remained more upright but still near the ground.

I rolled over and noticed with pleasure that Goncalo, like the other men, was kneeling. The whip was still clenched in his hands, its tips stained with blood. My blood.

"What has this woman done then?"

At the condescending tone, I looked up. A man sat atop a black horse, dressed entirely in black leather. He was bathed in the firelight, a glisten bouncing off of the metal on his pointed hat with the wide brim. My gaze was drawn to the hand clutching his horse's reins. The light bounced there, too, off a metallic bangle around his wrist. In the light of the fire, the bangle seemed golden, the sole sanctuary of color amongst the black silhouette.

His face was so alluring. His cheeks protruded so, I suspected the bones would cut my fingers should I touch them. His nose was so sharp and straight, it was almost unsettling. His fine brows were drawn together.

There wasn't a flame in his irises, yet they glistened strongly with a fire unseen.

The thought came to me at once: There was no curse over the men in this version of the village. If anything, it was the women who were cursed and tormented.

And this is "Lord Elric" unmasked, without a veil. But no, it can't be him. I just saw him, and he kept his face from me.

Pain shot through my fresh wounds, and I banished all thoughts of longing from my heart. *Why have I come here? What's the point of this?* A tear escaped from one of my eyes. I clenched my jaw and pressed my teeth into the grating muzzle tightly.

"Theft," said Goncalo. "Self-mutilation."

"Oh?" asked the lord. His voice, before so bored, carried with it some hint of interest. It reminded me of my recent conversation with the lord, when the things he said proved so callous, even if his words carried with them a slight trace of charm.

He jumped down off of his horse and crossed the short distance between us.

"And add 'failure to bow before me' to her list of trespasses," he said.

All eyes turned to me. Even the girls and women lifted their heads ever so slightly to get a look.

I felt the pressure exerted from all directions. Instead of succumbing to it, I stood and glared at the lord as he strode over toward me. He was taller than me. But only just.

Women and girls gasped and the men cried out, appalled. Goncalo moved one leg forward to stand, his whip shaking violently over his head.

"Kneel!" called the lord.

Goncalo instantly slid his leg back into position. I didn't move.

Still more whispers and gasps. A flash of anger shot across the lord's face. "Silence!"

All tongues halted. I remembered my muzzle and reached back, my muscles searing in pain with the simple movement. Even as my open flesh smeared against itself and the remnants of the dress I wore, I slid off the muzzle and tossed it on the ground.

The lord straightened his shoulders. He let a flicker of a smile grow on his face.

"Who is she?" he asked, looking straight down at me and not speaking to me at all.

"Was she not at the castle with you tonight, my lord?" asked Goncalo from behind me. "We found her coming out of the woods, holding the stolen blade."

"No, no," said the lord casually. "I would remember *her*. And besides, this blade is unfamiliar to me."

He pulled a short, glowing blade from a too-large sheath at his side. Elgar. So the men had brought it to him after all. He raised it into the air, turning it this way and that, letting the moonlight bounce off of the violet embers. I wanted to rip it out of his grasp.

"A strange blade," said the lord. "Smaller than I am used to, but somehow compelling nonetheless." He shifted his gaze from Elgar to my waist. "Ah. She wears the sheath still."

The man kneeling next to me grew alarmed and tore the sheath off of my waist. The movement stung against the wounds on my lower back, and I flinched.

The man held the sheath toward the lord with both hands. The lord seemed amused. He grabbed the sheath and slid Elgar into it, belting the sheath to his waist. Although his build was thin, the belt was just a bit too small for him; his face strained at the realization, but affix it in place he did, looping it tightly. He placed both hands on his waist as he finished, his elbows extended.

"Well?" he said. "Does the blade become me, girl?"

My leaking blood boiled over.

"My name is Noll," I said, my tongue bursting against fresh sores with each movement. "But only my friends call me that." I thought of the name that had drawn me there. "You will address me as Olivière."

The women and girls screamed. The men jumped to their feet, drawing their blades, shouting. The lord did not stir.

"Silence!" he said again. The women instantly went mute. The men stood beside me and behind their master. Never before then did they so remind me of the men of my village.

The lord tried to intimidate me with his stare, but I wouldn't let him. There was no flame within his dark eyes, and that fire that glistened unseen would not have power over me.

The lord broke the stare first and then laughed. He extended a black leather-gloved hand toward me and fingered the tips of my ears. The men relaxed slightly, and the grip on their hilts eased.

The golden bangle slid from his wrist to his forearm as he rubbed my ear tenderly. I shuddered at the touch and tried to draw back, but the lord seized my arm with his free hand and squeezed tightly.

"Olivière," he said. "I see what he meant about self-mutilation. What have you done to your beautiful ears?" A friendly smile beamed across his stunning features.

My stomach clenched. His face was just the mask of a heartless monster.

"Nothing," I said. "I was born this way."

Women and men alike whispered to their neighbors. The lord laughed, but the joy that spread across his face soon turned cold. He shoved me to the ground before remounting his horse.

"Lying to me gets her a day in the stocks."

He galloped off, leaving the men free to advance on me, their expressions twisted with both joy and fury. These were not the men of my village. They sheathed their swords, and I shut my eyes tight as dozens of hands set out to grab me.

≥ Chapter Eleven ≤

I couldn't wake from this dream. I was still living it. Hours had passed, and I was still here. *I'm home but not home. That lord, so pompous, so haughty.* I bit my lip. He was the lord I knew and not the lord I knew. But both versions made my blood boil.

The women wouldn't look at me. A young girl would sometimes glance as she passed, her face full of both curiosity and terror—*Nissa*, I'd think in my delirium—and then a woman standing next to her would shield her eyes and push her forward. *Not Nissa.* Nissa would be comforted by Luuk, not a mother.

My mother is dying, and I'm lost in a dream.

Most of the women went out to work in the fields or the quarry. Some piled crops into wheelbarrows and strained to push them into the heart of the village, toward the marketplace and the castle. Some of the women went into the village first thing in the morning, their arms full of tools. A rolling pin. A sewing box.

A gouge and a chisel. *Alvilda.*

Men would sometimes stumble their way into the commune, either intoxicated or merely bold and hungry. They'd enter a shack, or just grab the nearest woman and take off with her, back up the dirt path to the better homes within the village. Some of the men were laughing, some angry. Some were old, others could be no older than fifteen. Every woman looked terrified. Most of the men let their gaze fall over me in the stocks briefly, a few reaching out to caress my ear as they passed. Some would say things I couldn't hear. One licked his lips and smiled wickedly. I didn't fight back. I was too weak to care.

My throat burned with thirst. And my arms, tongue, and back ached with a feeling stronger than the ache of my heart all these past few months.

No one had attended to my wounds, and I felt my energy draining with each breath. From time to time, I would slip blissfully into unconsciousness, but I would wake again what seemed like moments later, my stomach growling and my head pounding. The sun felt hot and heavy over my head and at last, after what felt like days, I fell asleep and did not wake for quite some time.

***

My eyelids fluttered open. It was nighttime and the full moon had begun waning, but light from moonbeams lit the commune. The dying embers of a fire cast shadows over the empty area in the center. No one stirred.

I heard a rustle behind me and realized that my back no longer stung. It felt warm and soothed as the ache was leeched from deep within me. My eyes grazed the ground and saw my shadow; I was being bathed in a violet glow.

A moan leaped from my lips, and I craned my neck as much as the stocks would let me. A small figure moved in the dark, the violet glow surging and receding with its movements.

116

"Who's there?" My lips cracked, and my tongue bled again.

The figure jumped.

After a moment, it crawled forward. A little boy.

Jurij.

No. I had never seen Jurij unmasked so young. I had never seen any boy so young unmasked. He was seven or eight years at the most. Unless it was a trick of the night, his skin was even darker than a grown man's.

The boy lifted his hands toward my face, and the violet light fled outward from his fingers. My tongue strengthened, my lips moistened, and the sting on my cheeks receded. I even stopped feeling thirst and was no longer bothered by hunger.

I closed my eyes and bathed in the warmth of the light, hesitant to open them even after I felt the light fade. And then I remembered. I was home, but not home. I'd seen this boy's face, and he was all right. No men hid in this place that was and was not my village. My eyes flew open.

"Thank you," I said. The words were not enough. He had ended all of my pain.

The boy nodded and fell backward to sit on the ground. He stared at me, questioning.

"What's your name?" I asked.

"His name is Ailill," said a woman's voice that stirred something joyous in my heart.

A tall, dark woman strode into my sight. I recognized her as one of the few women who had stood alone in front of the fire the night previous. Her features were unfamiliar, her face too young, but I saw a trace of my friend Alvilda in her expression.

"My name is Avery," she said. "And I want to know where you come from."

It was hurting my neck to look up at her from the stocks, so I let my head fall and focused instead on the boy on the ground. He tensed a bit at my gaze and pulled himself over to Avery, hugging her leg and burying his face within the folds of her apron.

"How did he heal me?" I asked.

Avery crouched in front of me, careful not to disturb Ailill much in her decent. She swept him into the crux of her arm.

"I'm the one asking questions," she said.

"I … I don't know how to explain where I come from. Other than I don't come from here."

"Obviously," scoffed Avery. "Despite what men think, we're not stupid. All of us knew immediately you had never been in the commune before, that you weren't one of our members who had run off, stolen a sword, and lopped off her ears. But few of the men care to remember our faces, so it's no surprise that not a single one noticed that you were new."

These were not men. At least, they weren't the men I knew. I tensed, thinking of the whip and the muzzle. The stocks and my stolen sword. And Lord Elric. "Will you alert them?"

Avery sighed. "Your secret is safe. For now. None of the women have spoken to the men about it, but I recommend you go easy on your revulsion, lest you draw even more attention to yourself. There are ways to work around a man's orders without defying him outright."

Ailill adjusted Avery's apron so that he could peek just a little over the material. I smiled at him. He ducked immediately back under the apron.

Avery watched our exchange and hugged Ailill closer. She kissed him atop his head and rustled her hand through his short black hair. She stood and pulled Ailill up with her.

"You'd better get home," she said. "It'll be sunrise soon, and they'll notice you're missing."

She tapped him on the back and pushed him forward toward the dirt path through the village. Ailill stopped a few paces from us, pausing to look back.

"Go on," encouraged Avery. She waved him forward.

Ailill did as bidden, walking up the path until he disappeared into the darkness.

Avery put a hand on each hip. My head fell and I stared at her legs, which stood slightly apart.

"Now listen," she said, every bit Alvilda again. "If there's anyone who understands hating men, it's me. But there's a way and a place for certain things, and I don't want you to ruin what we've started."

She sighed. "I'll show you around tomorrow after they free you. If you have any skill with a blade, you may be able to work with an ax. I'm the woodcarver, and tomorrow I'm heading to the woods to chop down a tree."

My heart ached, hopefully, for the ax, the chisel, and the gouge—for home.

***

"Stay quiet," murmured Avery out of the corner of her mouth. "Keep your eyes on the ground and move forward quickly. Stick to the side of the path."

I found it hard to follow her orders, but I kept my head down, my hand clenched tightly on my ax. Disappointed I was no better at the thread and the needle than she was, and reluctant to speak to the other women about me, Avery had done a halfhearted job at sewing up the gashes in the back of my dress. They had few frocks to spare, and she thought it best I not attract attention with my healed back exposed. Even so, it was barely holding together, and I had to walk stiffly to keep it from popping open.

From time to time, my gaze wandered upward, and I caught a glimpse of men laughing and eating, drinking and dancing on the streets and through the building windows. And women and girls, their eyes always on the ground, serving food, sitting on laps, and being pulled and pushed and forced about among the revelry.

When we finally broke free of the village and started down the path toward the woods, I opened my mouth to speak.

Avery hushed me with a slight movement of her hand. "Not yet."

When we stepped into the woods, and I felt the cover of the trees hide us from view, I spoke. "What's—"

"Be quiet," murmured Avery.

I followed her down the path.

Some of the men in chainmail lined the path in the midst of the woods ahead of us. They chatted and leaned against trees or sat on the side of the dirt road. I remembered Avery's instructions and snapped my head back down.

"Off for more wood today, Carver-woman?"

"Yes, sir," replied Avery.

She set a foot off of the dirt path and into a familiar route through the trees. I followed after her.

"Don't go far," said one of the men.

"Yes, sir."

A hand reached out to grab my arm and pull me backward.

"It's her!" cried a man's voice. Instinctively, even against all I knew in my own version of the village, I looked up at him.

He seemed surprised to see my face. A look of anger and something far more salacious warped his features.

Avery appeared beside me, her eyes locked onto the ground around our feet. "I needed a sturdy hand to help with the chopping, sir," she said.

I dropped my eyes again.

"She's a feisty one," said the man. "Already up and moving. I can see why you'd think she was suited for hard labor."

"Yes, sir," replied Avery.

"Carry on," said the man. He let go of me, but as I turned, I felt a strong slap against my backside and heard the echo of the men's laughter. My face flushed red, and I bit my tongue so as not to scream.

Avery led me through the unmarked path that I knew led to my secret cavern. The farther we got from the dirt path, the faster she moved. Finally, just before the cave entrance, she gave a tremendous whack to the nearest tree, letting her ax rest in the trunk, and walked into the cave.

I gripped my ax tightly and followed Avery inside.

When we finally reached the pool and the violet glow, Avery faced me, one eyebrow slightly raised. "You walk through a dark cavern sightless with a sharp and deadly weapon in your grasp?"

I shrugged and laid the ax down on a nearby spike. My chest tightened for a moment as I looked at the pool. It could lead me home. But I couldn't jump in with her watching.

"I've been here before," I said.

"So I see." Avery sighed. "All right, no more games. Who are you and what are you doing here?"

"My name is Noll—Olivière, as I said, Woodcarver's daughter. I don't know why I'm here exactly."

Avery scoffed. "The woodcarver's daughter? I'm the woodcarver, and I have no children, much to my delight."

I cocked my head. "And Ailill?"

"He's my brother, not my son. Do I look old enough to have a child that grown?"

I looked her over, bathed in the violet light. I supposed, as much as I kept comparing her to Alvilda, she wasn't as old as my friend. She was perhaps more Elfriede's or my age, although her hardened stance and the muscles that rippled over her arms despite her small stature seemed to indicate a much more weighty life than ours.

"You didn't really answer my question," said Avery coldly.

"I'm a different woodcarver's daughter, obviously," I said, trying to meet ice with ice. "I trained under Alvilda the lady carver and observed the work of Gideon, my father."

Avery tensed. "Your father works?"

The grip I had on my elbows loosened. "Yes. Doesn't yours?"

Avery cackled. "No man works. And my father, whom I thank the skies is now dead, was the most indolent of all."

I shifted from one foot to the other uncomfortably. "And your mother?"

Avery glared at me. "Dead as well. But in her case, I thank the skies for the end of her suffering. She wasn't sturdy enough for this world. And she was far too beautiful. That makes you stand out too much."

She thanks the skies, but not the goddess. But what love have I for the first goddess myself?

I nodded, thinking of the women grabbed by the men during

my day in the stocks. Instinctively, I swept tendrils of hair over my ears, thinking of the hungry looks to which I had already been victim due to their discrepancy. I looked at Avery. She was pretty in her own way, but I wondered if she purposefully kept a sour look on her face to distort her features.

"My mother is not well," I said. "But even before her illness, she never had to work like the women here. And Father's always eager to help her with the housework."

Avery came a few paces closer, her gaze fixed down on me. "Then you are definitely not of this land," she said. "I don't know how you crossed the mountains or what exactly there is that lies beyond. All I want to know is if you can take us back with you."

I swallowed and glanced guiltily at the cavern pool behind her.

The chorus of voices calling my name was but a whisper now. "*Olivière.*"

I watched Avery to see if she wondered why the cave echoed my name, but she didn't move. Her eyes betrayed hearing nothing but the undying echo of the trickle of water.

Can I, alone, hear it? Do the voices call only to me? The chorus of voices had led me here, and they were no longer shouting my name, demanding me to come. They whispered, letting me know I could go home, but the pool didn't want me to go just yet. *But I do. How can I stay here, when Mother is ill?*

"No," I replied.

Avery sighed and stared hungrily at the ax I had propped against the spike. "Then there's only one hope for us."

I followed her gaze and asked a question I had wondered since I first entered this dream version of the village. "Why don't the women fight back? The men seem open to a surprise attack." It felt appropriate to have a real battle here, a battle like that from stories, where there was such wrongdoing.

Avery scoffed and picked up my ax, turning it backward and forward in her hands. "I cannot rouse enough of them. The men seem lazy—and they are—but they have quick reflexes and brute strength. Our only advantages are in our numbers and the men's smugness. But most of the women will not even entertain the idea of revolution. They're too scared."

"But surely they can see that with enough of us and a directed attack, the men will fall."

Avery smiled. "*Us*? So you'll help us?"

"Of course!" I lied.

Avery put the ax down and leaned on it, much like the men did with their swords. "Perhaps you're not so bad, outsider. Then there is just one more thing you'll need to know. The men of this village have a gift in their blood."

"A gift?" I asked. "Like Ailill's healing?"

Avery nodded. "They all can heal. But you'll only find little boys willing to use it for our aid before they get too corrupted and their hearts turn black. In their lives of luxury, men have little need for healing for themselves. If you want a man to die, you need to take him by surprise so he and his companions won't be able to heal him in time."

She spoke of killing a person like it was a possibility, like people would ever think to do that outside of play and stories. *Perhaps I'm living a story right now.*

She sighed and leaned the ax back on the rock. "Let's go chop down a tree. I'm sure you'll find it relieves a lot of tension."

It probably would. But this wasn't my fight.

As soon as she disappeared into the darkness, I dove back into the pool.

Chapter Twelve

My mind was blissfully blank as I walked back through the village—yes, this was my village, it had to be—and onto the path home. It was all a dream. My clothing, ripped and torn, dripped from the pond's water. Ripped mostly on the back. But that had to be a coincidence. I'd probably torn it on some sediment. Maybe I'd been sick under water, even unconscious. I could have died. I'd been stupid. I'd lost the sword I'd demanded from the lord in that water, but I had no desire to search for it. I needed badly to go home.

"*Olivière*," the pool had whispered as I put it behind me. But I ignored it. To believe what I'd dreamed was real was more than I could bear. *Everyone already thinks I'm an oddity. First I'm nobody's goddess and then I'm the veiled lord's. I don't even want to think of what I could be after having such visions.*

I had to prove to myself I'd just been dreaming. If I closed my eyes, I could still feel the pain of the whip across my back. But my back was smooth now. Unhurt. There was no proof I was ever there.

At the edge of the woods, I breathed a sigh of relief. My home was there. I'd reached the flattened grass where the carriage had turned around day after day. I took note of a few broken lily petals that had floated across the dirt road, still vibrant and purple despite their pressing fate.

The door to the house was cracked open. "Mother? Father? Elfriede?"

I pushed on the door and heard the creak of the hinges echo against the silence inside. There was no light, and the fire was dead, but thanks to the moonlight that crept inside, I could just make out a figure in the chair at the table that faced the doorway.

"Mother?" I whispered.

Bit by bit, the lantern light revealed the figure. The eyes, dark with just a hint of the flames that ought to have burned brightly. The scowl on the lips of his strained face. And in one hand, on the table, the same blue dress I'd seen Mother wearing before I'd visited the lord. It felt like days ago, but I knew it to be just a few hours earlier.

"I hope you're happy, Noll," said Father. His voice cracked and strained with each syllable. "You wouldn't help her. And now she's gone."

Elfriede shrieked from where she sat atop the bed she and I shared; she buried her head into the shoulder of the man, *her* man, who comforted her.

I stumbled, the breath completely sucked out of me. There was no one there to catch me.

***

Six months went by in a blur of numbness and woodcarving.

Every day the memory of the world in my drowning dream faded. Every day the memory of the lord doing nothing, caring only about his Returning, grew stronger. I told Father I'd tried to get the lord to help us. He didn't care. I didn't act soon enough. I wasn't there when she died and faded into nothingness—neither were Elfriede or Jurij, apparently, but they didn't merit Father's blame. So I didn't bother telling them about my dream. Why would they believe me? Why would they care? I hardly believed it myself.

The first thing I carved after Mother's death was my own interpretation of a heartless monster. It was a beast like the beasts of legend, a wolf, a bear, and a snake, all in one. I left an open cavity over the left side of its chest to show that there was no heart within it. Father didn't notice it. Elfriede gave me an uneasy smile and told me it may do some good scaring off rabbits from the garden. And that's where she put it, half-buried in leaves and dirt.

The day before my seventeenth birthday there wasn't enough scrap wood in the land for my trembling fingers. I finished the last few dozen projects I'd started—wooden animals, trees, and flowers—by adding a few more details than necessary. I ruined more than one, but my fingers wouldn't stop peeling away at the layers of wood. I started new projects I knew I would never finish, but it was just as well because the most I could think of carving was a blob of mud or a wooden rock.

My effort wasn't lost on Elfriede. Although, despite my better hopes, I thought she may have been more upset about the piles of sawdust all over her kitchen table than the reason for the mess. "Clean that off, will you? Father will be home soon."

"Here, let me help." Jurij released his hand from around Elfriede's shoulder and the one being became two. I didn't say anything as I set the carved pieces on the mantle, next to a wooden lily. Far better work than mine.

As Jurij wiped the dust into a rag, I numbly placed bowls and spoons for four people at our table. A brief jolt of pain brought me to life as I placed Jurij's setting down next to Elfriede's, and I thought of who had once sat there. "Ah. Good day, Jurij," came a slow, slurring voice, a croaking echo of what it had been. I glanced up to see Father in the doorway.

He stumbled his way to his chair, a shade of the father I had known.

Father had the same features, but they were muted somehow. His strong, dark chin poked through a rough, unkempt black-and-gray beard. His curls drooped and stuck out in all directions, although somehow the pointed tips of his ears made a slight appearance through the wild tangle of knots. His eyes sparkled, but in a different way than they once had. The flame within them burned as lightly as a candle in its final few moments before the wick withered away.

Perhaps that described my father. He had lost his sunlight and was left only with the dimmer echoes in the children she left behind. What room was there for happiness with the sun's light gone forever? The moon alone could never be enough, not after years of dancing in the sun's delight. It was just a matter of time. Nissa's father had died the same evening as his wife. They rarely lasted beyond a year.

"Good day, Gideon," said Jurij. He tore himself from Elfriede long enough to put his hand on Father's shoulder. "How're Vena and Elweard?"

"Huh?" asked Father absently. Often these days you had to ask a question more than once.

"*The tavern masters*," I reminded him. Father practically kept them in business since Mother's death.

"Oh, fine, fine." Father's eyes glossed over.

"Father?" I asked, covering his trembling hand with mine. He looked at me, the smallest of smiles edging onto his lips. The light flickered in his eyes. It was still there. Of course it was. But only just.

Jurij picked up Father's and my bowls and brought them over to the fire. Jurij and Elfriede worked in perfect harmony, one ladling the stew and the other holding the bowls out to receive it.

"Vena asked about your wedding last night," said Father as he withdrew his hand from mine. For a moment, my heart nearly stopped.

"And what did she want to know?" asked Jurij jovially. He

placed the stew bowls in front of Father and me.

I felt a rush of relief. Of course. *Their* wedding.

Father smiled, his face almost as warm as it had once been, his eyes growing brighter. "How much ale you'll need for the festivities, of course!"

Jurij shook his head as he grabbed the empty bowls for himself and Elfriede. "You know we only want a few bottles at the most." He paused a moment as he slid soundlessly next to Elfriede. Even from the table, I could see the lines burrowed deep between her brows.

"Or maybe none at all," muttered Elfriede. She plopped the stew into their bowls with a little less tenderness than was her custom.

My father's face fell. "I'll be on my best behavior. I promise you."

No one spoke.

Father and I sipped from our stew for a few moments longer, and Jurij sat down next to us, placing the bowls on the table and picking up his spoon.

Elfriede lingered back at the pot for a few minutes longer, stirring and stirring. Out of the corner of my eye, I saw her dab her cheek with her apron.

"Noll," she said tentatively. She stirred the stew with a little too much interest. "Would you be willing to help Darwyn deliver the bread to the castle?"

I drummed my fingers on the tabletop. "I didn't think the bakers were so busy they couldn't spare a few dozen members of their family to deliver bread to His Lordship."

"Noll. Help Darwyn deliver the bread," interrupted my father. He tried to take a sip of his stew, but his hand shook and the stew slid off the spoon, spilling onto the table. Whether because he had now gone a short while without his bottle or because he could barely contain his rage at me, I wasn't sure.

He only managed to truly seem among the living these days when it came to rejoicing in Elfriede's wedding and lamenting my unspoken opposition to my own.

I glanced out the window. Newly unmasked Darwyn stood

in front of our house next to his cart full of bread. Father had no doubt come straight with him from the village and had let Elfriede know ahead of time.

"I promised I'd meet Alvilda after lunch."

"Noll, you need to stop with that woodworking—"

I didn't let Father finish. I grabbed a chisel and a block of half-carved wood and bolted out of the door, walking straight past Darwyn—no doubt fuming with impatience to be done with the task and back in his goddess's arms. I headed down the dirt path, my head held high in the western direction.

The wheels on the cart squealed. Darwyn had no interest in waiting for me to change my mind. Just as well. I wasn't going to.

Arrow bolted up the pathway from where he'd been playing nearby to lick me goodbye. I pulled the chisel out of his reach so he wouldn't hurt himself and kept marching forward. Arrow followed me for a bit, jumping and yipping and straining against all hope that the wood I carried would prove edible. Perhaps to him it was.

"Arrow! Here boy!"

As I came over the hill, Arrow's mistress echoed his name, and he went running. How like the master of the golden dog who'd birthed him.

Goodbye to you, too, Elfriede. I felt like a nuisance in my own home. Jurij had taken Mother's place. Mine was practically taken by a dog.

It took me longer than it should have to cross the small distance to the Tailor's. Weariness invaded my feet as the shop finally came into focus. My palm crushed against the uneven surface of the chisel handle, which showcased an elegant carving of a string of roses through which a series of butterflies fluttered their fair wings. It was one of my father's better works, from back when he loved woodworking so much he even carved his tool handles. I could probably carve handles. But I wouldn't forget the thorns on the vines and might include a few butterflies whose wings had ripped as they passed by them.

I stopped and took a closer look at the Tailors' sign, which Father had carved some years ago. I would have put the image of the thread and needle looping through the letters in the word "Tailor." I wondered if Alvilda would have a large piece of wood I could use to design my own sign for practice. If not, I could chop some down.

A shiver ran down my spine as the thought of the ax brought up faded memories of Avery from my dream. I'd left her before the dream had finished.

Anyway, signs take time. And you're out of time, Noll.

The door to the shop opened abruptly, revealing the tired face of Mistress Tailor. Bow scampered out past her feet and jumped up to greet me. I placed the chisel and wood on the ground so I could take her head in my hands and rub her ears.

"You're late," said Mistress Tailor, not even bothering to greet me. "Why didn't—" She glanced around and the corner of her mouth twitched ever so slightly. "Oh. Noll. I thought Jurij might have been coming home. For once."

"He's at my place," I said, although that was probably obvious. "If you'd like, I can tell him—"

She eyed the things I'd left on the ground and waved a hand. "No. Don't bother. If you're heading to Alvilda's, send my husband over. There's enough work around here for ten." She turned to Bow. "Come on, do your business. Clothes aren't going to sew themselves."

I tucked my tool and wood block into my sash and started down the village path, but as I passed her, Mistress Tailor had one more thing to say. "I wish you the best tomorrow. Whatever 'the best' may be."

I was taken aback. Mistress Tailor, the stout and surly woman of few words, had said what no one else would. And she seemed to honestly mean it.

"Thank you."

Mistress Tailor practically growled. "All right. No use crying over the broken thread. I'm sure Alvilda will have some nice words for you." With that, she and Bow went back into the Tailor Shop, and I was left to face the onslaught of people between one end of the village and the other alone.

If I thought I attracted attention before I became the lord's goddess, for being a rambunctious child or for having no man to call my own, I had no idea of the type of interest I would have to deal with as the day of my supposed Returning approached.

"Blessed be your birthday tomorrow!" An unmasked man next to a stand of produce tilted his hat at me, the grin on his lips a sign he had no idea how his words cut me to the quick.

I mumbled my thanks, spinning to get out of the way of the tanner and his cart of hides, itching to get away from the busy path that led to the center of the village.

"Watch where you're going, you foolish girl!"

The woman startled me and I nearly fell, flinging my hands out to steady myself. My fingers smacked against a wicker basket, my nails catching in a dark gauze laid over it. The gauze began to shift and I realized with horror what I'd done.

Not a basket. A bassinet.

"I'm so sorry, Ma'am!" I hurried to readjust the gauze, grabbing my finger with the other hand and carefully untangling the jagged nail from the thin material, all while not daring to look down. "Is he all right?"

"Oh. It's you." The woman struggled to balance a baby in the crook of her left arm with the handled bassinet slid across her right. The baby sucked its fist and leaned into her shoulder. She had powerfully dark brown eyes slightly covered by a mess of dark brown curls. "I apologize for yelling at you." The mother bent awkwardly to tighten the gauze over the baby in the bassinet.

"You needn't apologize," I said. "I should have looked where I was going. I put your baby in danger." I stared at the girl, the only type of baby I'd ever seen. "Twins?"

"Yes. The first goddess blessed me with both a girl and a boy, with a daughter to take care of me and my husband in our later years and a son to do the same for his goddess's family, to learn the value of love." She bounced her baby girl higher and shifted the bassinet onto her elbow once again. "It's fine. It was an accident." She smiled, falteringly. "We're so looking forward to tomorrow. My husband is one of the men playing the music. We've already gotten the copper for it." The baby on her left arm cried out suddenly, her face twisting in fury. "Shh, shh," said the woman, rocking her back and forth.

I didn't want to tell her there was nothing special "tomorrow." Besides, *I* hadn't gotten an invitation to my Returning. He must have assumed I'd go, but I had no plans to be there.

"Noll, praise the goddess!" A hand touched my shoulder. Elweard. He had a barrel under one arm and a grin that took up half his face. "Vena and I were just talking about you. We received so many coppers for the Returning—we're so looking forward to finally meeting him, and thanking him for all his orders—and the invitation asked us to provide enough for the whole village to drink." Elweard laughed, but he wasn't one to wait for responses, which was just as well. "But he paid us far more than that! The village couldn't possibly drink that much, even if there were enough wheat and grapes to make enough ale and wine, and we wondered if it would be wrong if we kept the copper and sent the two of you and his servants free drinks for life, or if the lord would need it back—"

Elweard droned on, and the woman curtseyed at me best she could with one screaming baby in her arms and the child's twin joining in the cacophony from beneath his veil. Stepping aside and putting the bassinet on a bench in front of a nearby shop, she tugged at the gauze gently, shifting it so slightly I could hardly believe it moved at all.

"Noll?" Elweard's voice drew me out of my reverie. "*Do* you need Vena to stand up for you and the lord? I know you probably have another in mind. Alvilda, maybe, since you've been helping her with carving, or your sister's man's mother—"

"No!" I gritted my teeth and fought hard to keep the anger buried within. The woman stood up, tightening the gauze over the bassinet, a deep breath visibly escaping her lips. I clutched my skirt with both hands as the woman disappeared into the crowd, that black gauze on the bassinet threatening to drown me in memories of the veiled lord, in images of me and him where Elfriede and Jurij had once stood, in him removing the veil, in what I would find beneath it … "No. Thank you, Elweard, but no."

Elweard scratched his head. "All right. Vena thought we ought to offer, that's all. But about the copper … "

"I have to go." I spun around, almost smacking into another woman. At least this one carried bread in her basket instead of babies.

"Oh my! Noll!" Mistress Baker placed a hand on her chest. "Just the woman I was about to go visit. I thought maybe I should ask which of these breads you want served at the ceremony and which we should just send home with everyone." She shifted the loaves aside in her basket, producing one roll after another. "The lord sent us enough copper to feed the village three times over, so we've been working hard and making everything, but we simply can't carry it all to the Great Hall tomorrow. My husband hasn't slept a wink in days, I swear—"

I swirled around as if in a dance and darted through the crowd, leaving poor Mistress Baker to her breads and probable confusion once she looked up to find me gone.

Relief flooded my body when I finally made it across town to Alvilda's. I almost tore the door open, but then I remembered her visitor and knocked before I entered. Alvilda told me to wait a moment, and then to let myself in.

"Good day, Noll!" called a cheerful voice as I entered. Master Tailor's worn down owl mask greeted me from Alvilda's ever-dusty eating table. "How goes the woodcarver's daughter?"

I sighed and slipped into the seat next to him, placing the chisel and the wood on the table, where they seemed right at home. Alvilda was by her workbench, lost in the task of whittling a chair leg. I could see the as-yet-unfinished headboard propped up against the wall in the corner. She said nothing.

"The same," I offered. I didn't bother to ask whether he was inquiring about the daughter in front of him or the one who made his son's life worth living.

Master Tailor answered for me. "I bet she's excited about her wedding in the spring!" Even though everyone in the village was excited for the Returning, the most important things remained the same. Their own men, their own goddesses. Their children and the goddesses and men belonging to their children. I was just an excuse to have a celebration. Copper in their pocket, a day off from work.

Alvilda dropped the chair leg she was carving and shook her head in disbelief. She threw her gouge on the workbench, marched across the room, and whacked Master Tailor on the back of his head. Sawdust went flying with each movement.

"Ow!" Master Tailor rubbed the back of his dark curls.

"Go home!" barked Alvilda.

"What?" asked Master Tailor quizzically. "I'm excited about Noll's Returning, too, of course. Nissa has been so helpful in making the lord's new garments. Not that they're much different than the usual garments he orders, but Nissa does such a good job, they look better than—"

Alvilda crossed her arms. "Out."

Master Tailor shook his owl head and stood up from the table. "Sometimes I wonder if you think you're my goddess instead of Siofra."

Alvilda tapped her foot. "That's a disturbing thought. At least you can choose whether or not to obey my orders. Although I do suggest you choose wisely."

Master Tailor waved his hand lazily in her direction. "I'm going, I'm going."

"Mistress Tailor asked me to tell you to come home," I interjected.

Master Tailor tensed and moved so quickly out the door that I could hardly believe he'd had time to cross the room.

Alvilda shook her head and filled the seat that Master Tailor had just emptied. "You have to watch how you word your orders from a goddess to her man. They're almost as effective as direct orders from the woman herself, so long as they have a basis in truth."

That was true. I felt a little guilty messing around with that kind of power, even if I hadn't intended to. "Sorry."

She shrugged and began playing with her fingers, concerned with picking out some of the sawdust stuck under her nails.

"So," said Alvilda, finally giving up her futile quest to clean her nails and slapping her palms against the table. She picked up my half-block, half-rock piece of wood and examined it. "How goes the carving?"

I thought back to the ruined sculptures and other blobs of wood that looked no better than the piece Alvilda turned over in her hands. "Spectacularly," I lied.

Alvilda put the wood back on the table. "And how goes the carver?"

I waved a hand. "He's the same as always."

Alvilda shook her head and grabbed my hand that rested on the table. I flinched. "I meant the *other* carver in the family," she said.

I started bawling.

Alvilda got up from her seat and swooped in to embrace me, but that only made me cry harder. She let me cry a few moments more before she took my face in her hands and put on her most stunning smile. I wondered if this was how Jaron saw her when he first knew she was his goddess, and my heart ached for the pain he must be feeling even at that moment, to know that he would never hold her in his arms as I did.

"So, what would you like to do today?" asked Alvilda. I hadn't actually told her I was going to come over.

I glanced toward the work area of her home and the fallen chair leg. "Don't you have work to do?"

Alvilda shook her head and began shoving a few buns, some cheese, and a bottle into a picnic basket. "Nothing that can't wait another few days," she said. I noticed with some pleasure that her picnic basket's handle featured what I thought might be swords and daggers.

"A picnic sounds wonderful," I said.

Chapter Thirteen

Alvilda's choice spot for a picnic wasn't my own, but I imagined she didn't want me to head back home before I had to. We enjoyed the meager meal in silence under a tree just a ways from the commune. My eyes guiltily wandered over the moaning, wretched men sprawled out on the ground or walking about, lifting one foot after the other slowly, aimlessly. It was an odd choice for my last day of freedom, but I had no place else I'd be welcomed. After a little while, Alvilda went inside her home to grab my chisel. She gave me a new block of wood, and I'd started carving a flower. A lily.

It felt good to eat, to carve, and to not think. To feel less alone but to not have to answer to anyone.

The feeling didn't last beyond a few hours.

"Siofra sent me!"

I craned my head behind me lazily to see Master Tailor half jogging, half walking from the village toward our shady retreat. The closer he got, the louder his panting grew. The owl mask blocked his features from me, but I could almost imagine the strain on his face. He doubled over as he reached us, resting his hands on his thighs.

"What is it, Coll?" asked Alvilda. Her hand had tensed around the picnic basket, and she looked ready to jump up and run.

Master Tailor waved impatiently in Alvilda's direction.

"Siofra sent me ... "

Alvilda rolled her eyes. "Yes, we got that part."

Master Tailor took a few more gasps of air through the horribly confining small hole that opened over his mouth. I wondered briefly if death superseded a goddess's commands or if a command gave a man the strength to overcome even death to see the order followed through.

"Take it easy," she said. "You can't follow your goddess's order if you're dead."

Master Tailor nearly choked on his breaths mixed with laughter. For a moment, my muscles relaxed, but Master Tailor's troubled laugh still made me nervous.

"Mistress Tailor sent you?" I asked, rather impatiently.

Master Tailor took a great swell of breath and stood erect. "There's been an earthquake."

My stomach churned. Alvilda looked as panicked as I felt. *With Ingrith gone, who would dare look at the castle?*

Master Tailor continued, oblivious of the discomfort of his audience. "We were sewing. The kids were helping out." He nodded his owl head. "That Nissa's going to be a fine tailor. I'm so happy Luuk found the goddess in her."

"Coll," said Alvilda. "The earthquake."

Master Tailor pointed east. "We heard a tremendous noise in the direction of the woods. It was like the earth was groaning, and we could feel it moving beneath our feet. It caused Siofra to drop the shirt she was sewing and tumble clear off her chair." Master Tailor paused, perhaps in pain at the idea of Mistress Tailor tumbling, even though he was under orders to continue speaking.

I had more pressing concerns. "Who looked at the castle?

Master Tailor didn't respond to my question. "We went outside, and Siofra told me she saw a black carriage come out of the woods and stop in front of the woodcarver's home. I wanted to go check on Jurij and Elfriede, but Siofra stopped me. She said I had to explain what happened to Noll first, and then tell Noll to go." He directed his owl mask at me. "Go."

If Mistress Tailor hadn't worded her commands exactly right, he was liable to scream at me to go like a crazy person without any further explanation. If Alvilda thought it odd that her brother would turn into an unthinking being to speak Mistress Tailor's tale, she didn't indicate it. I wondered if Mistress Tailor often used her husband as a sort of messenger.

The black carriage. But it was too early in the day for it to come, waiting for its passenger.

Waiting for me.

But someone had caused the earth to shake. Elfriede wouldn't have been so foolish, would she?

Alvilda started gathering the basket and blanket. "Let's go." She shoved the items unceremoniously at Master Tailor, and he scrambled to catch them. "Drop these off at my home and then go comfort your wife. I'll send word as soon as we know that Jurij, Elfriede, and Gideon are well."

Master Tailor stood silent for a moment, shifting his weight from one foot to the other. He was finally free to do as he pleased, and he clearly seemed uncomfortable with the idea. Alvilda stepped up to fill the void that Mistress Tailor's fulfilled command had left behind in the man. "You've done as Siofra asked," said Alvilda, although she didn't turn to look at her brother. She grabbed me by the wrist and started dragging me toward the village. "Get going."

I wasn't entirely sure Alvilda didn't have as much power over him as his goddess because Master Tailor got his second wind and parted from us, jogging toward Alvilda's home.

As we entered the middle of town, Alvilda let go of my wrist and put an arm around my shoulders, pushing me slightly forward so that I could keep up the pace. The closer we got to the Tailors' at the east end of the village, the more people were out of their homes and shops and murmuring to one another. Almost every one of them would glare at us as we passed, a few whispering to their neighbors. I suddenly felt protected under Alvilda's tight grip on my shoulders.

"If someone looked at the castle by my house, why would the ground shake this far out?" I asked Alvilda quietly.

Alvilda shook her head. "I'm not sure. It seems that the farther east we get, the more people were affected."

She was right. The crowds grew larger as we moved on, and we had to fight our way through the center of the road, sometimes only able to shove our way through after a few curt exclamations of "Excuse us!" from Alvilda.

At last we broke free from the village horde, nearing the Tailor Shop at the very end of the line of houses. There stood Mistress Tailor in the open doorway with Luuk, Nissa, and Bow.

"Alvilda!" cried Mistress Tailor. Her voice had a frightening quality to it, one I wasn't used to hearing from the taciturn woman. She broke free from her grip on Luuk's hand and rushed forward, practically shoving me aside to embrace Alvilda.

Alvilda jumped, and her arms hung to her side limply. Her eyes flickered from left to right and then focused over Mistress Tailor's shoulders at the kids and Bow. She gave Mistress Tailor a quick pat on the back.

"Coll told us," she said. She gripped Mistress Tailor's shoulders, and she pushed her away so she could look at her. "He's on his way back."

Mistress Tailor's eyes glistened wet with tears. Her face seemed almost girlish. She stepped back and cradled one arm tightly against her chest. No sooner had she done this than Master Tailor's voice came booming from the crowd behind us. "Excuse me!"

Alvilda grabbed me by the wrist. "Come on!"

As we made our way up the first hill, Alvilda's ashen face turned a more sullen shade of olive-gray. I tugged my wrist free and ran in front of her.

My lungs, though ready to burst, inhaled the cool air imbued with an eerie fog that appeared as I came over the hill.

The fog burned in my throat and likely kept the castle entirely from view. I was too afraid to check.

When my home emerged through the fog over one last little hill, I nearly stumbled forward. Arrow gave a low-toned growl from the mist beside me. The poor pup was tied to a tree at the very edge of the woods a few yards away, his muzzle wrapped in what appeared to be fine black silken twine. But more arresting than poor Arrow's plight was the black carriage blocking the doorway of my home.

On top of the carriage in the driver's seat sat one of the specters with his cloud-white hair tied neatly into a tail, a few curls framing his face, which at first glance appeared to be eerily alluring, but on closer inspection, was flawed and wrinkled. The men may have been much older than I had first guessed them to be. Still, his hair was not the gray, dirty white of the older men in the village. It was a pure, unblemished white hair that retained its youthful silkiness.

The specter looked forward, his hands tightly grasping black silken reins. He didn't so much as glance in my direction. The four pitch-black horses that stood erect in front of him were surprisingly silent. I hadn't seen many horses, not outside of the livestock, but I knew that I ought to hear snorts or whinnies, see them shuffling their feet or shaking their manes—*something* to indicate that they were bored just standing around. These horses gave me the impression that they were above showing such crassness, or perhaps they viewed it as weakness. *How have I never noticed before?*

Arrow let out a pitiful whine. For a moment, I thought of going to free him, but my heart was pounding, and I was eager to get inside.

I walked past the coachman without a word. Circling the horses, I stepped back as another specter appeared before me. The red in his eyes overwhelmed me, but just for a moment. I moved to step around him. The specter anticipated the movement and stepped to block me. I moved back to push through on my original path. The specter blocked me again. Daring him to try again, I stared into his blood red eyes.

"Let us through!"

Alvilda sprinted up behind me. I hadn't realized I'd put so much distance between us. Her face contorted in fury, and she breathed hard as she slipped in beside me. "What's going on here?" she snapped, taking a quick look at the carriage, the horses, and the specters in turn.

The specters said nothing. But I knew they wouldn't.

"They won't answer you," I said, as much to myself as to Alvilda. I didn't tear my gaze from the red eyes of the specter in front of me, waiting to see if he would prove me wrong. He didn't move. He didn't blink.

"This is the young lady's home," said Alvilda, slowly and with a hint of threat behind each word. "Let us in."

The lord's servant didn't move. Alvilda and I did the dance with him again, trying to move as one past him, but he blocked us. We gave each other a barely noticeable nod, split apart, and tried to pass by the specter via both sides at once. He moved to block me. Another specter appeared like a phantom from the mist at the side of the coach and blocked Alvilda.

"This is ridiculous!" shouted Alvilda, throwing her hands up in the air. She stood on her toes and attempted to shout over the specters' shoulders. "Jurij! Gideon! Elfriede!"

A lump formed in my throat. Somehow I knew Alvilda's impassioned screaming would prove useless. It was my words that were needed.

"Elfriede! Father!" I called, my voice trembling. "Jurij!" I stomped my foot. "Oh, let me through!"

The specters parted.

Facing each other inward, they extended their arms nearest the door to my home to point the way. The mist cleared in the pathway and the door parted slightly.

I stepped forward. The specters quickly took their places again behind me, blocking Alvilda's path.

"Let me through!" she snarled. She forewent all hope of decorum by launching herself at the specters, wrestling with them as best she could. Sadly, it looked about as effective as a kitten attacking a mountain. The specters barely moved in response to her attack, other than to continue to block her.

"It's all right," I told her, more confident than I felt. "Wait here."

Alvilda stopped struggling and grunted. "Just scream if you need me."

I laughed quietly. I didn't think she'd been able to reach me even if I was screaming as if my life depended upon it, but I didn't tell her that.

I stepped forward, willing strength into my legs to keep me steady. They still ached from the run, but there was more to my body's apprehension than mere exhaustion. The walk from the path to my doorway took an eternity, but eventually I found myself standing before the front door, my shaky hand on the surface. I pushed forward.

I didn't know what I expected to see inside my home, but it wasn't what I found. The fire roaring, the pot of stew still boiling. Elfriede stirring the pot, ready to serve the same stew for dinner that she had for lunch. I caught Jurij's eye as I entered. The knuckles of his hands atop Elfriede's shoulders were almost as white as the specters' skin.

Father sat at his usual place at the table, as if he hadn't moved since I'd last seen him. His hands were gripped tightly together atop the surface. His gaze was locked in front of him. Elfriede, even over her stirring, stared at the same place. Only Jurij would glance in my direction, but his eyes kept flickering back to the table.

A man sat there.

As if "sat there" were words enough to describe the effect of his presence. Two more specters stood at either corner of the man's chair, unblinking and unmoving.

"Olivière," spoke the lord. "I have been waiting for you."

He was as still as the specters around him at first. Eventually, he unfolded his hands and gave what appeared to be an attempt at a welcoming gesture, a diminutive open embrace meant to indicate that I sit in the chair across from him.

"Well?" The lord's hands tapped impatiently on the table.

I raised an eyebrow and looked from one person in the

room to the next. Only Jurij's eyes would meet mine, albeit briefly. He seemed as puzzled as I.

Only I wasn't entirely puzzled. I hadn't gone to him in months. So he had come to me—even if he claimed he couldn't leave the castle. *Well, that was obviously a lie.*

A loud clang. Father, Jurij, and I all turned to look at Elfriede. Tears ran down her cheeks as she swooped down to pick up the ladle she had dropped, spilling bits of the stew across the floor. Jurij bent down quickly to join her.

The lord and the specters did not turn. "That will not be necessary," said the lord. He raised one hand. "Please clean up that mess."

His voice was so arresting, I almost moved to help Elfriede clean the mess myself. But the words were not yet fully spoken before the two specters were bending down to mop up the mess with rags they pulled from within their jackets. Elfriede and Jurij stood up and backed away warily, clutching one another's hands for support, the ladle back in Elfriede's possession. One of the specters withdrew a miniscule broom and a small metal pan from his jacket and briskly brushed the floor once the stew chunks were missing. The other pulled out a black, silken sack and emptied his pan and the rags into the sack, almost soundlessly.

The first specter restored the broom and pan to his jacket and pulled out a new rag. He grabbed the ladle from Elfriede, eliciting a small whimper from her, wiped it clean, and handed it back to her. Elfriede took it but required Jurij to wrap his free hand around hers to support the ladle in her grip.

The specters glided back into place behind the lord. It had taken longer for me to understand what had happened than for the actual event to take place. The specters seemed unchanged from mere moments before; the only difference now was that one stood holding the silken bag slightly to his front as if it were a freshly caught rabbit. There were surprisingly no visible wrinkles to the bag's smooth surface.

"Olivière," repeated the lord, a force not unlike a blast of blizzard air behind his words, "be seated. Please."

I did as asked. The black hands shifted, intertwining the fingers lightly beneath the bottom of the veil.

"Thank you," he said. His head appeared to shift slightly and he waved an arm behind him. "Please, join us. Your stew smells wonderful, and I did not come to delay your dinner. My retainers will serve you."

Elfriede and Jurij exchanged a concerned look, perhaps a little surprised to be further noticed. An unspoken message passed between them and they shuffled over as one, Elfriede taking the remaining chair and Jurij standing protectively behind her.

"A chair," spoke the lord with another wave of his hand.

"No, that's all—" began Jurij, but the specters were already in and out of the home, returning with a cushion-laced stool instead of the black silken bag. *Did they bring that with them in the carriage?* They placed it down next to Elfriede, and one put his hands on Jurij's back in order to guide him to sit atop the stool. "—right." Jurij looked from Elfriede on one side to me on the other, as if hoping either one of us could explain what had just happened.

The specters were already gone, over by the stew pot, ladling stew into white glass bowls they seemed to have pulled out of their pockets.

No one said anything as they worked in fluid motions, setting out white bowls of stew and silver spoons before first me, then my father, and then Elfriede and Jurij. They went back to their guarded posts behind the lord.

Elfriede was the first to pick up her spoon, and Jurij soon followed. Elfriede's hand twitched. "Won't you dine with us?"

It was a silly question, considering the lord's veil. The lord didn't stir. "No, thank you, my dear. I am sure it tastes delightful, but your cooking is meant to enrapture a man other than me."

Elfriede blushed and turned her attention to a floating chunk of potato. Jurij spread his arm on the table, trying to hide his now empty bowl. Usually, he seemed to feel nothing but delight—or at the very most, indifference—to others noticing his love for his goddess. The small gesture of him hiding the bowl from view felt odd to me, like there was a part of him that had enough free will to think negatively of the lord. To think *anything* of the lord. My heart was a flurry at the idea that Jurij might dislike the lord because he'd steal me from him, like that were possible. But that just reminded me that I was expected to accept the lord.

I looked at my own overflowing bowl. I couldn't summon the will to lift the spoon. I shoved the bowl forward.

"I left Alvilda out front," I said, anxious to change the topic. "She was blocked from entering by ... " My gaze traveled to the statue-still specters.

The lord waved his hand, cutting me off. "I will take but a moment of your time this evening. Are you feeling well, Olivière? You have not yet touched your food."

All eyes—visible and not red eyes, at least—fell on my full stew bowl and me. Even Father, I noticed, had finished at least half of his.

"I already dined with Alvilda." It was at least half-true.

Elfriede furrowed her brow and pursed her lips but said nothing.

"Alvilda?" asked the lord tensely. "She is?"

My father moved to open his mouth, but one of the specters bent down and perhaps murmured something where I imagined the lord's ear to be. *So they can speak?*

"Ah," said the lord. "The lady carver. I can see now why there are so many ... interesting ... wooden trinkets about." He motioned to the mantle above the fireplace, where I had haphazardly dumped this morning's creations.

Ugh. Those weren't my best work.

"Do you really think her a wise companion, Olivière?"

I felt a roar of fire grow in my stomach. "Alvilda has talent. She may get most of the village's carpentry and carving work these days instead of my father, but I assure you it's by his own deeds that he suffers in his trade as of late." I sent a pointed look to Father, but he did nothing more than pick up another spoonful of stew.

Another wave of a gloved hand. "I refer more to the detail that she refused her Returning."

My jaw dropped. "What business is it—"

"I've told her time and time again that I agree with you, my lord," interrupted Father.

My blood boiled. *Really.* I opened my mouth to speak.

"It matters not." The lord began to rise, and the specters slid smoothly behind him to make room. "The morrow is Olivière's Returning, and after the ceremony she will reside with me in the castle."

I shot up, sending my chair flying backward and crashing. "Excuse me?"

"Noll, listen." Father spoke quietly.

"I didn't agree to a Returning!"

There, I had said it. No one had asked my opinion before.

Elfriede dropped her spoon onto her bowl. The silver hitting the glass made a strange *clang*, not like the wood-on-wood of our usual dinnerware. Jurij seemed stunned, and I noticed his hand twitched nervously on his thigh, his chair half pushed backward, whether readying himself to jump up or forcing himself to stay seated, I couldn't be sure. Father's face glazed over, his eyes darting from corner to corner, probably looking for a bottle.

The lord stood unmoved a moment, towering about a head over me. I tried to imagine where I might find his eyes behind the veil and I stared, daring him to correct me.

The lord's hat shifted, and he made a quick motion in my direction with a gloved hand. For a moment, I thought the specters might move to grab me. I tensed, ready to put up as fruitless a fight as Alvilda had. Instead, they righted my fallen chair and exited the house through the doorway behind me.

"I assumed you would be ready by the morrow," said the lord after a brief moment of silence. "I gave you time to prepare yourself. Even if you chose not to visit me. Besides, your father and sister assured me just now that you would be ready."

A pain shot through my chest. I glanced at Father and

Elfriede in turn, but neither would meet my gaze. Jurij, at least, seemed in genuine shock at the revelation. Perhaps he'd been dreaming of Elfriede when they'd had the discussion. "I can see now that I was mistaken. The ceremony should be canceled," continued the lord. He traced the table with the tip of a gloved finger as he made his way past my father to join Jurij and me at the other side. He held the finger up to his veil, examining the small traces of sawdust. Then he flicked away the dust with his thumb and grabbed my hand in his before I could stop him. His grip was harder than I remembered.

"But I will come for you on the morrow nonetheless."

He slid my hand under his veil and pressed those cold, damp lips of marble to the tips of my fingers.

Chapter Fourteen

I didn't speak for the rest of the evening. I couldn't look at my father or Elfriede, and it was just as well for Father, who used the opportunity to stay long into the night at Vena's. He didn't appear again, not even in the morning to bid me farewell.

Elfriede busied herself first with freeing and washing Arrow and then with all manner of outside chores until the chilly air forced her to enter the home and pull herself beneath the bed covers. It wasn't our shared bed that she entered, but our parents'. She needn't have bothered. I didn't use a bed. Instead, I curled up against Alvilda's side, and we shared a quilt wrapped around our shoulders on the ground before the dying fire. She said nothing, only ceasing her gentle squeeze on my shoulder to stroke my hair on occasion.

Jurij gave me a sorry look and a pat or two on the shoulder before he disappeared outside with Elfriede. *Some friend. But then, the command must have worn off after the Returning.* When she came back inside, he wasn't with her. I'd hoped to see him in the morning, but the carriage came bursting through the woods at the first fleck of light over the mountainous horizon. I felt the urge to flee, and I searched restlessly for some clue in Alvilda's expression that I should follow the urge to run, that I could still hope for the choice that was my gift. The choice that was my right.

Alvilda wouldn't meet my eyes.

Elfriede shuffled out of the house, her face red and puffy. She nervously embraced me. I didn't embrace her back. I half wondered if she was secretly happy to see me go, so I could no longer distract Jurij from his goddess. Because I had no doubt that Jurij had told her of how I begged for his love. He wouldn't have thought it mattered at all. And to him, it didn't.

"Good tidings," Elfriede whispered. "Joyous birthday."

I turned away.

Six specters appeared beside me, two grabbing my arms, the others before and behind me. They moved me toward the carriage as if I were a ragdoll.

"Wait!" called Alvilda. "I have to say goodbye!"

The carriage door shut behind me. I peered out the small window to watch as Alvilda chased after us for a bit, and Elfriede stood frozen in the doorway. Then they were swallowed by the trees, and the breaking light of dawn was replaced by the shades of darkness.

"*Olivière.*" I heard the whisper of my dream even then. Even when there was no hope for me to escape to it.

***

"Is the venison not to your liking?"

Since he had already noticed, I let my fork fall abruptly to the plate, taking a little perverse pleasure in the drop of gravy that spoiled the delicate roses embroidered into the too-white tablecloth. I tore at the trencher meant for scraping the plate of the meat's juices and swallowed a chunk of the white loaf. It crumbled too easily in my throat.

"Olivière?"

I continued chewing and stared across the far-too-long table at the speaker. My dining companion. A set of black-gloved hands attached to a hazy outline obscured by a sheer black curtain. Actual sunlight was allowed into this castle, even if it was only the orange tint of twilight and not the bright white of true sunbeams, but it could do little to help me make out the lord behind the curtain. So this was how the masked ate when their goddesses couldn't perform the Returning. At least this was how this one ate. I couldn't picture Master Tailor bothering with this elaborate set-up in his home. I believed he ate only with Jurij and Luuk, or maybe at the Great Hall with other men or with Alvilda. And never with his goddess.

But this masked lord wasn't one for propriety.

It was hard to decide when the lord looked most inhuman, walking around with a veil wrapped around his head showing me this or that room in the castle, or sitting leagues away from me at a dining room table, that long curtain hanging between us, for our first breakfast, lunch, and dinner together. The masks on the boys and the few masked men of the village seemed almost human in comparison, although they never actually resembled humans until the day of their Returnings.

I thought of the lord from my dream, and how he thrust his face in mine.

I nearly choked on my trencher.

The lord took great care to lay down his knife and fork so that the plate only clinked with the most dulcet of tones.

"Olivière? Are you all right?"

His hand motioned upward behind the veil, and one of the specters standing still at the far edge of the room came to life and arrived swiftly at my side to pour wine into a crystal goblet. I hated the foul taste of wine, but I grabbed it roughly from the specter and downed an entire glass until the bread worked its way free of my throat.

"Are you all right now?" The hands clutched the edge of the table. "Olivière? Answer me!"

"Yes!" I slammed down the goblet, hoping it would shatter, but it remained intact.

The hands let the tablecloth go and picked up the knife and fork again to cut the rest of the meat still on his plate.

I felt a bit light-headed. This was why I hated wine. I shoved the plate away from me. The flank of brownish meat was even more disgusting now that my nose was full of the stench of alcohol.

"Would you care for another dish for dinner?"

One hand stabbed at a piece of meat with the fork, and then the fork and the hand vanished behind the curtain.

I shook my head and used both hands to push against the table. "I'd like to be excused now." I stood up.

Half-a-dozen specters surrounded me on either side before I could take one step.

"Sit down," said the lord behind the black curtain. "Please."

I did not. "I'm not feeling well," I said through clenched teeth.

"You have not eaten enough. Food will improve your temper."

A few well-placed stabs from Elgar the Blade to his abdomen might "improve my temper." I took a deep breath. Just because I dreamed of a lord even more foul didn't mean this one deserved my anger. I moved to sit, but I caught myself halfway. And why wasn't he deserving? When I thought of how he'd acted when I'd begged for help, or how he assumed I'd perform the Returning ... I had power over him. It was time he remembered that.

"Let. Me. Leave."

The fork fell to the floor with an echoing thud. One hand gripped the tablecloth again. I found it strange to observe the specters looking almost lifelike all around me. They didn't move to pick up their lord's fork. They didn't move to block me. In fact, a number of them stepped backward, clearing a roundabout way to the dining hall doorway. I smiled.

The lord loosened his grip on the tablecloth and picked up a napkin from beside his plate. "She means to let her retire from the dining hall for the night. And so shall I." The napkin disappeared behind the curtain.

The specters swept into a state of activity, having regained their composure. As expected, one swooped down by his lord to pick up the fallen fork. The others stood in two facing lines, forming an enclosed path between the doorway and myself.

But I wasn't satisfied.

"No, that's not the full extent of my wishes," I began, emphasizing each word with a strained attempt at Elfriede's own pretense of innocent sweetness. "Let—"

The lord flew into motion, knocking his chair backward into the waiting arms of one of the specters. The curtain in front of him shook rapidly with the movement.

"Do not speak further!" he bellowed.

The words echoed in the cavernous dining hall and died only after a series of repetitions.

I could see the two black-leathered hands clench into fists below the surface of the fluttering curtain.

I clenched my own fists. "I don't think you understand how this works—"

"Silence!"

"No! Who do you think you are? What do you think you're supposed to mean to me? I don't even know you. I don't want to be here, and you're expecting me to perform the Returning!"

The black fists pounded on the table. "Was it not *you* who first sought me out?"

I gestured at the ridiculously large, cold, and empty room around me. "Not for this! I never asked to be your goddess! I just wanted—" I bit my lip. There was never going to be any going back.

"You wished to free your friend so you could steal him from his goddess." He made a gesture toward the line of specters, and the two closest appeared at my side, their hands wrapped tightly against my arms. "How unfortunate that I was unable to help you with such a generous act." I struggled to break free, but I felt powerless in their tight grip.

The lord turned sharply. Before he took more than two steps, a series of specters appeared from the line, one to pick up his plate from the table and then one who fit the lord with his black veil and hat even as he walked. He appeared in mere moments from the side of the curtain.

"Come with me!" He exited the dining hall doorway.

The specters dragged me after him. I kicked and screamed, and, thinking of Alvilda, even tried to reach the specters' hands in order to bite them. They dragged me forward without hesitation, and other specters broke from the line to open the doors for the lord.

"Stop!" I screamed.

The lord stopped.

"Let me—"

"Silence her!" he ordered before walking again, and one of my pale captors produced a black veil-like material and wrapped it over my mouth, tying it at the back of my head. My eyes welled with tears. But not from sadness. No, this was a rage I'd felt only once before. *He's just like the men from my dream.*

Staring straight ahead into the back of that black-veiled head was no different than staring right into the front. It made me realize that there was no loss of honor to stab this man in the back if need be. The thought gave me comfort, and I let the specters drag me, soon willing my feet to keep up with their pace so that they wouldn't be so sore. But try as I might, I couldn't quite match my pace with them or with the lord in front of me.

He led us through the main entryway and up a flight of stairs. From there, we marched down the long hallway that contained an empty set of guest rooms—one of which the lord had shown me earlier and told me would be mine, an opulent room that retained the chill of the castle air despite the tremendous fire in the fireplace and the bear-skin rug spread before it. I had spent the afternoon after the "tour" and lunch nestled deep within the fur, and still the chill sliced down inside of me.

As we passed a hall window, I noticed that the sun had set. The dull torchlight and the slit of a moonbeam were all there was to light the way. But the lord moved through the near-darkness unheeded, as comfortable navigating the twists and turns of the path before us as I had been in my own dark secret cavern. Only I at least knew a violet glow awaited me at the end of that journey. What would await me now? A prison? A shackle for my arms and legs to match the muzzle over my mouth?

The lord led us up another flight of stairs and across a hallway. My heart sank at my speculations nearly proven. This had not been on the "tour." The specters had even blocked me from coming this far my first time to the third floor. The lord's shoulders twitched as we passed the throne room, its doors opened, the room darkened. But I'd never been past this point.

At the end of that hallway—the coldest place yet in the castle, a blast of icy air blowing in from the few windows—stood two more specters, immobile before a large wooden door.

"Let us in!" barked the lord. One of the guards pulled a set of keys out from his front coat pocket and turned the lock. He stood back and both specters pushed open the thick, heavy door; even they strained to do so at their usual rapid pace.

This was it. I was to rot in his prison the rest of my days. Probably "graced" on occasion by a visit from the lord, asking me if I would like some more wine or venison or if I found the cell cold enough or if I was ready to break down and perform the Returning.

Or why I'd "mutilated" my ears.

The nausea that spread over me was met halfway with something deeper. A force of sheer will lent steadiness to my shaky legs. I could let him think he had broken me. I would let him remove the muzzle with his leathery fingers, and with all of my might, even if they proved to be the last words I ever spoke, I could tell the lord to climb up to the roof of the castle or the tallest mountain and to jump to his death. I let the words form on my trapped tongue, ready to pounce the moment he removed the muzzle.

And then the specters dragged me into the room after the lord. He stood in our way for a moment before shifting to the side and pointing to a bed. There, in the middle of the room under a thick quilt, lay my mother.

Chapter Fifteen

I tried to scream, but the veil muzzle gripped too hard against my tongue. Its movements were heavy and impeded.

"Do you understand now? Do you understand what I am to you?"

My eyes darted around the room. I did not understand. I didn't understand at all.

My mother lay in a large wooden bed atop a plush mattress. Across her body, the thick quilt was tucked tightly below her neck and hid everything from view but her face. Aside from a roaring fire in the nearby stone fireplace, the room was empty. I wanted to know how she still remained visible after death and why he would have her.

She moved. I had to squeeze my eyes shut tightly for a moment to make sure I wasn't dreaming. But there it was. Ever so slightly, the area of the quilt over her abdomen rose and fell.

She was alive.

The mother I thought dead months prior had been alive all this time.

But why? How? Why had we held mourning? And why

was she sleeping? Why didn't she wake after hearing all of the ruckus?

"Will you think twice about abusing your power now?"

My gaze shifted from my mother's peaceful shape to the harsh, black-covered lord. He stood beside the bed, his elbows akimbo, his legs slightly parted. He awaited an answer.

I had more than a few choice words to give him, but I couldn't speak. I did what I thought would rectify that situation and nodded.

My eyes still betrayed some of my intentions. The lord nodded, and one of the specters' hands released its grip on my arm and removed the muzzle. However, he stood holding it beside my head, ready to slap it back on at a moment's notice. And his other hand wouldn't release his painful grasp.

I said nothing. Nothing was to be gained yet until I knew what was going on.

The lord had no qualms about filling the silence. "We should have had the Returning today. And the wedding. I would have let your father and sister come to see her." He paused. "I gave you almost a year to get over that *boy* you thought you loved. But, as ever, you prove too stubborn."

It was difficult to bite my tongue and not respond to his comment about Jurij. I forced myself to remain calm. "What's going on? You said you wouldn't help me."

"I said I would do what I could." The lord stirred slightly, seeming to fight something within himself. Then he relaxed. "Her survival was to be a Returning present."

"What?" So much for calm.

The lord crossed both his arms tightly across his chest. "I would have told you, but only upon the Returning."

"But since I refuse the Returning, why did you tell me anyway?"

"Because you have acted so imprudently. You are taken with the power you have over me!"

"The power *I* have over *you*?" I gave a pointed look first to one of my trapped arms and then to the other before glaring in the lord's direction.

He must have nodded, if only slightly. His shiny metal hat tipped forward and caught a small sparkle from the firelight. The specters released me but remained close. The one holding the muzzle tucked it into his front coat pocket. I had the feeling that even though they had set me free, it would take only a slight wave from the lord and I'd find myself ensnared again.

The lord's voice was hard and cold. "You know of what I speak."

I laughed. I was his goddess, but the thought didn't make me rejoice at my power over the lord. It was a mere illusion, like the power of my choice.

My mother was alive and the lord had her in his grasp.

I crossed over to her and felt her cheek. Ice cold, like the rest of this dreaded castle. I wished against all hope that I could turn back time and listen to her and the other villagers. That I had never so much as looked at this place.

I ran a finger across her golden hairline, noticing the touches of gray that framed her face, and watched the barely noticeable twitch of her nose as it took in and let out the frigid air around us.

I faced the lord, one hand still resting atop my mother's head. "How is she alive?"

The lord moved closer, the hollow echoes of his hard-tipped boots reverberating across the room. Without even thinking, I jumped up, sliding between the bed and the wall and clutching the headboard tightly with both hands. Although thin, the lord was more broad-shouldered than I. He wouldn't be able to follow me.

He almost tried it regardless, but he paused and walked slowly in the other direction. He ran a black-gloved hand along the length of the quilt covering my mother and stood opposite me at the foot of the bed.

"I expected to be thanked," he said.

Forget the lost blade Elgar. I wanted a few of my chisels and gouges. Perhaps I could carve him a new face so I could stop directing my anger at an empty black void.

"*Explain*," I uttered slowly, "why my mother is here."

"I had her brought here," replied the lord, "after you asked for my help."

So Father was right. He could have done something. But what had he done?

The specters snapped back into imitating statues.

He was careful with his words, this one, saying not a grain more than bidden. I had never seen a man not yet Returned so reluctant to obey his goddess. But he wasn't like the other men at all; the power he went great lengths to hold over me was more than enough to prove that.

I couldn't help but think the men I'd met in my dream were a warning, something my subconscious had picked up on the few times I'd met the lord.

The lord moved casually now toward the fireplace, the fingers on one hand running over the edges of the footboard.

"I would be careful," he said before pausing. "Just how freely you use that power."

He faced the fireplace now, folding his hands behind his back. One finger pointed outward briefly and the four specters flew in, two on each side of the bed. From their coat pockets, they each removed a small blade and held it out over my mother, ready to strike.

"No!" I screamed, my arms flinging forward, trying vainly through the holes in the headboard to block the nearest blades from my mother.

The lord stepped to my side at the edge of the headboard. He flicked his hand, and the specters put their blades back into their inner coat pockets. They remained hovering over her.

I fumed. "Don't hurt her!"

The lord shrugged. "I am not hurting her."

I pointed at the specters. "Don't let *them* hurt her."

"All right." He waved his hand.

The specters retreated through the doorway. Six more specters marched in. They were all so similar in appearance and in gait that I had yet to put my finger on whether they were identical or merely brethren.

The six shuffled in on either side of the bed, and each removed a blade from his inner coat pocket.

"Stop!" I yelled.

The lord tensed and didn't move, but the specters stirred just a little, glancing first at me and then at the lord. After a moment, the lord moved closer, running his hands slowly over the top of the headboard, almost within reach of me.

I clenched my jaw. "I can play this game all night."

"As can I."

I backed away from his encroaching fingers, not caring if that put me closer to one of the specters and his extended blade.

"I could think of a way to word it," I said, not bothering to pretend any longer, "so that I would *win*."

"And win you would," said the lord. He stood upright and made a slight wave of his fingers. The nearest specter grabbed me and pulled me out from behind my small sanctuary behind the headboard, the blade gone from his hand and both hands gripping tightly on each of my arms.

"But you would also lose."

The rest of the specters lowered their blades toward my mother and I screamed.

Chapter Sixteen

Don't look before love. What if I agreed to the Returning and then he simply vanished at the unmasking? If Ingrith wasn't crazy, no one would even remember.

No. It was too late for that. The lord knew I wasn't able to Return to him. And besides, what if he was needed to save my mother? There had to be a way to word it. To win the choice that was owed to me but to save my mother at the same time. Could the specters still respond to those little hand gestures if I commanded the lord to slice off his own fingers? Had they already been ordered to rush to my mother and kill her if I so much as dared? Would it end there? Would they go to the village and slaughter Father and Elfriede, Alvilda, the Tailors, and Nissa? And Jurij? Would it end with my own death or would they drop me in the commune, forcing me to live with the endless trail of blood my choice had wrought? Would the lord's death be worth it, when with his death, I'd lose all control over the one who held command over the specters?

You sound like a bloodthirsty monster. No different from the men in your dream.

I didn't have to kill the lord to come out on top. The specters gave me some hope. They seemed different when I gave my orders. They obeyed him, but in that brief moment, they at least appeared confused. That could prove to be my opening, if I could just figure out how to take advantage of it. But before I could risk my mother's safety, I would have to practice, to push and pull with inconsequential orders and figure out how I could stop the specters from acting, even as I prevented the lord from noticing what I was doing. But he noticed every order. He anticipated it. He must have spent all this time since he met me planning for my refusal, even as I lay ignorant in my bed beyond the woods. If the stories were to be believed, he could have spent a millennia preparing for my refused Returning.

The lord of our village. He who never stepped beyond the woods surrounding his castle. A lord whose birth and parents no one could remember. There were those whispers that he was proof of the tale—that men who couldn't find their goddesses among the village women would live forever until they did. For if no one remembered when he was born, was it possible that he was older than everyone who lived?

I shuddered to think of an old, wrinkled, spotted man taunting me behind that black veil. To unmask him upon a Returning might be more chilling than seeing him now hidden from view.

My mind swam with faded, unreal memories of the village that was and was not my own.

You said you would help them. And then you left them.

I shook my head. It wasn't real. My hands reached out for a phantom sheath at my waist. But even if it had been a dream, it lingered with me all these months later.

Because even if I'd seen that lord's face and not this one's, they seemed more and more alike the better I came to know him.

What if that was him in his youth?

An immortal man, whom I visited in the past in my dreams? Ridiculous, but my mind swarmed with questions. There had

161

always been something eerie about our village lord. He was a man most of the village could hardly believe existed, but for the small but steady supply of food and other essentials the boys and men delivered to his castle—which, conveniently, had been stopped now that I had moved in. Until I performed the Returning, the lord's servants would go out into the village and bring home the necessary wares directly. No one—no woman, no man, no child—could set foot in the castle.

The villagers wouldn't object to dealing with the mute servants more often, especially since I heard nothing of the lord demanding his coppers back from what he paid for the Returning preparations. I'd seen the specters all my life. A hint of a white back turning around the corner here. A glimpse of the black carriage in front of the tavern there. There were actual monsters roaming about the village, and I was off fighting lambs.

Who were these servants? Why didn't they speak? Why were they unmasked? They couldn't be married. Or perhaps they had been or at least had been Returned to, but their goddesses lived elsewhere.

The women who lay beyond the cavern pool. A pool that was a path to the past.

Did it matter? I wasn't leaving the castle, that much I knew.

My mind grew tired with all of the thinking. For there was the question, too, of how much my friends and family knew about my mother. How much the entire village knew. Was I alone left in the dark, or did only a few of them know the truth of the matter? Did those closest to me know, and was that why they all seemed so anxious I perform my Returning? Had I broken my father's heart all over again by delaying his meeting with his one true sunlight? Did he truly believe I would experience the Returning with the lord without knowing what it was I put at risk—or that I could even do so once I had known all that was at stake?

That was the worst of it. Now that I knew, at least a part of me thought that it would be wise to give up the fight. But my heart would simply never be up to Returning to the lord. Even if all the will had gone out of me. I was cursed by the gift of choice.

What I would give to be Elfriede, whose heart shifted so freely from distaste to love after the initial shock of the confession. What I would give to be Elfriede, just to be with the one I loved.

But that was fine. I could live without love. I'd accepted that by now. I wasn't sure I could live without freedom.

***

Yet another day passed. I'd lost count.

At first, I filled my days with thoughts of my dilemma and ways to escape my trap. It made the time pass quickly, but it produced no results. Each idea ended with the lord's gruesome death, followed immediately by the equally horrific deaths of those I loved.

I began to resent the idea that my mother was alive after all, that she had not died from illness, and that the specters had stopped their blades a mere hair's breadth from touching her. And I hated myself for that. Especially since if it wasn't her, it would surely have been another loved one.

My mind went numb after a while.

I didn't see much of the lord. We dined together in the dining hall for breakfast, lunch, and dinner—at his orders. He tried to ask me about myself, about my thoughts on the castle, but he'd get frustrated at my silence and storm out. Eventually, he resigned himself to the same silence in which I had found refuge. We ate together, neither one of us saying a word.

I was given free reign of the castle, except I wasn't allowed to set foot on the third floor. The top of the second staircase was guarded by five specters anytime I thought myself alone and able to sneak up the stairs. Morning or night, they just stood there, staring above my head, their legs slightly parted and their hands clutched behind their backs. They moved only when I attempted to climb under their legs or fit between them—then all of a sudden they were fast as hares, blocking my path. At last, I gave up. The obstructed entryway meant I couldn't visit my mother, whose prison was the only place I could possibly wish to go in the dank and dreary castle. This made me even angrier and more eager not to please. I shut myself away in my room between meals.

When the snows came and blocked even the view of the village from my room's window, it felt fitting. I was trapped in a place from which I could reach no one I loved.

And even that dream world never came back to me. Without the blade, without the pool, I'd never know if I'd seen a vision of the past.

I saw the specters often. They brought me tea between meals and built a fire. At first they also brought things I assumed were meant to amuse me: old books, art supplies, and embroidery. All things to which I had never taken and had no desire to practice still. My mind was numb enough without drudgery. Several weeks into the snows, the servants saw to my fire, but they no longer brought me anything.

There were dresses in the chest at the foot of my bed. At first the specters would choose one—a different one each day—and lay it on my mattress. My hands dared to touch them and found them finer than anything I had seen on any woman, but rough and cold to the touch—and far too heavy. They also immediately brought to mind images of Master and Mistress Tailor, whom I assumed would have made them, as they were the only true tailors in the village. And thoughts of the Tailors brought up thoughts of Jurij. I wouldn't wear them.

Eventually, the specters delivered a strange package to my room that contained the clothing I'd left behind at home. I sorted through the pile, my heart nearly stopping when I came across the dress with the fine embroidery flowers on the back. I fingered it, familiar with the dress but the needlework new to me. It was the torn dress I'd worn that day I fell into the pool. She'd fixed it at some point, and I hadn't even noticed. It was clearly Elfriede's handiwork, done to mask the ripped material. The rips down the dress like the cracks of a whip. My finger stopped at a single crooked thread that Elfriede had failed to cover up.

This dress was first stitched by Avery. And that dream was no dream at all.

I burned with the stupid idea that this was more proof I'd met the lord in the past. In a past so long ago no one else even remembered it.

Not that it mattered. I wasn't allowed to leave the castle.

As soon as I slipped into the dress, the specters swooped into the room and took the dress I'd worn to the castle from the floor. I nearly screamed upon their sudden entrance.

The dress was given back to me later the same day, washed and folded.

For some reason, it felt like I had lost in a game I hadn't intended to play.

***

When I woke up one morning, a surge of warmth hit my face. I lay in bed for a moment, picturing myself having risen from a nap on the hilltop where I'd often picnicked with Jurij. But I couldn't feel grass and dirt beneath my fingers, only cold silken plush.

I remembered where I was. My eyes opened reluctantly.

A sunbeam trickled onto my bed from the window. It actually warmed me, and I felt a stirring in my heart. Cautiously, I sat up and then took the few steps over to the window. I peered out and my heart soared, if but for a brief moment. The snow had melted. A gentle haze permeated the horizon, but I could still make out the village below. Perhaps spring had finally come.

Before I could be summoned for breakfast, I dressed, this time in the worn-down dress that I often wore when I'd been carving. It had been cleaned before it was presented to me and was cleaned every time I wore it since, but I still imagined it carried the scent of sawdust.

I bypassed the untouched vanity and the white hairbrush I knew would be lying out for me. Although I didn't brush my hair myself, the specters had started brushing it for me before meals. All the better reason to leave before they got there. Perhaps I would find a knife with which to chop it all off and leave them with nothing to make pretty.

Gently, I pushed the door open a crack. I sucked in my abdomen and squeezed through, quietly pushing the door shut behind me. No one was in the hallway, but I stood still for a moment anyway to see if anyone stirred. I knew from the "tour" that the lord's chambers were located on the floor above mine, but I wouldn't put it past the specters to be on guard. But no one came.

I slipped across the hallway to the staircase and took one step down at a time, cautiously peering through the banister for signs of the specters. There was no one.

I came upon the grand entryway and my heart skipped a beat. This was where I'd had my first encounter with the lord, more than a year prior. I could picture myself now, bathed in a moonbeam, following it to its source.

A sunbeam had replaced that moonbeam. The rays of dawn were peeking through the cracks in the door that led to the inner courtyard. I shuffled quietly over to it and peered through the space in the door as I had the first night I'd foolishly ventured to the castle. A garden. When I'd been shown the place on the "tour," it was but a drab collection of stone and branches. Now, almost overnight, the sun had breathed life into the place.

Feeling suffocated inside, I grabbed hold of both handles on the wide double door and pulled. I stood still for a moment and closed my eyes. They couldn't adjust to the brightness, and I felt blind, but the light that seeped in through my closed eyelids was enough to make my heart race and my mind come to life.

My thoughts flew instantly to the field of flowers that covered the hills near my home in the spring and how I'd run as a child, giggling with Jurij, Darwyn, and my other friends as we kicked up petals and rolled down the hills. I remembered looking up one day and seeing Elfriede sitting quietly atop the hill as she looked after us, careful not to disturb the passionate purple of the flowers that framed her peaceful little body. She weaved together lilies into a circlet for my hair, crowning me "the little elf queen." She'd first named me that, taking a title from one of Mother's stories, although I'm sure she didn't remember. There was no mistaking the vivacity of those hilltop blossoms, flowers that could both robustly cushion a tribe of lively little adventurers and still yield to the gentle movements of a weaver girl's fingers.

The garden in the castle featured only white roses on carefully manicured bright green bushes. Save for the large space immediately in front of the two large wooden doors that led back into the castle, the rose bushes linked together in an unbroken circle framing the entire garden. Cobblestones lined the rest of the garden ground, and there was sign of neither dirt nor grass.

It was no hilltop, but it would have to do.

I shivered. The winter air was retreating, but there was still a nip of cold in the spring morning. The closest thing I could find to a comfortable seat was on one of the two benches on either side of a stone table to the left of the entrance. I sat down on the bench that would give me a full view of the garden and stared again at the odd water fountain at the middle. Two streams of water still spurted from the eyes of the pointed-eared child, his arms outstretched towards the skies. My heart ached for his torment. He seemed to be reaching for something—and weeping because it would never be within his grasp. He and I, we shared much of the same feeling.

A tray with food appeared on the table before me.

I started. A specter stood next to me after dropping off the tray on the stone table, but I hadn't noticed him enter. Despite my best efforts, my movements in the castle hadn't gone unnoticed.

I felt ill.

But the specter soon retreated, leaving me alone in the

garden. The empty feeling in my head and the rumbling in my stomach won out. I picked up the spoon on the tray and began eating. No one disturbed me. The sun rose ever farther over the horizon and the light made the water pouring from the child's eyes sparkle a brilliant blue. It was the first meal I'd enjoyed since my stay began.

Chapter Seventeen

Whenever the sun was out over the next few weeks, I took my breakfasts and lunches in the garden. Even when it was overcast and a chill swept through the air, I went to the garden. Only rain disturbed my sanctuary. And dinner, for that was the one meal the lord ordered that I eat with him. He didn't tell me that—we still didn't speak—but the specters always appeared at dusk, their hands clenched tightly around my arms, and I was whisked away. I always knew it was coming shortly after they came to water the roses.

I began to feel. And that feeling, I was upset to find, was boredom. I almost wished for the books, the needles, and the paints again, if only to find some way to make each day pass by. But I didn't want them enough to break my vow of silence. I hardly wanted them at all. Instead, I took to staring at the fountain or pulling out the petals of a rose one by one.

As if hearing my thoughts, the specters started bringing things again. Paper, quill, and ink. A board decorated with black-and-white squares and thirty-two odd-shaped figures made of bone set on top. I laughed one time when they brought me a flute. I didn't touch it.

Once, they brought me a few blocks of wood and a set of gouges and chisels. I ached to pick up the items and numb my heart with them, but I refused to acknowledge the gift he got right. I didn't touch them, I wouldn't look at them, and they didn't appear again.

Drawing wasn't my strength, but I picked up the quill and ran it back and forth over the paper. I thought about writing a letter home, but I didn't know whether I would be allowed to send it, nor if I could even begin to express my feelings at their betrayal. There was no way I could write a letter to Jurij, and even if I could, I wasn't sure I wanted to. I held the different bone figures in my palms, running my fingers across the cold, smooth surfaces. I liked the one with the multi-pointed crown the best. It reminded me of the elf queen.

One afternoon, the specters brought a letter.

I looked at it warily where it sat on the stone table, at first afraid and then enraged that it might contain a message from the lord. But I felt a stirring in my heart that I hadn't known in ages as I looked at the script that wrote out my name: "Olivière, second daughter of Aubree and Gideon, Carvers." It was Elfriede's hand.

I turned it over and grew hot with fury to see the seal already broken.

I hope this letter finds you well. Jurij's birthday is next month. Enclosed is our wedding invitation. I hope you can come. His Lordship is welcome as well, if he would like.

I had to laugh at Elfriede's attempts to act as if all was well. To her, perhaps it was. I was gone and out of her hair, after all.

My fingers ran over the embossed edges of the invitation. A wedding in the hills beyond our home in the first full month of spring. So it was only a month until the wedding now.

I didn't know what to do. I didn't know what I wanted. At the very least, perhaps I could look out my bedroom window and watch the specks of people gathering in the hills that day. But what would be more painful, to watch or not to watch? To celebrate a sister's happiness or to keep pretending that happiness didn't exist for others because it never would again exist for me?

But a thought struck me. I didn't want to watch—I wanted to go. Not just to see if I could sneak to the pool and test my theory. Not just because any freedom, even for just a day, was better than whatever this was. A wedding may not be the best opportunity to air a deep and terrible secret, but Elfriede and Father at the very least owed me an explanation.

I would just have to do my best to pretend the groom wasn't the only person I knew who made life worth living.

But to go would be to open my mouth.

But would an order to let me go, even if just for the wedding, incite his anger? I knew that it would. I would just have to find some way to pretend that I had no power over him and to ask permission. Even if it meant locking my feelings away.

***

Every second at dinner, my heart threatened to jump out my skin. From time to time, I would open my mouth to speak, only to quickly grab the goblet or fork and stuff wine or food in to silence myself. I couldn't let the opportunity pass. Still, it bothered me that he'd read the letter and still he didn't say a word. He wasn't the first to lapse into silence, but he wouldn't be the first to speak.

I cleared my throat. The air felt like knives in my raw airways.

"I assume you read my sister's invitation. The seal was broken."

I hadn't intended to start off so antagonistic, but I found the words and tone tumbling freely from my hibernated mouth. I stabbed at some meat and began chewing to cover some of my indignation.

A small cough came from behind the curtain, and a black

glove reached for his goblet of wine. The goblet appeared again in view but remained cradled freely in one hand.

"Yes," he spoke at last. "Her wedding is next week."

The fork fell from my grip. "Next week? The letter says next month!"

"It is already the first full month of spring, Olivière."

I bit down on my lip. Hard. If I hadn't, I would have started screaming and said more than one thing I'd have regretted. Even if they would have satisfied me immensely before I later regretted them.

I grabbed my goblet from the table. After a large gulp of wine, I slammed it down.

"I would like to go."

"You may not."

My jaw dropped. Was the letter just to torture me, then? Why not just give it to me after it was over, and I had completely missed it? I tried to cover up my frustration by grabbing my napkin from my lap and wiping my face. At least the cover allowed my lips to turn freely into a sneer.

"And why not?" I asked.

The goblet disappeared behind the curtain for a while before reappearing, this time settling back on the table. The sip took far too long to be anything but intentional.

"You know why," said the lord. A finger ran across the jagged edges of the crystal goblet. "Unless you intend to order me to let you go?"

I forced my mouth into a thin line before putting the napkin back on my lap. My eyes fell to the napkin, suddenly interested in seeing that I smoothed it just right.

"I thought not," said the lord confidently.

"You may come with me," I said quietly. "If you like."

I didn't know how I would speak to my friends and family alone if he were with me, but the distraction of the lord of the castle out among his people might provide enough cover for an opportunity or two.

The lord behind the curtain laughed. It may have been as close to a joyful laugh as he could muster, but I heard it laced with traces of ridicule and contempt.

"How very gracious of you!" he said. "But I am afraid the answer is still no."

He stood up, his chair scraping backward. Some of the specters flew into motion, cleaning his dinnerware, putting on his veil and hat, and then settling against the wall as always.

"Good night, Olivière," he said as he came around the edge of the curtain. "It has been a pleasure speaking with you."

I stopped myself from saying something more explicit in response that would drip more venomously with that very same edge of disdain he displayed.

***

I tapped my fingers impatiently on the stone table as the specters cleared away my breakfast and brought out the board and figures. I snatched the white elf queen off of the board as soon as they set her there and started rubbing my hands over her smooth surface. If I rubbed hard enough, what would break first, the bone figure or my skin?

I could hardly see straight. The garden was spinning around me. Try as I might, I couldn't think of a way to get to the wedding that would leave my captor happy. The worst part was that I knew that was precisely why he tormented me with it in the first place. Because it was the first time in months that I felt anything more than boredom—and I felt powerless. And angry.

I began tapping the elf queen against the board in her vacated spot, watching the black elf queen, her mirror image, across the board in the same position. And then I was struck. Two queens. Two kings. Four ... horses? Four castles. And other pieces I wasn't sure I knew. But this was a game, obviously. A game meant for white and black. A game meant for two.

I jumped up from the bench and ran into the castle entryway, looking for any specter within reach. A dozen appeared from the shadows at the edges of the room and lined up before me.

***

"You seem a quick learner, Olivière. I have to admit myself surprised."

I did my best to smile. However, I knew from experience that my best attempt to smile when a smile was unearned could send livestock running. Still, I had to try.

"Well," I began, "I am when I actually *want* to learn something."

Surely I could get away with unspoken contempt. He wouldn't really have expected otherwise.

The figure in black sitting on the bench opposite me laughed. He began gathering the scattered pieces, dropping each one on its place on the board. Chess, he had told me, was his favorite game. But it was a bore since his servants always let him win.

I'd told him it would be my pleasure to make him lose. That had made him laugh, too.

"Are you ready then?" asked the lord.

I nodded.

The gloves gestured toward me. "Ladies first."

My hand gripped the white velvet of my skirt, and I fought to keep a surge of heat from reaching my face. I'd told the specters to help me dress in one of the fine ball gowns before I asked them to tell their master what I wanted. They had even gone so far as to intertwine white ribbons and roses throughout my dark locks.

When the lord appeared in the garden to join me, he stopped, nearly lost his balance, and then stood straight again. He laughed, and I could almost picture the amused look on his face. The face I imagined was alarmingly like Lord Elric's from my dream.

I was trying too hard. And I was ashamed to know that it fooled him not in the least.

I started with a pawn. The pawn, I'd learned, was practically powerlessness, a mere echo of the seven other identical pieces. It could only move forward, one slow step at a time, breaking its pattern to move diagonally only in the incredibly unlikely event that it was able to catch a more worthy piece off-guard and capture it. When there was enough action on the battlefield, the pawn might just get away with it. But to begin the game, the pawn's one-time ability of moving forward not one, but *two* spaces would have to be most I hoped for from the pathetic piece.

"So," I began as my fingers left the ivory pawn in the middle of the empty battlefield. "Why only white roses?"

The lord commanded a bolder first move, guiding one of his black knights to leap over the unbroken chain of black pawns guarding his king.

"Do flowers interest you?" he asked curiously as his leather glove retreated to the fold of his arms.

I gripped another pawn tightly as I guided it two steps forward. The pawns could only hold on to such bravado when the battlefield seemed relatively clear, so there was no sense in wasting the weak figure's unwarranted enthusiasm.

I shrugged. "Not really. But I like *color*."

He moved a black pawn one space forward lazily, forfeiting its one-time chance to leap forward double that amount. "What flowers do you imagine should live in my garden?"

Annoyed by his smugness, I moved my white king forward one space to where a pawn had just been. "Violet lilies grow on the hilltop by my *home*."

He didn't remark on my emphasis. "And where should we plant the lilies?" he asked, sending a black pawn one step forward again.

"Perhaps around the fountain." I took another white pawn and let it jump forward its first single space. "If pulling up some of the stones to allow the dirt in would be all right."

"Perhaps," he said casually, guiding a black bishop out on

a long diagonal trek to the thrust of the battlefield and taking the life of one white pawn with no more guilt than a chicken devouring a worm.

"It would be a shame to lose any of the white roses," I said, flicking another white pawn two steps forward. "Which is why I suggested adding new space for flowers."

The lord nudged a black pawn forward two paces to match mine. "Perhaps we can pick some of the lilies for transplantation during the wedding. Is that what you would like me to say?"

I smiled sweetly. "Oh, but I'm not allowed to go to the wedding." I guided another white pawn two steps forward. "Apparently."

"You are, as you so rightly point out to me, a woman. You are free to come and go as you please." His favored black knight jumped from behind, slaying another white pawn.

"Let's not lie to each other." I sent another pawn two steps forward, not pausing to think of the danger it might face. "We are, after all, the only two people who can keep each other company in this castle. Since the rest are silent—or sleeping."

"It is not *my* speech that has the power to command *your* actions." His knight jumped again, pouncing on another white pawn that hadn't yet left the last line of defense. "You need only order me not to stop you from going, and you will find yourself able to walk out my front door."

"And I will also find a knife sent straight into my mother's chest." I sent another white pawn two spaces forward without much thought, eager to let it sacrifice itself and get the worthless piece out of my way.

He laughed and sent the black queen out into the battlefield to take the bold white pawn that had ventured too close on its own to the black army. "Well, well. It appears that you are not the only one in this coupling with power."

I bit down violently on my tongue for a moment. I moved a pawn one step closer to the black stronghold, sending it deeper into danger. "It's a pity you weren't born with yours."

"Was I not?" He sent a black pawn forward one space to take the white pawn head-on.

"I don't think even being born the lord of the castle equates to the power of the lowliest woman in the village." I suddenly noticed a white pawn with the opening to take a black pawn off-guard and slew the pawn before it could do any damage. "Oh, I would have to disagree." The black pawn that had just recently entered the battlefield avenged its fallen ally by taking the white pawn that had dealt it such a swift blow. "After all, doesn't everyone in the village say the lord is always watching?"

I wrapped my hand around a white bishop in the last line of defense and paused, a chill running up my arm to my shoulder. I thought of how long my mother suffered, and he hadn't done a thing until I'd asked. "Watching, perhaps, when it strikes his fancy."

The lord shrugged and crossed his arms. He wouldn't take my bait. "In any case, I seem to be the only fool with the wherewithal and the means necessary to stand with his goddess as her equal."

"As her equal?" I lifted the bishop and moved it one careful step diagonally. "I'm surprised you give me that much credit."

"I have no choice but to admit your power." His black queen sped diagonally from one side of the battlefield to another, spearing a white rook without my ever noticing it had been in danger.

I yanked up a white knight and let it leap closer to the action. "And that bothers you, doesn't it?"

The black queen zipped horizontally and took out the white queen in one blow. How stupid I had been. I had lost my most powerful piece before she even set one foot upon the battlefield.

The lord laughed, but I knew he wasn't scoffing at my foolish move.

"I have to admit there was quite a lot to celebrate in being so long without my goddess," said the lord once his laughter subsided. "There was no need to concern myself so much with the needs of another." In the sunlight, I saw the embroidery on his jacket clearly for the first time. Roses and thorns. "Check."

So much for the lord's altruism and concern for the villagers. I picked up the white king and moved him one small, pathetic step forward out of harm's way. After the pawns, the king was actually the most useless piece, I was glad to notice. Why were all of the other pieces fighting so valiantly to protect this man too powerless to defend himself?

"Well, there was plenty *I* enjoyed before you found your goddess, too."

"Whether that is true or not, I am afraid you have lost far less than I." He left the black queen to hover dangerously close to the white king and entertained himself by sending a black bishop across the field. It felled the white knight that had so recently entered the fight without even one kill to its name.

"I find that hard to believe." I grinned. I'd nearly forgotten the pawns that managed to survive the brutal slaying by more powerful enemies actually had a hidden power that made their existence worthwhile after all. I moved one of the last white pawns forward one small space.

"You know nothing, you silly girl!" His black knight leaped again to slay an unsuspecting white bishop, a powerful casualty, but a piece I could do without now.

I pushed my pawn forward one more space. "I know that you leave behind no family, no friends to be with me. I know that it is *you* who demands I be here rather than setting me free and moving to the commune."

His hands clenched the edge of the table, like he dared to hope the stone would crumble underneath his pathetic grasp. "The lord of the village does not *move into the commune.*"

I drummed the fingers of my right hand on the stone table and cradled my cheek with my left. "That's right. Because you are a man with *power.*"

"Are you so selfish?" He slammed the table with the palm of his hand. "That you would rather see a man wither than simply be with him? I could give you anything you desire. You would not want for comforts. I do not need your heart, I just need you!"

I bit my tongue and let the sting of pain shoot through

me for a moment before releasing it and gesturing toward the game board. "It's your move. I can't let you win without at least a proper fight."

A black-gloved hand grabbed that black knight again, and it jumped around the board searching for prey, landing in an empty patch of the battlefield. His voice grew quiet. "You were born to torment me."

"I think the same of you." I pushed the sluggish pawn one more space forward, passing up an opportunity to take out an overconfident knight that had yet to join the fray in order to make it to the edge of the board without notice.

I ground my teeth together until they hurt. "I'd like that pawn to become a queen now. And checkmate."

The lord stood, upturning the game board with both hands. The bone figures went flying across the garden, the captured white queen caught tightly between the roses' thorns.

Chapter Eighteen

When the day of Elfriede and Jurij's wedding arrived, I expected nothing. The air was clear, and I thought I might be able to watch from my window at the very least. But I decided that would be more painful than not looking. If I was honest, it wasn't the wedding I truly wanted to see, but the groom, even if for just a short while.

I hadn't seen the lord since our chess game almost a week prior. He didn't show even for dinner. The specters brought food to me in the garden or in my room.

That morning, the specters didn't retreat from my room after they set down the tray. I asked them to leave me, but they didn't. I yanked the spoon off of the tray and ate my fill, watching the specters warily. Only once I finished did they stir, a couple cleaning the table of my breakfast, and a few more heading to my chest full of dresses. They withdrew a pale lavender gown that I hadn't remembered seeing before. But I'd paid such little attention to the fancy dresses.

A couple of specters appeared at my side, forced my arms up, and began to tug at my nightshirt.

"Stop! What are you doing?"

The specters shifted backward, and I thought I could see a flicker of flame in the red pools of their eyes. Then the spark died out and they were back beside me, tugging on my shirt.

I slapped at the nearest hand. "All right! But I'll do that part myself, remember?"

The specters let go, and I walked behind the small screen where I could change into a slip in private. It was what I had done the week before, when I had asked them for help in dressing in that white gown.

I sighed and stepped out from around the screen, letting the specters fly into action. They slipped the gown over my head, then brushed my hair and worked in violet ribbons and lilies through the black tendrils. Purple lilies. Like the ones from the hilltops back home.

When they were finished with their work, two specters began tugging on my arms, and I struggled to break free. "Let me go!"

Both sets of hands loosened slightly. Then they tightened and started propelling me forward again.

"I'll follow you, I promise, just let me go!"

They stopped. After a moment, they began walking in front of me. I straightened out my sleeves and followed behind them.

We walked down the stairs, through the empty entryway, and out the front door. The black carriage waited for me, its doors wide open.

The specters paused before the carriage, spread to either side of the pathway, and gestured inside. I took a deep breath and propelled myself up the step, using one of the specters' extended hands to steady myself. A surge of panic implanted itself deep in my chest as I peered inside.

But the carriage was empty. He had let me attend the wedding, and he had not even spoiled the day by appearing himself. I didn't know what I'd done to "deserve" the courtesy of attending my own sister's wedding, but I was going to make the most of the opportunity as it was presented to me. I sat down, the doors shut, and I heard the quiet clop of the black horses as we headed down the dirt pathway.

***

I heard rehearsing musicians first, followed by the chirping of birds. The smell of the baker's bread and something sweet tickled my nostrils. Quiet murmuring like a hive full of bees grew louder—and all of that noise suddenly snapped into silence.

The carriage stopped. The door opened. A white hand extended inside. I grabbed it and pulled myself out.

Nearly the entire village was gathered in the knolls among the lily-strewn hilltops. There were chairs, benches, and blankets arranged into rows along either side of the dirt road into the village. Of course, the ceremony took place in the opposite direction of the castle. Too many girls and women would be watching to chance one glancing upward if facing east. At the top of the westernmost hill stood a wooden arch and Elweard, Vena's unmasked husband and the tavern master, if only in name. He was the most popular choice for village witness to a union. It had to do with the discount you got on ale as a result. Vena liked to have Elweard feel important, as long as it didn't interfere in the running of her business.

At first I didn't see any of the faces I'd hoped to see. And then Alvilda, looking stunning in a red gown, jumped up from the front of the left row of chairs. "Noll!"

I saw a wooden duck-face and a beaming smile below a mop of bushy dark hair pop up on the chairs next to her. *Luuk. Nissa.*

Alvilda picked up her skirt slightly and ran down the hill toward me, not noticing or caring that she kicked up dirt in the nearest seated people's faces.

She crossed the distance in mere moments, almost as quick as any of the specters could, and wrapped me tightly in her embrace. She pulled back only to kiss me atop the head.

"I'm so glad to see you!" She grabbed my chin in her hand and turned my face to and fro. The calluses on her hand irritated my skin like sandpaper.

"You look well fed." She moved her hands down to meet mine and pulled my arms outward, observing my new garment. "You look like a lady. Elegant. Beautiful." She leaned in to whisper, "And not at all like yourself."

I smiled and squeezed her hands. "I'm so happy to see you, Alvilda. It's been a long winter."

Alvilda put her arm around my shoulder, guiding me up the dirt path and toward the arch. I heard the specters and the black carriage move behind me, but when I turned to look, they had only moved to the side of the path and were still close enough to keep an eye on me. Alvilda propelled me forward and kept her voice low, but countless pairs of eyes—human and animal-masked ones alike—drank in every movement we made as we ascended the dirt road.

"I imagine you're anxious to see your father and your sister," she said. "And Jurij," she added in a lower tone. "But you've arrived mere moments before the ceremony is to begin. Come sit with Siofra, the kids, and me, and let's surprise them."

The kids jumped out of their seats and ran to hug me both at once, screaming, "Noll!" The duck beak on Luuk's face poked into my chest.

"Careful, Luuk," said Alvilda, gently pushing his shoulders back. "You'll stab Noll through the heart with that beak."

We laughed. I squeezed them both back, ignoring the poke. I tapped Nissa on the back of the head, and then bent one hand upward awkwardly to pat Luuk's curls that stuck up and out above the duck mask.

"You've certainly grown!" I let my hands fall, feeling sort of stupid for petting the kid atop the head. Another half a yard, and he'd be as tall as his brother.

"Thanks," said Luuk, tucking both hands into pockets in his fine dark trousers. Even through the muffled sound of his duck beak, I thought his voice sounded lower. And without so much as a hint of the quivering that used to accompany his every word.

Nissa, a little beauty in a cream-colored silken dress, put her arm through Luuk's. "Isn't he getting to be so handsome?" That made Alvilda laugh, but she was quick to bite her lip and cover it with the side of her hand, pretending she had a sudden itch beneath her nose.

"Yes, of course!" I'd have said I'd have to take her word on that, but I knew since he was still breathing that Nissa had never seen his face, either. Still, the way her young, dark eyes drank in the wooden duck, I might have been able to believe she saw beneath it to the wonder she thought lay inside. "And I love your dress, too."

Nissa blushed. "I made it with Siofra."

So they were on a first-name basis. I supposed it made sense since she was to be her future gooddaughter, the same as Elfriede. Nissa finally tore her eyes off of Luuk long enough to look at what I was wearing. "We made yours, too!"

"Did you?" I turned in place and let the skirt swish beneath me with a sudden appreciation for the fine skirts and dresses I'd refused before. "It's lovely. You're so talented."

Nissa beamed. "Thanks. We made it last month. The lord paid so well for it, too. We had enough copper left over to buy silk for my dress and for Siofra's, and for Alvilda's too."

At the sound of her name again, Mistress Tailor finally decided to join in the conversation in her own curt way. "Luuk, Nissa, be seated. It's about to begin."

Luuk and Nissa sat back down in their chairs at the end of the row, their hands clasped together. Alvilda guided me a tad forcefully into a seat between her and Mistress Tailor, who looked as pretty as I'd ever seen her in a muted green dress. Mistress Tailor didn't seem happy to see me, but I supposed I *was* unintentionally making a fuss at her elder son's wedding.

My stomach clenched. I'd been so happy to win this bit of freedom that I hadn't quite faced the fact that the man I loved would move beyond my grasp for a second time. But that was unfair. I already knew that he was long, long ago swept away out of my reach.

Alvilda squeezed my hand and pointed to the arch towering over Elweard. "How do you like my gift to the coupling?"

The arch looked familiar. "The headboard?"

Alvilda laughed. "It started off as one, but I had a burst of inspiration that told me this just had to be a wedding arch." She lowered her voice even further and whispered in my ear. "That and I love to tease Siofra. She hates useless gifts. When she saw it, she thought I wasn't going to make them a headboard at all, and I got an earful about always forgoing common sense to suit my poor choices. It was fun." She smiled, and I witnessed an odd flash of something I didn't recognize cross her features.

The music started, the dainty tune that heralded the bride and her parents' arrival at the ceremony. The bride's mother usually stood among them to emphasize the maternal cycle, an act the groom's mother did not share with her son. I thought of Mother lying in the castle for a moment and felt ill. Then I shook my head to clear the stirring of venom and turned with the rest of the villagers to watch as Elfriede and Father came down the first hill and ascended the second, being sure to keep my eyes downward, off the horizon. *I don't want to see the castle anyway.*

She looked beautiful, as fair as ever in a deep-violet gown I imagined to be the work of Mistress Tailor's. It was not unlike my own, although Elfriede's had real, live lily blooms woven into the material. Father stood beside her, a man-face mask hiding his face from me. Elfriede's features fell when she noticed me. Then she smiled, only a slight touch of pain remaining on her face.

They reached the top of the hill, and Father removed his mask and threw it at the ground. His eyes wandered in my direction briefly, his features as cold as stone, but his gaze was quickly drawn away to the hill.

The music switched to the hearty march that signaled the arrival of the groom and his father. Jurij and Master Tailor came over the lily-covered hill, both wearing masks. Jurij's was the man-face mask like the one he'd worn to his Returning, and

Master Tailor's was also man in form, a mask I'd never before seen him wear.

When they arrived at the top of the second hill and took their places beside Elfriede and my father, Jurij removed his mask and tossed it on the ground, leaning in toward Elfriede for a quick kiss. Master Tailor removed his man-face mask to reveal his favorite owl mask underneath. The villagers laughed. Mistress Tailor shifted uncomfortably beside me.

Jurij, his back toward me, didn't seem to have noticed me. There was nothing in all of the land that could tear him from Elfriede. The happiness on his face slipped only slightly when he noticed the furrowed brow on Elfriede's expression. But she soon regarded her pain in his reflection and put on her best smile. Unlike me, she could genuinely and completely shift from pain to joy. But she had Jurij, and I had nothing.

I watched the ceremony and felt the pain of the Returning flood back. Once they exchanged the last of their vows and the final kiss of the ritual, they headed back down the dirt path together hand in hand. As their feet disappeared over the hilltop toward my home, my heart sank, and I wondered if he was watching. If this was indeed why I'd been able to go, if this was what he'd wanted me to see.

My clapping slowed, even as the rest of the crowd grew more jubilant. Alvilda's expression grew sour next to me, and she grabbed me gently by the hand. "Let's go," she whispered. She tugged me gently toward the back of the archway. I noticed Mistress Tailor's bitter expression as she watched us go; Luuk and Nissa leaned in toward one another, smiling girl forehead plastered against wooden duck crown. *It never ends, this wretched cycle.*

"Congratulations," Alvilda said softly to Master Tailor as we passed by him. She patted him on the back with her free hand. Master Tailor turned briefly and nodded. I thought I could hear him weeping, but the sound was hollow beneath the owl mask.

We walked around Elweard and stood behind my father. He saw us coming and pointedly turned back toward the jubilant crowd, digging into his front coat pocket and pulling out a small bottle. Before the bottle could quite reach his lips, Alvilda let me go and moved her hands to block it.

"Come, Gideon," she said. "Come and speak now with your daughter."

Father sighed and slid the bottle back into his pocket. The cheering crowd began to make its way toward us and the village.

"Let's go," said Alvilda, taking hold of Father and me, one in each arm. "We can talk at my place. We can pay our respects to the happy coupling later."

We headed down the hill and toward the village. The specters in the distance stirred and jumped atop the carriage.

**

"Tea?" asked Alvilda, already pouring the hot water into the mugs she'd placed before Father and me. She put down the kettle and went back to her cupboard. As she rummaged around for leaves, Father snuck a sip of ale out of his bottle. Alvilda dropped the tea leaves into the water and took a seat at her sawdust-covered table between us. She looked from one of us to the other. I grabbed hold of my mug.

"Gideon," said Alvilda, when no other voice was forthcoming. "I think it's time you have a heart-to-heart with Noll. It's actually high past time."

Father sighed and began fumbling at the outside of his coat pocket. "What does she know?"

I felt the heat of the tea almost singe my palm through the mug. "I know that my father is so ashamed to face me that he won't even speak directly to me."

Father wiped a tired hand across his gray and black hairline. "I'm sorry, Noll. When I saw you'd showed for the wedding … I just didn't know what to say."

"You should have started by asking how Mother was doing."

Alvilda gasped. Father's eyes widened. "She's well, then?"

I slapped my palms atop the table. Sawdust went flying, probably landing in my tea. "I can't say how well she's doing, fast asleep in the care of a monster!"

Father pulled his ale bottle out of his pocket and took a swig. Alvilda didn't stop him.

"I knew he had her," said Father at last. "I didn't know for certain if she was still living. I thought I'd feel it if she ... well. I couldn't be sure."

My eyes couldn't meet his, couldn't stare into the budding ember of flame I knew I'd find there.

Alvilda looked from one of us to the next. "So you've seen her, Noll?"

I shifted in my seat uncomfortably. "Just once. My first night there, he took me to see her in a guarded room, sleeping. She didn't wake. And he made sure that I knew the consequences of abusing my power over him: Her death."

"The cheat!" Alvilda banged her hands across the table.

"That evening when you were gone, Aubree took a turn for the worse." Father gulped the ale for a moment, slamming down the empty bottle. "She was breathing so heavily. She could barely speak, but she couldn't stop moaning. Sweat poured off her like she'd just come in from a torrent of rain. Then she stopped moaning. That was scarier than when she *was* moaning. She was still breathing, but barely."

Father drummed the shaky fingers of his free hand on the table. "I heard a sound outdoors. I thought it might be you or Elfriede come home at first, but it was louder than that. The door burst open. It was the lord's servants."

He picked up the bottle and tried to take another sip. When he came up empty, he leered at the bottle and put it back down. "I told them you weren't there, to be on their way to find you, that I had a dying wife to worry about. Then they came to the bed and picked her up, carried her right out the door without so much as a word to me. I jumped in and followed. 'This was all I wanted from Noll,' I told myself. Just to *ask* the man. Ask him if he could help us. Since he'd do anything for you."

"I *did* ask him. That same night. You wouldn't believe me. But that's probably why he finally sent for her."

Father shook his head. "The lord greeted us in the entryway to the castle, wearing his black veil and hat. I dropped right down to my knees, even as the pale servants lay Aubree on the floor before me. 'Have mercy, my lord,' I said. 'Do what you can to spare my wife. I'll do anything.' 'And where is Olivière?' he asked. 'Why has she not come with you?' Well, I wanted to say it was just that Noll is such a—" Father stopped suddenly, held the empty bottle to his lips and spat. He wagged a finger at me. "She's a *stubborn* girl, but I thought better than to insult a man's goddess right in front of him, so I said nothing."

But you don't think better than to insult your own daughter in front of her. Not that that was surprising. I took a sip of my tea. It tasted a bit of sawdust.

Father plopped his filthy spit-bottle down on the table. "The lord, he waited a bit for my answer. I suppose he finally figured I had nothing to say to him on the matter, so he bade me to rise. 'That woman continues to aggravate me,' he said, which is why I thought you hadn't visited him. I thought he'd tell me if you had. 'I can heal your wife. It will take time. Tell no one she is here, not even your daughters, and do not come here yourself. You can see your wife again on the day of Olivière's Returning.'"

If he could heal her, why wasn't he certain until he'd sent me away? "He told you not to tell me? How could he—"

Father cut me off, letting go of the bottle in order to wring his hands. "I dared to ask if he was certain he could save her. I regretted the words as soon as they were out of my mouth. He gave me a warning. 'The lord of the village does not make promises he cannot keep.' I begged his forgiveness. I just didn't know what to believe, what with the talk of immortality and how it was his lack of a goddess that had made him master of death. But I knew beyond a doubt that the lord had never found a goddess among all of the women in my lifetime, so maybe it was possible. I just worried that having found Noll, he'd have lost whatever it was that made him keep death at bay."

Of course. Another excuse to blame me.

Alvilda sighed and stretched her arms up over her head. "I hope you didn't say that part aloud."

Again, Father tried to drink from the empty bottle. "No, of course not."

"So you've heard it, too," I interrupted, putting the mug down. "The title the 'heartless monster.'"

Alvilda let her arms fall gently to the table. "People have never liked to talk much about the 'always watching' lord and his servants. A whisper here, a tale there—the things one could piece together are downright laughable." She sighed. "The 'heartless monster.' A strange way to put it, but it means that he's inhuman, an immortal whose heart never found its goddess and so he lives forever."

I felt something strange clutching my heart, like I could feel the man watching me. "Mother told me it was just a story." *But if that dream was real, and that was the lord when he was younger, it'd have to be long ago. So you're actually certain you went into the past. Through a pond.* I knew it was crazy, but it felt true. Maybe spending so long alone in the castle had made me lose my sense of reason.

"I have to admit," said Father, running a nervous finger over his palm, "it seems to be the only explanation. No one can remember when he came to be."

"Nonsense," said Alvilda, waving a hand. "All of this talk of immortality in our blood is merely an old wives' tale."

I cocked my head to the side. "And what of the men and the masks? And the power of their goddesses?"

Alvilda looked thoughtful for a moment but then shrugged. "That's just the way things are."

I mulled that over. What was in front of us was fact. What we couldn't prove was nonsense. But still I didn't understand why men and women were so different. Or why men and women were so different in such a very different way in my drowning dream.

"So you really don't know more about him than the whispers I've heard myself."

"Did you believe those whispers then?" asked Alvilda. I shrugged. "Maybe. There are far too many things about the man in the castle that set him apart. You have no idea of the lengths to which he goes to offset the power I have over him. I wasn't exaggerating about his threat to kill Mother. It's like he can't stand that he loves me. I'm not even *sure* he loves me. Not that I *want him* to love me."

"Kill? A person? Like the animals we kill for meat?" Alvilda shook her head thoughtfully. "No. I'm sure not. But even so, I can't picture a man who had found his goddess who would do anything other than agonize and wish to please her. Younger boys can manage to engage themselves in different pursuits from time to time because their hearts haven't yet given up hope. But once a goddess turns seventeen, a man pretty much knows whether or not he'll ever have her—in one form or another."

She sighed. "For a man to actively plot against his own goddess seems something altogether new. I know men can be torn between their own desires and the desires to make their goddesses happy, on the rare occasion that those desires don't line up. But for one to grab hold of his own wishes while knowingly making his goddess so unhappy goes against everything we know. If that were true, maybe there could be hope for men without the Returning to find happiness in another form. But that simply is not so." She stared over my father's head at the art on the wall. It always came back to her brother.

"What if I told you I have reason to believe he's different? That he *has* lived a long time. Longer than he ought to have."

Alvilda seemed genuinely curious. "What do you mean?"

"I ... " I bit my lip. "Did anyone—your grandparents, talking about their grandparents maybe—tell you of a time when men walked around without masking their faces?"

"No ... " Despite the flush on Father's cheeks, he seemed to think I was the one who was drunk.

"You mean, like the tales of the first goddess?" Alvilda asked. "That's just a story, Noll. A way to explain why thing are. But there's no proof things were ever any different."

Father shook his head. "Maybe they were. Long ago. But the legend of the first goddess must be a thousand years old."

We three sat silently for a while. I felt stupid. *A thousand years? You really think you traveled back in time a thousand years, and that the lord lived then and has lived to this day? How? It just can't be. It felt real then, but now it's just a memory.*

Finally, Father let out a deep breath. He didn't seem interested in my visions of the past. Not when his goddess's life hung in the balance.

"Whatever you think of the lord, Noll, he saved your mother's life."

Both Alvilda and I turned toward Father.

Father traced a pattern in the sawdust on the table with his finger. "Everyone who got sick from that illness died, Noll. Every single one. And I think all of her stress over your refusal to love your man made Aubree susceptible."

I grimaced. This revelation explained much of the unspoken strain between us after Mother's "death." My mother was his goddess, and whatever I was to him, nothing could match the worth he put on her health and happiness. He could feel free to blame me. I no longer cared. "Mother understood. She didn't want to rush me. She wanted me to be happy."

Father licked his dry, cracked lips. "But that's only because she assumed you'd eventually Return to him. Like decent women do."

Alvilda reached across the corner of the table and smacked Father on the back of the head. She sent me a satisfied smile.

Father rubbed his head and looked at Alvilda wearily. "That wasn't a comment on you, Alvilda."

Alvilda pounded her fist on the table. "I don't care. It's a darn careless thing to say about your daughter. What about a woman's *choice*?"

Father shook his head. "What worth is a woman's choice when it comes to the lord of the village? I'd hoped she would learn to love him. At the very least, that she wouldn't wish for him to be as wretched as those in the commune."

"The lord of the village does not *move into the commune*,"

I said. Alvilda and Father both looked at me with puzzled expressions. I sighed. "And did Mother know what you had done?"

Father rubbed his cheek and stared at his empty bottle. "No, she was already beyond consciousness by then." A tear trickled out of the corner of his eye; that eye seemed dark and lifeless with its dying flicker. "I didn't know for certain until today that she truly still lived."

"And does Elfriede know?"

Father continued to scratch his chin. "I think she knows enough. She probably pieced some of it together. She spent more time around the house than you after I told you your mother died."

Probably because I spent most of my time outrunning carriages and deliverymen's carts. And because she was there, almost always with Jurij.

I'd had enough of the tiresome discussion. I would say my goodbyes and be on my way. Back to that chilling castle, the closest thing I had to a home now. I stood to leave when the door burst open. Jurij and Elfriede appeared in the doorway, and before anyone could speak, Jurij swept me into his arms and held me tightly.

"Noll," he whispered. "I didn't know you came. We missed you."

My hands moved numbly to squeeze him back. Elfriede, still in the doorway, wouldn't look at me. She stood there, her eyes on the floor, one arm cradling the other against her chest. She hadn't missed me at all. In fact, I imagined seeing her new husband in my arms was enough to make her wish she had seen the last of me when I rode off in the black carriage.

They never cared about me. Not Father, not Elfriede. They wanted me to stuff away all my hopes, all my feelings. I tried. I did. But if I'm going to accept that I'm the veiled lord's goddess, as they want me to, then at least I'll have one thing to remember before I lock all my happiness away.

I ran my fingers through the back of Jurij's hair and kissed him.

Chapter Nineteen

The ground exploded. It cracked and groaned and roared to life. And I knew, just a moment too late, that it wasn't the euphoria of my first kiss that made me feel as if the earth moved beneath my feet. It was actually moving and I was sent flying.

"Alvilda! Are you all right?"

I looked up to see a masked man in the doorway. He crouched near Alvilda, who must have fallen off of her chair.

"I'm fine, Jaron." Alvilda pushed away at his chest even as he extended his hand to help her. "How is everyone else?"

I took in the shambles of Alvilda's home and shop. Furniture tipped over, carvings fell off the mantle, and some of the artwork was on the floor and split in two. Her tools lay scattered about the room. On the ground, Father rubbed his elbow. Jurij lay on Elfriede's lap beside the doorway. Elfriede wept. Jurij was moaning and a trickle of blood ran down his face.

And I was clear across the room, dazed but uninjured. It was as if the ground had moved solely to split Jurij and me apart.

And as I thought that, I knew that it had. That he had made it so.

Why did I do that? Goddess help me. I'm sorry, Jurij. I'm sorry, Elfriede.

But when I thought of how much the lord had overreacted to my inability to Return to him, I wasn't very sorry to have hurt him.

Although only two specters had brought me to the wedding, half a dozen filed into the home now. I blinked and swore I saw even more of them piling into the road outside.

Alvilda scrambled to stand beside me, elbowing Jaron as he tried to restrain her. He didn't succeed, but he trailed after her, only one step behind.

"What's going on here?" Alvilda demanded of the specters. She still hadn't learned that she couldn't take them in a fight.

"Alvilda—" began Jaron.

"Be quiet until I tell you to speak again!" snapped Alvilda. Jaron spoke no more.

The specters moved around Alvilda and seized me, propping me up. Alvilda launched herself at them, but the specters weren't bothered in the slightest. Jaron wrapped his arms around the kicking, snarling Alvilda but had no choice but to let her go when she ordered it. Two specters took Jaron's place and grabbed Alvilda to restrain her, if only to stop her from yipping at them.

"I apologize for being so late to the celebration."

Alvilda ceased struggling. Even Elfriede stopped weeping. All eyes but those of the specters turned toward the black figure that had entered the room.

"Congratulations, my dear," said the lord, extending his hand downward toward the weeping Elfriede. She looked back at him, confused, her eyes still swollen with tears.

The lord pulled his hand back, not bothered by Elfriede's lack of reaction. "What an accident!" said the lord. My gaze fled to the fallen Jurij on Elfriede's lap. The blood I'd noticed earlier extended clear across his left cheek. His left eye was swollen and clamped tightly shut. A bloodied gouge lay on the ground beside him.

The lord waved his hand in their direction and a few more specters entered the already crowded home to sweep Jurij from Elfriede's lap and carry him outside. Jurij moaned as he disappeared from view. Moments later, a black carriage passed by the open doorway, silently slipping away from sight.

What have I done?

"Fret not, my dear," said the lord to Elfriede. "My servants shall attend to him." He crouched down and cupped Elfriede's chin in one gloved hand. "There, there. You have to smile. Today is your wedding day. And was it not kind of me to allow your sister to attend?"

No. What has he *done?*

Elfriede's mouth cracked upward in a hollow echo of her smile. She opened her mouth to speak, but she bit down on her lip quickly. Was it the idea of our mother in the castle that kept her from asking the obvious?

Well, I wasn't afraid to ask the monster a question. "Where are you taking him?"

The lord released Elfriede and stood now, facing me. He adjusted first one glove and then the other, tugging on the leather cuffs.

"Well, well, good day, *my* goddess," he said. "Did you enjoy the wedding, Olivière? Or did you find the reception afterward more enticing?" His words gathered an extra edge toward the end of his latter question.

Heat swirled inside of me. "I enjoyed the reception very much."

The lord placed his hands on his hips and stood immobile for a moment. Then he motioned a hand toward me and turned to exit. "In any case, I can see I just missed the last of the festivities." He nodded at Elfriede, the tip of his hat bobbing down and up. "I dare say your sister will be glad to see us leave. The lord of the castle and his goddess alike. Wherever they go, no mere bride can compare. It seems we have stolen all that was owed to her this day. It is, after all, her wedding day."

"Noll, how could you?" Elfriede screamed as the specters pulled me toward the second black carriage. She was weeping, barely able to speak between heavy, quivering sobs. Her voice grew quieter, the words catching in her throat. "How could you be so selfish? You won't be happy until you have Jurij for yourself. You'd rather he die than be with me."

"Friede!" I shouted back, doing all I could to break free from the tight grips on my arms. I had more to say, but I wasn't sure what it was. I hadn't wanted this. I hadn't wanted her to hate me.

The lord seemed amused. "My, what a joyous family reunion." He nodded at the specters, who pulled me inside the carriage like they were lugging in a sack of grain. The lord grabbed hold of the sides of the carriage doorway and heaved himself inward. "You must be so delighted that you came."

***

My fingers dug into the black leather seat. It was my first time in the carriage with company.

The lord sat across from me, his hands folded tightly in his lap. I imagined his eyes attempting to bore through the veil to shoot daggers straight into me.

"That was not very nice," he said at last.

I gripped the leather harder, imagining that it was the arms of his leather jacket instead. "What have you done with him?"

"Are you going to order me to answer you?"

"Will you not answer me otherwise?"

The lord moved his hands up, stopping shortly below where the veil began.

"I feel compelled to answer you," he said. "I feel compelled to do anything I so much as think you want done. It is a battle within me not to slit my own throat at this very moment."

I smiled sweetly.

"But I will not let you have power over me."

I scoffed. "I don't think you have much of a choice."

"No, I do not," he said, his head tilting slightly toward the carriage window. "But still, I have the power to fight it. And I will fight it until my last breath."

Don't tempt me.

I bit my tongue and followed his gaze out of the window. We were entering the woods now. I had missed the chance to bid my childhood home one last farewell.

A surge of wickedness came over me. There was one place nearby that was still home. And it could save me, if but for a moment. *You promised them you would help. Dream or not, I've got to know.*

"Were you alive long ago? Say, a thousand years in the past?"

The lord's head snapped toward me. "How could you—"

"Answer me!"

The lord spoke before he could stop himself. "Yes."

I'm not crazy. It wasn't a dream! "Don't move," I said.

The lord tensed.

"Have them stop the carriage."

He knocked on the window and the carriage halted instantly. "Olivière, if you remember—"

"Stay still," I said. "Don't speak. Don't move."

If I can go back, I can stop him before Jurij was ever hurt. Before he ever took my mother. Before she ever fell ill. What if he caused the illness somehow? I didn't understand how or why, but it seemed to be too much of a coincidence since it happened right after I met him. *Maybe he planned to make me grateful to him from the start.*

I have to go back. Before this village ever became cursed with men and their goddesses.

I pushed the carriage door open and ran trembling off of the dirt path and deep into the woods.

My legs burned. My dress snagged on branches and tore. Lily petals fell from my hair, withered already by a day without earth and water. I hiked up my skirt and kept moving.

I reached the cavern and tore inside. I had no candle to

light my way, and my feet stumbled from time to time over a rock or a spike I didn't fully remember, but I made my way through the darkness.

And it was the violet glow and the cavern pool that awaited me, called me home.

Even my wild and racing heartbeat seemed suddenly subdued, quiet, and calm. There was something in the pool that wanted me, a gentle vibration, an unrelenting reminder of life. It was as if until that moment I hadn't realized that even among the voluble pounding of my heart, there had been gaps every other beat. Moments of silence in which my heartbeat echoed here, in the pool, in the depths of the secret cavern.

Little droplets of purple rose up from the surface and spread out to banish the darkness trying to invade the corners of the cavern. I moved closer to the edge of the pool, dipping one hand into the water to grab a droplet of violet. But they were too quick.

Can I do this without Elgar? Was the blade the key?

The violet light came from a sphere, large as the pool, covering the bottom. I scrambled to my knees, shoving aside my skirt and scuffing my legs on the cold stone, and bent as close as I could to the water's surface. The little droplets tore off from their shells and rose up to the surface, but as many droplets as there were, the sphere grew no smaller. It seemed to be contracting and expanding, like the beating of a heart.

I took a deep breath and submerged my head beneath the water. The violet droplets soared toward me, and I fell in. The sphere drew me in like a man to his goddess. I would swim to the heartbeat that called mine and embrace it.

I can do this. Even without Elgar.

I snapped awake. A familiar feeling. I felt the sudden shock of the water being disturbed and a moment later a strong arm pulled me violently upward. The figure next to me struggled. It thrashed with such force that eventually, I pulled away from the light. My heart ached as I saw it grow smaller in the distance.

Black leather gloves. A pale arm.

My lungs exploded to life again with a strong slap against

my back. The watery violet blood of the beating sphere spilled from my mouth and burned my throat as it left my body. I hacked and choked and sputtered for air while that strong arm remained wrapped around my shoulder, my back to the man who supported me.

"Do not fight the reflex," said the lord from behind me. "You must purge yourself of the water."

I've been here before. Not just in this place. In this very moment. The first dream in the cavern, when Jurij saved me from drowning.

And now he has stopped me from going back to where I was needed. Where I wanted to go.

The hand slapped my back again, and my throat widened, letting the water flow out in a steady stream. Despite the part of me that was reluctant to see it go, still glowing violet even as it poured from within my body, it came easier with each blow.

The hand reaching across my chest slid softly to grasp onto my left shoulder just as I felt the hand that had struck me grasp hold of my right. The hands were wrapped tightly in gloves of black leather—wet leather. But I had already guessed as soon as I heard his voice. There was no one else to rescue me now.

"Olivière," he said. "You could have died."

I felt gentle pressure across the back of my head, the tickle of breath as it whisked past my ear.

"Do not try that again," he said. His hands squeezed my shoulders harder. "Please."

His arms wrapped tightly across my collarbone, his hands coming to rest on the opposite shoulder. He still wore his leather jacket. The smell of wet leather made my stomach rise with a sharp new wave of nausea.

He rustled slightly, thanks to the telltale squeak of his wet leather pants. I felt soft, damp feathers against my cheek and then a light pressure against my right ear. His hair, his lips … he wasn't wearing his veil. And he had kissed me!

I lurched forward, hacking again. I met some resistance from him at first. It annoyed me to find that even with all of my strength I couldn't push his arms off of me. But he let go of my shoulders and let me fall loosely forward. His hands caught me again around the chest before I could hit the ground. Nothing came out of my throat, but I couldn't stop retching.

"Let go ... of ... me!" I managed to sputter between hacking. Falling forward, I tried to use the small window of time my command afforded me to flip around, to turn my body to face him and let my eyes assault the sanctity of his face, but within moments, I felt a hand push hard against my shoulder, forcing me to lay face down.

"DON'T!" His voice seemed all the more commanding as it echoed with the life force of the cavern.

We stayed still a moment longer, locked into our positions. With my cheek flat against the cavern floor, I faced the pool with my back to the darkness down the entry passage.

The hand released me. The cavern echoed with the steady pounding of his boots, which muted the sound of the rustling, wet leather.

"Rise," he said. His voice was once again composed, but there was an edge of iciness that conveyed everything.

I rolled over, fighting the pounding in my head. I sat up and stared at him. He'd retrieved his black veil from the darkness and had tied it around his head once more, placing the hat atop it. They were the only items of clothing he wore that weren't soaked. He towered over me, his arms akimbo, his legs slightly parted. I didn't see any of the specters.

I struggled to stand on my shaky legs. The lord's legs trembled slightly forward, but he stood his ground. Until I lost hold of mine.

He swooped in to steady me, and I pushed his chest, much like Alvilda had done with Jaron.

The sudden comparison brought fresh pain to the ache in my chest. Right after the kiss. Right before Jurij was taken by the heartless monster.

"Stand back," I told him, not bothering to disguise the bitter taste in my mouth. "The smell of wet leather is making me sick."

He let me go and took two steps backward.

I stumbled over to one of the spikes jutting from the ground and used its sharp edge as a grip with which to steady myself.

"You are nothing but ungrateful." Iciness.

I sneered. "Oh, I'm sorry. Thank you ever so much for injuring my dearest friend and then ripping him from my sister's arms on the day of their wedding."

The lord laughed coldly. "It seems to me that you and your *dearest friend* had done enough on your own to ruin the celebration before my arrival."

I scrambled to my knees and drew myself up to stand as tall as I could, trying to match his height and ignoring the wobbliness in my legs. "That's no concern of yours!"

"It is, my goddess, every concern of mine!" He started walking back and forth a few paces before the pool. "Have you no idea of the curse by which you have bound me?"

"I'm the one who's cursed," I shouted, "for I am denied a choice that was promised to me!"

He stopped walking and spun toward me. "You *never* had the choice to love the man who belongs to your sister."

"You're wrong! I'm a woman and I can love where I will, even where love will never find me!" I bit my lip. Even if it hurt others. Even if I was foolish. *I'm sorry, Elfriede. But I can't help but hurt you. Just like you can't help but hurt me.*

The lord started convulsing, his right fist struggling to find a place between pointing at me, resting on his waist, and being raised upward to the sky. "And I am a man! And I am *forced*, against my will, to love just the same!"

His fist unclenched, and he grabbed my left arm with a force I hadn't felt since his struggle against the violet glow's pull.

"Do not speak!" He echoed my words from the carriage. "Do not move against me, or I shall do more than wound your lover and safeguard your mother. I should have let you drown!"

I tried to tear my arm from him as he dragged me forward into the darkness, choosing the pain of struggling against his tight grasp over letting him have hold over me so easily.

"I should have *ordered* you to drown!"

He stopped. His grip tensed on my arm, and his weight shifted from one foot to another. I thought he might run past me and jump back into the water. Instead, he grabbed my other arm tightly with his free hand. "I do not want to hear another word from you!" he said. "Every word that passes through those twisted lips is poison enough to break me."

"Good," I replied. He said nothing for a moment, and I stared right into where I guessed his eyes might be, a hungry smile curling the corners of my mouth.

"Is your heart so cold and closed to me?" he said at last. His grip slackened.

I clenched my jaw and gazed straight into the void that his veil created in the violet glow. I hoped my eyes, flameless though they may be, would burn straight through him. "I do not need my words in order to answer that."

He picked me up, slung me over his shoulder, and carried me into the shadows.

⋛ Chapter Twenty ⋞

I could see by the leather-gloved hands just below the billowing black gauze of the curtain between us that the lord had little appetite. He picked at a piece of meat with his fork and had barely lifted any of the potatoes. My own appetite was surprisingly strong. I devoured every last crumb on my plate nearly as soon as a specter laid it in front of me.

A specter came to retrieve my plate the moment I put down the fork, and the black-gloved hands lifted slightly to call another specter to his side. The servant removed his plate and exited the room, but no one swooped in to place the veil and hat on their master. The lord remained seated, his palms resting atop the table.

He lifted the tips of his fingers again, and the specters filed out of the room, every last one.

The dining hall door closed. A gust of wind suddenly seized upon us through the open window, causing the curtain to flutter as if a giant hand had run itself across the gossamer surface.

"Speak now," spoke the lord. "They will not hear. They

will not strike."

My tongue was struck dumb. It was impossible. I couldn't trust him. He was always two moves ahead of me.

Fine, I would play along. But he would be surprised to see that I could play by his rules and still come out victorious in the end. *I'm going back to the pond. I have to stop him before it comes to this. I have to stop all the men.*

"Tell me where Jurij is," I said, my tongue suddenly snapping back into action.

"On the top floor," he replied. "In the room next to your mother's."

"What have you done to him?"

"I staunched and treated his wounds."

My lower jaw was grinding. "To the best of your ability?"

He didn't hesitate to answer. "No."

"What are you going to do with him now?"

"Nothing."

I sighed and rapped my fingers on the table impatiently. "Why did you bring him here?"

"To heal him."

I snorted. Really, he had been so eager to follow my orders for once that I had forgotten to actually form the words correctly. "Tell me why you brought him here."

"To heal him and to punish you."

There it was. I laughed and breathed a sigh of relief. "Release Jurij."

The black hands waved upward. So the specters were still able to follow his orders even when not within sight of their master. *Is this how he is always watching?* I wondered if somehow my wedding escorts had seen the kiss and had alerted their master from a great distance, or if it was the goddess curse that wreaked the pain of the kiss straight to his heart. I hoped it was the latter.

"Release my mother as well," I said.

Another wave of the black hand.

How simple. How dubious.

"Prove to me that they're going home."

A black glove gestured to the open window. I moved across the room, keeping a suspicious eye on his extended hand. I tore my eyes from the lord and let them fall outside the window, my body still facing the billowing curtain.

After a few moments, specters carried Jurij and my mother from the castle door to the two awaiting black carriages. Jurij, his face wrapped in bandages, shifted slightly, but my mother didn't stir. For a moment, I wondered if they were well enough to travel, but my instinct was to get them as far from the lord as possible.

Mother and Jurij were laid one after the other into the carriages. Without a sound, the black horses started moving, and the carriages disappeared down the dirt path through the middle of the woods. The specters who didn't drive the carriages walked in two steady lines after them. More and more specters poured from the castle door and out into the woods until finally, the last of the specters disappeared from view and into the trees. There had to have been a hundred at least, more than enough to keep watch over the entire village.

I faced the black curtain. There had to be a trick, a plan for the specters to strike when out of sight, or to wait perhaps, until they could capture Father and Elfriede, Alvilda, Nissa, and the Tailors, and everyone else within the village before they made their deathly blow.

"Command me to tell you if this is a trick," spoke the lord, as if reading my thoughts.

I wasn't willing to play the game just as he wished it. "Don't ever harm the people I love."

Something odd stirred in the lord. A black-gloved hand clutched the edges of the lace tablecloth, an unnatural dam causing ripples along its otherwise unblemished surface. "I will not harm the people you love."

"Don't ever let your servants harm the people I love."

"I will not let my retainers harm the people you love."

I clenched my fists together. "Tell me if you have already ordered harm to come to them."

"I have not."

He released his grip on the tablecloth. The ripples he'd made diverted seamlessly back into smooth waters of lace.

There had to be something I was missing, something he had planned to stay two paces ahead of me. Because now there was nothing holding me back.

"Tell me why you aren't fighting my orders."

"I never stood a chance against you, in the end." His voice was barely a whisper. His hands tugged carelessly at the bottom of the curtain.

My heart emboldened. Laughably, I felt that surge of pride that I had once known as a girl, when I was the little elf queen defeating monsters in the shadows of the secret cavern.

And here sat a monster, hidden in the shadows of that black curtain.

I stepped forward. "You will not harm me."

"I would never harm you."

"You will not seize me or grip me by the hands or arms."

The lord tugged at the curtain, and I heard a small rip among the clattering of the curtain's rings. "I will not hold you."

I started, my tongue stumbling for a brief moment. It was off, but it would do. "You will keep no servants in this castle, and no one under your control will ever harm me."

"They are gone. They will not harm you."

I nodded. "You will do nothing to stop me from leaving."

"I will not stop you."

I paused mere paces from his side, only a thin layer of billowing curtain between us.

"Remove the curtain and show me your face."

The black gloves didn't hesitate. They took the bottom of the curtain in their grip and pulled. Rings the color of Elfriede's and Mother's hair, only brighter and shinier, fell like shattered glass all around us, to the floor and to the table. *I've seen a ring like that before—a bangle around Lord Elric's arm in my dream—in the past.* I didn't flinch as the curtain fell, letting the elf queen inside of me revel in her moment of glory. Nothing touched me. The curtain floated briefly before me as it made its leisurely descent.

My chest was an inferno, and I could feel the flame spark on the skin of my breast. My cheeks blazed, and the very blood that ran throughout my veins seemed ready to light my body aflame.

For he was beautiful. And he stabbed me through the heart with his beauty.

His dark hair came down to his shoulders. Like his hat had often done, the hair caught the flicker of the flame in the fireplace and showed me that it wasn't black like the men in the village's, but a dark, succulent brown that only masqueraded as black.

Just as I suspected, he did so look like Lord Elric. But he was paler, much paler. Almost like he was halfway to becoming a specter himself. His skin had an odd, creamy, rosy quality overlaying the soft white. His lips were dark red, as if they had been stained by blood. His nose was thin and straight—and familiar somehow. His brows came together in an almost perfectly straight line, and the bones in his cheeks practically burst through the strange, alluring skin.

His ears were as I expected. They poked through the dark tundra of his tresses and rose upward into jagged points. I stepped closer, my hand extended forward against my will to finger the sharp edges. I stopped and pulled my hand back before I touched him.

A timid smile slowly splintered his faultless face. His lips parted, and I could feel the warmth of his breath cross the few paces between us.

"And so you have made your choice at last, Olivière."

The fire in his eyes burst into red flames. And then he was gone.

Chapter Twenty-One

Elgar must have proven essential to getting back to that place. Or it was all a dream after all, despite what I knew in my heart to be true. I tried jumping in again to no avail. Every time I came to the surface, I came back here.

Home and not home. But not at all that place I'd once been, that place with Avery and Ailill, with the darker lord and Goncalo.

So I'd given up. I lived among those who were lost among the living. I carved and I whittled, I sat and I stood, I walked and I lay. The few men who populated the commune did not disturb me, so lost were they in their own torment. We watched together daily as the farmers—men, women, girls, and boys alike—marched past from the village and into the fields beyond our heap of dilapidated shacks. They marched past again what felt like years later as the sun set, the women and the girls with their heads held high despite the fact they faced the east. They didn't look our way, and we didn't stir. And that was the most we could hope for of peace.

After the lord vanished, the earth trembled. My memory

turned black, and then I woke up in a large field of dirt.

A field where the castle should have been.

I dragged my feet forward numbly, cradling my arms to my chest in the chill of the moonlight down the dirt path back to the village. I paused at the edge of the trees where I usually broke off the path to visit the secret cavern. I'd try jumping into the violet sphere beneath the waters during the days that followed. But that day, I just wanted to be sure everyone was well.

I arrived at my home, recognizing the windows on the house on the horizon lit brightly by the flame of the fireplace.

When I opened the door, I was greeted first with surprise and then with warmth by Arrow, Elfriede, and Jurij. His face was untouched, not a scar or injury to be seen.

"Where's Father?" I croaked. "Was Mother brought home to him?"

The light fell from Elfriede's jovial face. "Mother and Father are dead, Noll."

She brushed her palm across my forehead. Jurij peered over her shoulder, his face full of concern.

"Were you out in that cavern again?" he asked. He touched my shoulder, and I shivered perceptibly. Still, Jurij didn't notice. "Did you swim? You don't appear to be wet from the pool."

Elfriede tugged gently on my elbow. The force was not one I couldn't fight against should I have wished to, but I had no such desires then.

She led me to the bed we shared and tucked me in.

"Rest now," she said.

She's forgiven me. I closed my eyes but didn't fall asleep.

Hushed voices held counsel over my questions.

"Why did she come back here?"

I should have known she was still angry.

"I don't know. She's acting delirious."

"Why did she ask for Mother and Father? How could she forget Mother died from her illness almost a year ago now?"

Impossible.

"Or that Gideon followed her shortly thereafter? I don't

know. She doesn't seem ... right." The way he spoke the last word made me wonder what the "right" me would be.

I flitted in and out of consciousness. A long time later, I heard the soft moans and rustles from behind me in my parents' bed, and I shuddered, pulling my quilt tightly over my head. In the morning, I glanced at the coupling intertwined in one another's arms, Arrow resting at their feet, breathing easily in their slumber. My gaze fell upon the delicate valley of lilies carved into the unfamiliar headboard. I left without a word, dragging my feet back down the dirt path and through the village.

I stopped in front of the Tailors', wondering if I might find shelter there. But I thought of Luuk and Nissa—the little Jurij and Elfriede in training. What room would there be for me? What place was there for me, among the sewing and the clothes? I walked westward.

I paused at Alvilda's door. *No. No, that wasn't home, either.*

The commune was just a few paces away. When the pool brought me nowhere, I had nowhere else to go.

And there it was that I sat now, carving life into a block of wood. At first, I left the commune only to speak with Alvilda, to borrow tools and to get supplies. She was as concerned for me as Elfriede and Jurij had been—perhaps more so because she wasn't lost in the bliss of Returned love as were those two. But she didn't pry.

I had but one question for her. "What became of the castle and the lord of the village?"

She ran her sawdust-covered palm over my forehead. I let the dust settle in my eyebrows. "What are you running your mouth on about now? What castle? What lord?"

There was no castle, no lord of the village. And there never had been.

I was nobody's goddess—odd, but not worth much notice in the village where all were concerned with their own exchanges of love and Returning. Maybe my man would be born a few decades later, they thought—it'd happened on occasion before. Old Ingrith didn't even have a man yet when she died, they said. Of course, I knew better.

She hadn't lied. She'd seen her man's face before she loved him, and with that, she killed him.

Pity she was gone now, too. She might have been the only one who could understand me.

For I knew now what she meant when she talked of killing a man no one else remembered. The fate worse than death that lurked around every corner for a masked man was that the eyes of a girl or woman upon his face would make him vanish not from life, but vanish completely from existence. It would be as if he never lived, forgotten to all but the woman who granted him that fate.

I had two visitors once, early on. And only once. Luuk and Nissa stopped by, the cart they dragged full of hides.

Nissa gasped when she saw me. "It's true! You're living *here!*"

Luuk's bear face tilted slightly. "Why?"

I looked up from my carving and opened my mouth only to find the airwaves cracked and coated with dust, my lips too dry to form words. The kids watched me expectantly. "I have no home," I said at last.

"That's not true!" said Nissa, her hands on her hips. "You were supposed to move in with Alvilda, the night of Jurij and Elfriede's wedding."

Alvilda told me that herself the first day I'd spoken to her. A new cot still took up a corner of her home, its quilt coated with sawdust.

Luuk pointed to the figure in my hand. "I thought you were going to become Auntie's apprentice. That you would take up a trade while you waited for your man to finally find you."

"My man did find me. I killed him. I killed him, and no one remembers."

One of the men from the commune tumbled out of a shack, his back slouched, his arms practically dragging against the ground. He moaned as he stumbled forward toward the bucket of water the farmers dropped off every few days for drinking, but his aim was off, and he bumped against the kids' cart, his outstretched arm brushing against Nissa's waist.

Nissa screamed, and Luuk jumped between her and the cause of her terror. "Let's go," he said, dragging her by the elbow toward the cart. The sight made me queasy—the thought of being pushed and pulled as I had been in another life—but Nissa let her man guide her without hesitation. As they pulled the cart away, she alone looked back at me.

Her expression reminded me of the look I'd given Ingrith when I thought she was just an old, crazy lady, before I realized the truth of what she said.

"Learned from Alvilda?" The voice was filtered and hoarse.

I turned my head slowly. The man scooping water up beneath his mask was Jaron, the only other commune resident whose name I had ever had cause to know. I recognized his worn-down animal mask from the quake at Alvilda's house, although I was certain he wouldn't remember the incident if I asked him, either in this life or my last. He stumbled forward and perched on a rock next to me, peering at my woodworking from behind his facial coverings. I couldn't make out what animal it was supposed to be.

I suddenly took notice of the shape of the wood in my palm. A rose. I ran the gouge brusquely over the petals, tearing them asunder.

"Yes," I said at last, not feeling that Jaron warranted my silence.

If he noticed that I now wrecked my creation, he didn't speak of it. Instead, he put a hand on my shoulder, his touch as light as a feather. "She will not come here."

She? Oh, Alvilda.

It was not Alvilda who was my torment. However, I knew instinctively that to this broken man, all torment was Alvilda. My heart tightened, and I wondered if Jaron and the other men in the commune had always felt this way. Even a tenth of my feelings for even a tenth of a second would be torture.

It was a wonder they did not die.

"That's good," I said. And it was true. I was in no mood for visitors.

Nevertheless, Jaron sat still beside me, his mask pointed toward the jagged wooden rose in my hand. I put the broken blossom on his lap and walked back to my shack in the middle of the commune.

***

After a couple of weeks, they didn't feed us anymore.

There were supposed to be pity scraps, weren't there? The rotted produce that didn't sell in the market. And the buckets were supposed to be refilled because someone remembered the men didn't have the strength to pull their own from the nearest village well. Because someone cared enough that we didn't die of thirst. But the buckets ran out of water a few weeks after I joined the men in the commune.

I saw a man vanish one morning, his rotted dog mask clattering to the broken stone tiles in the middle of the commune. I felt compelled to trace the fading pattern on the mask, the nose, the mouth, the long, floppy ears, one half broken. I hoped it wasn't hunger or thirst that had killed him. How long were these men going without food or water? How could I have been so lost in myself that I hadn't noticed? I'd hardly eaten myself.

The men were lying in front of their shacks, moaning. One man was half in a shack, half out, rolling around and pawing for an empty bucket. He scooped imaginary water with the scoop beside it, lifted the empty ladle up under his mask, and grunted when the ladle fell from his grip, clattering to the ground. "Water ... " It was the first word I'd heard him speak that wasn't the name of his goddess.

"Water," another man nearby joined in.

"Water," they all repeated.

I wanted to roll on the ground beside them. I wanted to not want water, to let myself vanish with the life I knew.

But thirst won out. As did the constant chorus of "water"

punctuated by the names of women from around the village. *Those women couldn't care less if you starved.* I knew it. What I once wouldn't have given for the problem of the lord to resolve itself without me. For him to suddenly vanish, for me to not know it was my fault.

I stood, fighting the weakness in my legs, and grabbed the nearest empty bucket. Without responding to any of the anguished cries, I headed toward the well at the center of the village, not caring if I drew everyone's notice as I dragged my feet through the crowd I knew I'd find there.

I drew no one's attention. And there was no crowd in the market.

Merchants' stalls were threadbare or empty. There was only a quarter of the amount of produce I expected to find and almost none of the cheese or fabric. The little things that no one needed, even if they were lovely, the gifts that men often bought their goddesses, were gone entirely. The rotting produce that would normally have gone to the commune was for sale at discounted prices, and it was only those cheaper items that the few villagers with baskets were buying.

"Come now," said one merchant. "Don't you have a young boy and girl at home? Don't you want to feed them the best? Look at the color on this tomato!"

A woman who seemed vaguely familiar grimaced and rifled through her basket for a single copper. "No. These." There was a pile of wilted vegetables in front of her, and she shoved them eagerly into her basket after the man accepted her coin, sighing as he tucked it into a pouch at his waist.

"I suppose no one can afford to pay for your husband's music no more." The man put his perfect tomato down gently with both hands in front of a sign that read, "High Quality Produce. Among the Last. 3 Coppers Each." He scratched his chin. "Why is that, you think? What went wrong? Seems just a few weeks ago, the farmers had more food for us than we knew what to do with."

The woman tucked a wilted head of lettuce on top of her basket. "I don't know." Her lips pinched into a thin line.

"Maybe you merchants pay them too little for their crops because you charge too much and no one's buying. Now they don't have enough copper to feed themselves anything but what they manage to hoard from the rest of us."

The merchant yawned and stretched a hand over his head. "But the prices aren't so different, are they? I know we charged more than this for quality goods just a short time ago. And we had no need to sell this wilted trash."

I didn't think the woman cared. "Good day," she said, curtly. She met my eyes as she passed and looked at me from top to bottom, but she said nothing. I realized my bedraggled appearance wasn't as out of place as I expected. The woman's dress was coated in white dust, and I wondered what a musician's wife was doing to get that way, and who was watching those children the merchant mentioned if she worked.

"No one has enough copper." The merchant stared overhead, not paying me any mind. "How could so much copper just vanish into thin air? Goddess help us." He kept muttering to himself and I pushed forward down the path, my eyes widening as I took in the line in front of the well.

They *were* all tired. No one was quite as tired or hopeless as the men in the commune, but there was something different in the air. Men still had their arms around women, and women still laid their heads against their men's broad shoulders. But there were fewer smiles and less laughter.

"Thank the goddess water is always free," said the woman in front of me to her man.

"Yes, darling." He kissed her forehead. "I'm sorry."

"It's not your fault the payments at the quarry have decreased." The woman bit her lip and traced a finger over the man's chest. "How can the foreman *forget* where he got the copper to pay everyone from when people weren't buying stone for building materials? How does he expect to replenish it with more copper if he can't pay the men enough to dig it up?"

"We'll find more." The man took the woman's hand in his.

"We all have our goddesses to take care of. So many of the men have children—"

"Thank the goddess we haven't yet had any." The woman smiled, but just barely. She didn't seem thankful at all. "I don't mean … Don't get it into your head that I don't want any. Because I do. It's just … " Her voice quieted as she played with her man's shirt. "I'd hate for them to be so hungry now, along with us. Someday it'll get better. We can welcome them then."

Someday it'll get better. It won't.

The bucket fell out of my hands and clattered to the ground. The coupling in front of me tore their gazes from each other just long enough to glower at me, but I didn't care. I crouched beside the bucket and hugged my knees to my chest.

They don't remember the lord. They don't realize it was him who kept this village running. I didn't even realize it was him, really. How could I? He never even came down to the village. He never spoke with the people directly. How could I have known he helped so many?

How could I have known what I was doing, when I yearned for my own freedom?

"Hey. *Hey.* Do you want some water or don't you?" The woman behind me kicked at my back lightly.

I saw the line that had formed behind me and realized I was some distance from the well and it was my turn. I didn't know how long I must have been lost in my thoughts. "Yes," I said, quietly, thinking of the men in the commune.

Every muscle ached as I dipped the bucket down with the rope to the well and pulled it back upward.

They all knew. Before they forgot him. They all wanted me to Return to him, to keep him happy because he was their best customer.

Because he kept this village going.

***

A couple of weeks later, I laid on the ground in my shack, telling my thoughts to quiet for once so that I might sleep and enjoy a brief moment of peace from my waking dream.

"Because you bring us water. And scraps. And for the rose."

A gruff voice. I struggled to open at least one eye, but my eyelids were heavy, and it strained me more than it should have. I blinked to bring the streaming moonlight into focus. A black figure stood in the doorway.

I shot up from my pile of hay on the ground. My heart beat harder, stronger.

And then I recognized Jaron standing before me.

It wasn't the lord. He was gone, and he'd taken everything I knew with him. My life was gone. I felt the violence of a torment that would not break, even across the jagged surface of my heart.

Jaron must have recognized the feeling in my face, for he was soon crouching before me with both hands extended.

He held a sheathed blade. *Does he even know what's in his hands?*

Before I could stop myself, I grabbed it from him, pulling it out of harm's way and removing the blade by the hilt. It sparkled with a violet glow that felt all too familiar. "Elgar? How … "

"Don't know what it is. Maybe a carving tool. Found it in a tree hollow in the woods," croaked Jaron tersely. "When cutting wood for Alvilda. Years ago. She would not take it."

Years ago? Of course. I just have to leave it there for him to find, all these countless years later.

I felt a stirring in my heart that wasn't quite like the pain it had known for the past month. It was mixed with great sorrow for Jaron and the truth of the longing I knew he felt even now for Alvilda.

I sheathed the sword and squeezed Jaron's shoulder. "Thank you."

Jaron's mask bobbed, and he stood up. He left the shack just as quietly as he had entered it.

I pulled out the sword, gripped my hair into a tail behind me, and sliced it off close to my scalp. Now that I was alone, I was free to be myself. There would be nothing about me for anyone to make pretty.

***

I brushed aside the last of the branches that blocked the cavern's entrance from view. Elgar, my blade, had summoned me here. The sheath hung from my waist, and I rested my hand comfortably over Elgar's hilt. I couldn't walk through this life anymore. My parents were gone. My sister and the man I'd loved were lost in each other completely. The lord had vanished, but he left behind a feeling of emptiness in my chest each time I thought of his face—and I hated myself for that. I didn't want the burden of remembering him. If my heart was empty after I had slain the heartless monster, I would let the blade and the violet glow guide me to where I would stop him from hurting others in the first place.

I was the elf queen—and I was nobody's goddess.

Chapter Twenty-Two

Elgar proved the key to getting back through the violet sphere, as I'd guessed. This time when I resurfaced, I knew immediately it had worked, even though I had no reason to believe the cavern was any different.

But there was an ax against a nearby rock. As I grabbed it, I noticed Elgar and its sheath were missing from my waist. The memory of the lord taking the blade away with him to the castle surfaced, more real than I had let myself believe it to be all these long, long months.

There's no going back now. Not without getting the blade back. Somehow I knew this, even though the pool had taken me back once without it. But that was just as well. I had no place to go back to.

When I exited the cave, dripping wet with water, I came face to face with Avery. She looked at me like a piece of animal dung she had stepped in. "I almost went back in to see what was keeping you. Did you fall in that pool?"

"I … " I studied Avery's face. "How long was I gone?"

"What are you talking about?" Avery raised an eyebrow.

"Just a few minutes. Did you lose consciousness?"

I shook my head.

"What did you do to your hair? Did you lop it off with the ax?"

I fingered my shorn tresses. *So that change made it through the journey.* To Avery, I'd walked into the cavern with long hair and walked out with short. It might have drawn attention away from the changes to my clothing—not that my dresses looked very different. But my back was missing the terrible sewing job Avery had done long ago. "Yeah ... it was getting in the way."

"If you say so. The men will *love* that." Avery shrugged. "And maybe next time save the swim until after you've worked up a sweat."

We worked for hours. I felt almost as if I'd never been gone. As if my home was the dream. This felt so natural, so real. Like I didn't have anything terrible behind or before me, just the whack, whack, whack of the ax. I wondered how we were going to carry all of the wood back to the village without a wheelbarrow, and whether we'd bring it back to the commune or to a workshop I hadn't yet seen, but Avery said not to worry about it. Some days she just felled the tree and left the collecting for another day's labor. She was far enough ahead in her work that the men didn't care how she paced herself.

It took us most of the day, and my muscles ached for Ailill's touch by the end, but we brought a tree down with a thunderous crash and a surge of pride and exaltation. We hugged each other in triumph as the ground shook. For a moment, I remembered the times I looked at the castle in that other life. My spine tingled.

Back at the commune, Avery guided me into her shack, which she shared with more women and girls than ought to be able fit inside.

"Sorry," I said as I nearly fell onto a woman nursing an infant on the ground.

The woman looked as if she were staring into the eyes of a monster.

I crouched down to face her, and she backed up as far as she could, practically willing the strength to knock down the wall of the shack so she could back away even farther.

"She's darling." I tried my best to put on a smile and pointed to her baby. "What's her name?"

Avery grabbed me by the shoulder, pulling me upward. "It's a boy," she said. "He won't be named until he's weaned and sent home to his father. Only the girls stay with us and get our names."

I let Avery guide me to a small open corner of the shack across the way. The nursing woman sighed with relief as I left, letting a small smile work itself onto her face as she looked down at her baby.

Avery crossed her legs, sat down on the ground, and tugged at my hand for me to do the same. There was really only room enough for one of us, but I grabbed my knees tightly to my chest and did my best to cram onto the little free floor space anyway.

"You have to separate those likely to fight from the weak," she whispered. "The ones likely to fight have fire in their eyes."

That's right. You promised to help lead a rebellion, not take on the lord by yourself. But that was even better. I'd have help. I'd stop him for certain this time. Maybe life would be different when I got home. Maybe Jurij would never have found the goddess in anyone.

There was no flame in the eyes of the women and girls around me, not like in the men back home. But I soon understood what Avery meant. Most of the women and girls huddled together, crying softly, staring blankly, or looking ready to fall over dead. In the three other corners of the room were the biggest and the strongest—which meant nothing compared to a healthy woman back home—leaning or standing against the wall, nodding over at me as I looked.

"It's not enough," I whispered back. "We've got to get them all—or at least most of them—to fight."

Avery snorted. "We've been trying for years."

"But there are more willing, right? In the other shacks?"

Avery shrugged. "A fair few more. But not even a tenth of our total number."

Two women and a girl sitting on either side of us looked over uncomfortably. They tried to back away as best they could, but their space was limited. Avery shot each of them a look. "Cower and hide, like you always do! It won't change anything!"

The few whispers and moans in the room stopped. Avery stood, heated, looking down on all of the women gathered.

"You heard me," she said, her voice quiet, but her tone strong. "We're the men's slaves and all of you—every last one of you—is the reason why the men think they own us."

"Don't give us trouble," croaked an older woman from across the room. "Just let us have peace."

It was my turn to jump upward. "You don't *have* peace!" Avery and the women in the corners seemed pleasantly surprised. The two who had been sitting stood to join us.

"I've come to help you!" I looked at some of the nearest faces, felt the pain and fear radiating from their eyes. "You called for me, in your hearts, I know it. You've suffered. Where I come from, it's the women who bring the men to their knees! It's the women who give the orders! Women don't have the power to heal, just the same as the women here—but we have something more powerful than that. We have a choice! And *you* have a choice! You can choose to be miserable, to give your daughters the same shoddy echo of a life that you enjoy, to labor and birth and die, or you can choose to fight!" I was lifting some of the sentiment from the lord's blessing. But what more suitable time was there than this?

The women gasped. Some hid their faces. The women standing in the corners gave a delighted cry, raising their fists into the air.

The euphoria spreading throughout my body came crashing to a halt.

"What is going on here, women?"

The sitting women screamed or buried their faces deeper into each other's bosoms. Those in the corners slunk back

223

down to the ground. I faced the entryway and saw Goncalo. Behind him stood a few more men, their hands locked tightly onto a number of bedraggled women.

Avery cut in front of me and bowed, immediately lowering her head to the ground. "Just trying to liven spirits with a few stories, sir."

Goncalo scoffed. "No need to sharpen dull minds with stories in the commune, woman." He grunted and waved his hand forward. The other men pushed the women they were holding forward into the shack and let them go. Instead of catching one another, they tripped and fell and screamed, trying in vain to move out of each other's way.

"His Lordship is done with these," spoke Goncalo.

The men started moving about the commune, not caring if they stepped on a hand, foot, or leg. They shoved women over, grabbing their faces, slapping through their clothing at chests and backsides. Some molested women were ripped upward into the men's grasps.

Avery tensed in front of me. She crouched down and stuck her hands out behind her, grabbing at my bodice and trying to pull me down with her. I followed, but I hadn't yet reached the ground when Goncalo spoke.

"You cut your hair?" He spat. "How unseemly. But you won't hide that way." I dared to lift my head slightly and saw he was pointing directly at me. "That one's coming with us," he said.

Avery rolled around to face me, pretending she was falling forward against me in the ruckus of the men moving about the shack.

"Find Ailill," she whispered.

"Are you coming?" I asked.

"No, they can't take me to the lord," she replied. "He won't speak—Ailill. But find him."

Before I could ask why, two sets of hands seized me and dragged me across cowering women and out into the night.

Chapter Twenty-Three

I recognized the black carriages straight away. However, the black horses that pulled them shook their tails and stomped their feet, unlike the ghastly horses I had seen before. I thought that we would all be shoved inside the carriages as I'd always been, but the men instead dragged us to the back of the last carriage in the procession and bound our hands together before hooking the rope on the hitch. Then they piled into and on top of the carriages and cracked a whip. The horses trotted away. We stumbled after them.

Some of the women fell straight away.

"Keep up!" I whisper-shouted. "Keep up or the pain will be worse!"

The fallen women grimaced and pushed themselves up.

We continued to stumble as we headed up the dirt road and through the village. A few women fell, but I was never among them. I kept coaching the other women to stand up, to keep up, to ignore the leering eyes and the whistles of the men we passed along the way. By the time we broke free of the heart of the village, the other women and I had gotten used to each other's rhythms, and we trotted evenly in a straight line.

We continued over the hilltops, maintaining our grit and determination not to fall even then, and broke through the woods in a single formation. The central dirt road through the woods made for easy travel after the ups and downs of the hills. And before we knew it, we were there—at the castle. I was still not used to looking at it so freely. Its spires seemed less menacing now, even if I knew what lay ahead was sure to be worse than what was inside the castle when I'd lived there. But it was still so large, even larger so close. It loomed tall above us, threatening to swallow us up.

The carriages stopped before the large open doors. Fire and candlelight poured forth freely from inside. Roaring laughter and music filled our ears. Men came back to cut the rope loose from the carriage. Goncalo walked down the line, inspecting each of us. I noticed too late that it was I alone who still faced forward. He was drawn instantly to me.

"You all seem more sound than the women usually are after this journey." He grabbed me by the chin again and peered down at me. He needn't have bothered. I wouldn't have let his gaze intimidate me into looking away.

"I thought I heard you saying something to the others as we traveled," he said.

It wasn't a question, but I answered anyway. "I just told them to keep up, so we wouldn't all be dragged down by ones who fell."

Goncalo's lips trembled.

"Sir," I added, too late.

He smacked my cheek with the back of his hand.

"Good," he sneered. "Then you are all well enough to entertain us straight away this evening."

The women gasped, and more than one sent a surge of loathing in my direction.

Goncalo finally released my face. "Freshen them up!"

A series of women, old or scarred or altogether plain, came out from the castle. They bowed slightly and then grabbed our rope by the lead, like we were livestock to be pulled onward.

We were dragged upstairs, and more than one woman stumbled and fell this time, whether from exhaustion or just to spite me, I didn't know. But the women not bound by ropes didn't stop.

***

Without a word, the castle women freed our hands and got to work making us over. They washed us from head to foot, put us in slips and dresses, and combed and styled our hair. I was outfitted in a white gown, not unlike the one I had worn that day so, so long ago for the chess game in the garden. The one difference was the black shawl the old woman in charge of me draped over my shoulders.

I had a strange feeling about the old woman. She said nothing, did nothing that would make me think "crazy old crone," but her large, dark brown eyes had been burned into my memory. I couldn't help but think of Ingrith.

The woman made one perceptible noise, a disgruntled sigh when she picked up the brush and took hold of my cropped hair. Her hands went to work, brushing what little hair I had left. In the end, she managed to make my jumble of locks look presentable—even attractive—which defeated my purpose for cutting my hair in the first place. She finished the job by wetting the tendrils that caressed my cheeks and pulling them back, tucking a fresh red rose from a vase on the vanity behind my left ear.

Then she did something I didn't expect. She bent forward and whispered into my ear. "What sets you apart will be their undoing. Don't hide it."

I met her eyes in the vanity mirror and opened my mouth to speak, but she silenced me with a pinch to the cheek that was not still stinging from Goncalo's blow. It brought forth a rush of darker color. "This won't do," she said, lightly touching the bruise.

She nodded approvingly to the other castle women and the women made up like playthings. "Send them down," she said. "I need one of the boys to fix this one first."

The women did as bidden, exiting and leaving the old woman and me alone in the room, shutting the door behind them.

She met my gaze in the mirror and squeezed my shoulders.

"I'm Livia," she said quietly.

"My name is Olivière."

Livia nodded. "A nice strong name. A bit similar to mine, if I may say so."

"My friends call me Noll," I said.

Livia shook her head. "Women here do not need friends. They need a leader. They need Olivière."

To be needed ... a leader. The women in my village needed no such thing, so complacent were they in how things were, how they perceived themselves to be in power. They couldn't even remember the leader they once had, the one who kept their lives so simple and easy.

The door opened just a crack, and a child squeezed his way through the opening.

"Excellent," said Livia, sweeping forward to greet the small figure. "They sent Ailill." She shoved the door closed quietly behind him and put her hands on his small shoulders, guiding him over to the vanity.

"Hello," I said, reaching my arms out to greet him. I hadn't seen him in so long, and he reminded me anew of Jurij as a boy. He may not have worn a mask, but he was just the same kitten in demeanor.

Ailill's eyes grew wide, and he buried his face in Livia's apron.

"He's a shy one," explained Livia. "But he's the most kind-hearted."

I smiled. "I've met him before. At the commune. He healed me after I was whipped."

Ailill rustled the edge of Livia's skirt and peeked over. Livia patted him on the back.

"Foolish child," she said. "Always off to visit his favorite sister."

I nodded. "Avery. She's the one who explained to me how things are run here."

Livia cocked her head. "So the whispers are true. You *are* an outsider."

"You didn't know? Avery said women knew who belonged to the commune."

Livia freed her skirt from Ailill's tight grip and gently pushed him forward. "Oh, no. I've spent most of my life here in the castle. I've never been a looker, but I can keep the place well in order. The present Lordship's father was the first to take advantage of that.

"Go on and heal her cheek, Ailill. Please."

Ailill looked cautiously first at Livia and then at me. At last, he extended both palms outward, and I felt that embracing, violet glow seep the sting out of my cheek. When he finished, Ailill stared at me and touched my ear cautiously, bringing some of the glow back to his fingers.

I took his hand in mine and pulled it gently away. "Those don't need to be healed." His eyes widened. "Thank you again, Ailill," I told him. "Avery told me to find you. I'm so glad I did. My name is Noll, by the way. But people here call me Olivière."

Ailill backed away, knocking into Livia behind him.

"Thank you, child." She patted his head. "You may go now."

Ailill nearly tripped over his feet in his rush to the door. It creaked open, and he disappeared, pulling the door closed behind him.

I turned to the vanity to see my unblemished cheek. Livia pinched it, bringing dark color to its surface. I wondered why she didn't just leave the slap mark.

"You don't speak to him with reverence," I said. "Ailill."

Livia sighed and placed her hands on my shoulders. "Not yet, anyway. It takes a while for the boys to learn to be heartless. For some, like his Lordship Elric, who made his father especially proud as a boy, it takes far less time than for others. Ailill is slower than most. He's been tormented, and like his father, he had such a fondness for his mother."

"Avery said she was very beautiful."

Livia nodded. "She was. She was a frequent 'guest' of the castle in her day. All the men were captivated by her, and she bore many children."

I cocked my head. "Many?"

Livia exerted pressure on my shoulders and directed me to stand. "Very few—only the hardiest—survived long. She bore more daughters than she did sons, and fathers care no more for daughters than they do for livestock. They only take special note of daughters and sisters to decrease the risk of inbreeding."

That's disgusting.

We walked across the room, toward the door. "Ailill was the last she bore, and they say she saw something special in him—perhaps a human heart that no other boy could hold on to. It ripped her to pieces when they took him away. Ailill, unlike most boys, was drawn back to his mother. He started sneaking back into the commune for visits almost as soon as he could walk."

"And none of the men knew?"

We had reached the door now, and Livia spun me around to face her. "It was known but looked at as little more than an annoyance. A weak boy, a boy with too great a heart, a foolish boy—it led to a lot of torment that halted the boy's tongue. When his father died, he lost all special treatment he had in their shared fondness for that woman. When hearing of his father's death, His Lordship Elric rode straight into the commune, caught Ailill in the arms of his mother, and ordered her dead by morning. He made Ailill watch it happen."

I gasped. Livia nodded.

"Be wary how you deal with His Lordship," she said. "There are few women who do not wish his downfall, but there are none with the courage to play his game and win it. Perhaps you will be different."

I clenched my jaw. I would do it. I had won before, when I had everything to lose, and I would win again, when we had everything to gain.

Chapter Twenty-Four

I stepped into the lit dining hall, easily willing each foot to move forward. It was a grand spectacle, and I was late to the festivities. Music blared from a corner in which several castle women plucked at their instruments grimly. Men danced, whipping their women partners to and fro. Other men sat around, eating and drinking, their arms wrapped tightly around one or two women. Castle women moved about, serving more food and wine. None of the women had food or drink. No woman had a smile on her face. There wasn't a man without one.

Except for the lord. He sat without his hat before the fireplace in a chair I recognized immediately. It was the chair in which he dined with me, although I had seen it only once, after the curtain fell, when so much of the color would be drained from the man who sat there now. Three women sat on the ground beside him, looking away. He cradled his cheek with his hand and tapped on the armrest impatiently.

There was no way to blend into the crowd, not with my late entrance, not with the rose in my shorn hair, and not with my exposed ears. Man after man turned from his women and companions to look upon me. The lord had not taken his eyes from the doorway the entire time; his gaze had been locked there before my entrance, as if he had been waiting for me.

He stood, not noticing or caring that he stepped on one of the women's hands as he did. The music stopped abruptly.

"Well, if it is not Olivière, the mutilated woman whose name I must use to address her. You made it to the celebration at last."

The men looked at one another and laughed. The lord held a palm out toward me.

Fighting the urge to flee or vomit, I pushed myself forward and let him take my hand. He brought it up to his lips and kissed it. A cold, dry kiss.

He cocked his head slightly. "What did you do to your hair? Short hair to match short ears?"

"What are we celebrating?" I asked, ignoring the question.

Men around the room whispered. A flicker of delight spread across the lord's face as he pulled my hand outward to the side, wrapping his other hand tightly around my waist. His golden bangle clashed against my wrist like a block of ice. I put my free hand on his shoulder.

"Why, your arrival, Olivière," he said. "And the end to all of my boredom."

He swept us both to the center of the room, and the music struck up again. Other men followed suit, dragging their partners to join us. I didn't let the lord drag me. Instead, I matched each of his steps with an echo, allowing us to dance as two, active and reactive partners.

It didn't go unnoticed. The lord leered at me, first concerned and then delighted. "You dance like no other, Olivière."

"You'll find I'm like no other," I said.

"That I can see. It is a wonder I did not notice you earlier." He freed his hand from my waist to run the coarse leather over the rounded edge of my left ear. "But perhaps it took your mutilation for me to notice your beauty." He gripped my waist again.

It would be mutilation that attracted your interest. I smiled sweetly, my gaze falling toward the lord's abdomen, where Elgar was sheathed. "The blade becomes you."

He laughed. "And yet I feel it drawn more to you—a woman, of all things. Would you care to delight me with the tale of how you procured it?"

"I'm afraid it's not much of a tale to tell. I was born to wield that blade against a heartless monster, and so it found its way to me."

The delight fell out of the lord's face, and we stopped dancing. "They say that each lord of this village finds a woman with whom he could not bear to part," he said. "I always thought it a weakness. I am not sure my mind is altered."

I made my best attempt at a grin. "But surely you, of all people, would delight in a change from the usual tedium?" I stopped myself from mentioning he would be less bored if he picked up a tool and worked once in a while.

The lord cocked his head. "I am no longer sure. What do you propose?"

His words shot through me like a kick to the stomach. Whatever he had in mind, I couldn't bear to give it, no matter what opportunities it might afford me. Besides, Elgar wasn't yet safely back within my grasp, and I felt that I couldn't properly confront a monster without it.

"The garden," I said, suddenly thinking of my old sanctuary.

***

Were it not for the red roses that grew in place of the white ones, and the lack of a statue on the fountain, I would have thought I was back within my version of the garden. I could have sat down at the bench and table and awaited specters to bring me playthings and food. Perhaps some paper and ink. A block of wood. Or a game of chess.

The lord pulled me into his arms the moment we stepped

onto the garden cobblestones, running his fingers through my hair, his lips over my face. I shuddered and convulsed and wanted to let him continue and also to scream and rip his eyes out all at the same time.

Instead, I put my palms gently on his chest and tried to push some space between us. "Do you enjoy chess, Your Lordship?"

The look of shock and anger on the lord's face at my gentle shoving was equal only to the joy that appeared now. He let me go and laughed, running a hand through his hair.

"Chess?" he said. "You bring me to the garden to play chess?"

I nodded. The lord's smile fell a moment, and he cradled his chin with his thumb and index finger.

"How do you know of chess?" he asked.

My heart raced. I'd said it without thinking, but a lifetime of labor wasn't suited to casual pursuits. That, and I was sure the lord didn't think a woman's mind capable of the intellect required to play.

"I taught her."

Both the lord and I faced the timid voice. It was Ailill, who stepped cautiously from behind a nearby rose bush to lie for me. I had to lift my hand to my face in order to stop my jaw from flying open.

The lord was not pleased. "What are you doing here, brat?" He yanked Ailill's elbow, dragging him across the thorns and ripping small tears in his flesh.

"And you taught a *woman* chess? Are you stupid?" The lord laughed. "Of course you are."

He dragged Ailill past him, shoving him to the ground, so he could drop his boot on the small of Ailill's back. "Still looking for *Mama*, Ailill? Your sisters and the castle hags not enough to comfort you, so now you're spending time teaching games to deformed women?"

I rushed forward without thinking, collapsing to the floor and tugging on the lord's boot. "Get off of him!"

His boot lifted without resistance. He looked down at me,

still as a statue, his anger transforming to confusion. My heart beat rapidly, and a familiar feeling swept over me.

I wrapped Ailill in my embrace. He looked up at my face, frightened, but I gave him a warm smile and pushed his head against my shoulder. He started chewing his thumbnail.

The lord placed his arms akimbo and laughed. He raised his head and laughed harder still, like the heartless monster I knew him to be.

"Looks like you found a new Mama after all," he said once his laughter died down.

"I'm not his mother!" I snapped. "I just can't believe you would treat him so cruelly."

The lord's smile vanished. "She is not a sister, is she?"

Ailill looked up slightly and shook his head no. The tension fled from the lord's body.

"All right, then," said the lord. "Let us play a game of chess. Ailill can help you."

***

We sat at the stone table, the chessboard between us. Once again, I played white to his black. Ailill sat tight against my thigh, watching the game intently, occasionally removing the mutilated thumbnail from his mouth to grab my hand and direct it to another piece. His choices were always right, and it was only with his watchful eye and guiding hand that I stood a chance of winning.

And winning I was. The lord's face soured.

"I tire of this," he said, when I stood but one or two moves from victory. He knocked his arm across the board, felling the rest of the bone figures and destroying my chances.

"You have a good teacher, Olivière." He stood and glared at Ailill, who buried his face in my side. "Too good. Although I admit it has been a pleasure playing against an opponent other than my feeble brother. Even if I think you owe more than a few of your small victories to him."

My heart skipped a beat. "Your brother?"

The lord gave me a look of bemusement. "You did not know?"

My jaw went slack. I couldn't form the words. "Then you … you ordered your own mother's death?"

Her own child killed her. I couldn't believe it. And here I'd been, thinking he was needed in the village, my heart half softening to him, even though I was still so angry with him. Until then, I'd pictured Ailill's mother as my own. Ailill nudged his face deeper into my side. The lord laughed.

"I did. She was nothing to me. I was rather annoyed by the hold she had over my father and this brat, to tell the truth, and once my father was dead, there was no reason to suffer her any further."

I choked. I couldn't find the words to speak the monstrous anger that spread throughout my blood.

"Get off of her," said the lord coldly. He reached a black-gloved hand into Ailill's hair and tugged hard. "This one is mine."

Ailill moaned. His face pulled backward, tears lining his cheeks.

"Let go of him!" I shouted.

The black-gloved hands let go.

Ailill and the lord both stared at me, their faces reflecting the same puzzlement I felt. And then I knew. I knew for sure what my heart had been trying to tell me.

I shot upward. "Give me my sheath and blade!"

The lord unfastened the loop, removed the sheath from his belt, and handed it to me with both hands. I snatched Elgar from him and tied it back around my waist.

"Lord Elric. I want you to listen *very* carefully. Set all of the women free from the castle and send them to the commune inside of the carriages. Tell the men you tire of them and do not want a single woman here for the rest of the night. Speak to no one of these orders—in fact, forget them as soon as you have followed my instructions. Now go. Go!"

The lord, his face as empty and nearly as pale as a specter's, turned and left.

I looked down at Ailill and smiled. He breathed heavily, his face flooded with tears as he gazed up at me. I grabbed his hand gently, but he tore it away.

"I think you should come with me," I said.

Ailill shook his head and stumbled back toward the rose bush from which he had first appeared in the garden.

I heard a loud ruckus coming from the entryway beyond the garden door. Voices, whispers, screams, and gasps. The thunderous clomping of the hooves of horses from outside.

"Ailill, come with me! Hurry!" I shouted.

Ailill shot out from the rose bush to my side. We joined the bewildered rush of fleeing women, the men still shoving and pulling them this way and that.

As we climbed into a black carriage, I caught a brief glimpse of Ailill's face in the moonlight. His eyes were wide with terror. He had seen a monster.

Chapter Twenty-Five

"**W**e strike tonight!" I shouted. "Before the rest of the men have time to think about what might happen with all of the women gathered here in the commune."

I stood before a roaring bonfire in the middle of the commune, still clad in my white gown and black shawl. All of the women and girls of the village crowded in a circle around me. Some still clung to each other, but quite a few more than usual now seemed ready to stand on their own.

Avery stood beside me with a few of the potential rebels. Ailill still wept into the folds of his sister's skirt, while one of his free hands clutched Livia's beside him.

"You have seen what I can do!" I said. "In my village, each woman commands the man who longs for her." I laughed. "But here, the men long for every woman! I can tell the men to do as we please!"

And I had. On the way back to the commune, I'd knocked on the carriage door and ordered the guard men to go door to door in the village, bringing forth any woman or girl taken for the night to be set free and sent back to the commune.

Remembering Alvilda's words about my passed message to Master Tailor, I ordered the guards to tell any questioning man they encountered that I had ordered these women set free.

And they had been.

"So why don't you order the men to slit their throats now?" barked one of the standing women. "If your words carry such power?"

"I could … " To tell the truth, the idea was unsettling, even if these men were not the men I knew from my village.

Avery shook her head. "No. We do this with our own hands." She shot me a sideways glance. "And rely on Olivière only if things go sour."

I smiled and turned back to the crowd. "I know you're scared. But I heard your voices calling me. I came from beyond the mountains." It was true, after a fashion. "I'm here to show you that you can fight, that you have the power to end this nightmare! I know what it's like to live without love. I know better than any other could. Never more! Never more should you labor and birth and die!"

A number of women raised their fists and shouted.

"Who's with us?" I screamed.

More and more women raised their fists and shouted.

Avery cupped her hands over her mouth. "Just don't forget to leave a few for breeding!"

Laughter broke the last of the tension that held tightly on to the crowd.

Avery grinned and placed her hands on her hips, satisfied. "Let's go!"

The women shouted and screamed.

"Olivière," Livia spoke quietly beside me. "Not all of us are able to go."

I looked at Livia, her face covered in wrinkles. My gaze fell upon a few women still with child or nursing and the little girls in the crowd. Some were still scared and moved nervously to the outside of our circle.

"If you don't feel you can fight with us, do whatever will keep you safest during our battle."

Ailill dropped hold of Livia's hand and Avery's skirt and took off down the dirt path eastward.

***

"Where did Ailill go?" I asked Avery as she strode to a tool shed in the commune and ripped the doors open. She started pulling out axes, knives, pitchforks, and hoes and passed them down to her comrades, who spread them throughout the crowd of women.

She shrugged. The furor coursing throughout her body was too strong for her to bother with the safety of her brother, even if he was the only one of the two she could possibly love.

"If he's smart, he'll head to that cavern we went to earlier," she said. "I've shown it to him before."

I nodded, the nausea rising from my stomach slightly cooled. But still, I felt uneasy. "Why didn't Ailill heal your mother?"

Avery grimaced and picked up her ax and gouge from the tool shed, the last weapons that remained inside. She turned them over in her hand hungrily. "He tried. She was too far gone."

"Does their power not work on all wounds and illnesses?"

"The deeper the wound or illness, the longer it will take and the more power it requires to save someone. He would have had a better chance with a serious illness, but it would take all of his power, and it would take a long time. Tear a person into too many pieces too quickly, and no man has the power required to heal all the wounds in time to save them."

I felt sick at the thought of Ailill weeping before his fallen mother. What did she mean, too many pieces? Had he removed her hands and feet? Her arms and legs? Did her small, innocent child—a boy who still had a heart—stand there, watching the blood pooling around the last recognizable pieces of her body until she vanished, free of her pain at last?

I'll never forgive him. Never. I don't care what role he played in my village. I had the sudden urge to fight.

"That's useful to know." I pulled Elgar from its sheath and held it before me, allowing the moonlight to heighten its violet glow. "We'll have to make sure we don't leave behind too few pieces."

Avery grinned.

***

We strode through the woods down the dirt path, my mob of women and I. Avery stood beside me, her ax raised high in the air, a battle cry escaping her lips every few moments. Every time we encountered a man between the commune and the castle, I ordered him to go inside a building and stay there until a woman came for him. I told him he was never to hurt a woman again. And I ordered him to pass along my message to any man or boy he came across in the future.

No, we would save our bloodlust for the castle. At least at first.

As we passed the area where I always broke off for the cavern, I sent my best wishes in that direction, hoping Ailill had done as Avery had said and that he was out of harm's way.

We left the last of the trees behind us, and Avery and I stepped forward. Avery lifted her gouge in the air to signal the mob to stop behind us.

Goncalo and his usual group of men snapped out of their lazy conversations and looked at us. They seemed surprised to meet with so many pairs of defiant eyes.

Goncalo fumbled with the back of his belt and pulled out his whip. As if a whip had a chance against a blade and an ax.

"What are you women doing?" he barked.

I smiled. "We're changing how things work around here."

Goncalo scoffed. "I'd like to see you try." He cracked his whip on the ground.

"Whip yourself," I said, devouring both words with my tongue.

Goncalo did as bidden, whipping the weapon across his legs. He yowled in pain. The men behind him murmured, pulling out their blades shakily and pointing them toward us.

"Settle down," Goncalo said to his men. "My fault. A rare mistake."

"Whip the man next to you," I said.

Goncalo did as bidden. The man jumped back and screamed. Blood dripped from an open wound on his arm. He lifted his other hand and pressed it over the wound, letting a violet glow pour forth. He looked at Goncalo with the confusion of an obedient dog kicked by its master. The crowd of women behind me burst into laughter.

Goncalo picked up his whip and strode toward me. The veins on his forehead throbbed to life, distorting his otherwise flawless features. "You insolent woman."

"Let us pass," I commanded. "All of you."

They could wait. It was time to say goodbye once and for all to the lord in black.

The men shuffled sideways, clearing the path before us to the castle door. More than one seemed lost in thought; others, like Goncalo, shook and trembled, doing their best to fight the orders given. But they couldn't move until my entire mob had passed through the door.

As the last woman stepped inside, Goncalo and the other men forced their way through the crowd, shoving women as they went.

I parted my lips to speak a command, but Avery thrust out her hand to cover my mouth.

"They'll get what's coming to them," she said coldly. "For now, let them think they have the upper hand."

I wondered how they would explain the whip and the way they let us pass. Perhaps they wouldn't be willing to admit that they had been dumbfounded and obedient at a woman's words.

"What is going on here?"

The lord entered the grand entryway from the inner garden

door. I wondered briefly if he had been looking for me there. Had my orders muddled his memory, caused him to remember leaving me last at the end of our chess game? The door shut behind him, but that large crack I had noticed the first time I ventured inside the castle was present even then, and a trickle of moonlight fled into the foyer. The fire still burned brightly in the open dining room hall, but there was no longer any music, no longer any laughter.

"Lord Elric," spattered Goncalo. "There are women walking freely out of the commune, disrespecting men, waving around those playthings—"

The lord lifted a tired hand. "Enough, Goncalo. I can see."

Goncalo's face burned darker, and he took his place standing behind the lord. His hand still gripped the whip's handle and not the blade at his hips. He would regret the choice later.

The other men were not so sure of themselves. Many of them drew their swords as they gathered around the lord and Goncalo, and the rest tensed their hands on their hilts uncomfortably.

The lord put his hands on his hips. "The question is *why* are these women here?"

I put Elgar back into its sheath so that I could mimic his stance, the one that had always stirred rage inside of me.

"We come bearing a message," I said. "And it's for all men, not just for you, Elric."

The lord raised an eyebrow. "You have never been one for courtesy, Olivière. I believe you are addressing your lord."

"I have no reason to give courtesy where there is none owed."

The lord laughed. "As disdainful as ever, *woman*— Olivière."

He looked puzzled. I smiled. He hadn't intended to speak my name aloud. I had ordered him to address me by my name, after all, even if I didn't know at the time what I was doing. "One day you will surely beg to forget my name, *Elric*."

Goncalo surged forward, cracking his whip. "You insufferable woman—"

The lord halted him with a wave of his hand.

"No, please," said the lord. "Let her speak. She went to the trouble of bringing all of her friends for a visit. Let us hear their message, and then we can be done with this mess and punish the lot of them."

The last of the men who had not yet drawn their swords did so. The women shook their tools. I caught Avery's eye beside me. She nodded and began slinking away from me, between Goncalo and one of the other men.

I drew Elgar again and pointed it toward the lord, closing the space between us. It bothered me that he didn't move, and his guards didn't stir from their posts. I stopped just a few paces from the lord, Elgar looming dangerously close to his abdomen. He looked amused.

"In your arrogance," I began, "you have treated the women of the village as your slaves. You have worked them to the bone while the men sit on their asses. You have plucked them from the commune at will, treating them like your playthings, all of you—fathering children like it was no greater deal than siring cattle."

I turned my eyes from the lord and let them wander over the rest of the men in the castle. I recognized a few from my day in the stocks. Those last few words would be especially suited to them.

I continued. "But you will learn what love is, and you will respect the power women can have over you. For where I come from, it is women who have the freedom to do as they will, and the men have no choice but to follow them."

The lord tapped his fingers against his elbow impatiently. Behind me, the women started shouting and spreading throughout the room. Many stared straight into the guards' faces, willing them to melt.

Still the men didn't strike. My blood boiled.

"I will not let you forget what you have done!" I cried. "What I say will be done by any man who has ever felt longing toward me."

A flash of pain marred the lord's stunning features, but

only for a moment. The women continued to circle the room. I felt moved by the lord's sadness, as I had the only time I had seen him before all of this, when he was drained of color. But then I thought of Avery, Livia, and the other women of this village. I thought, too, of Ailill watching his mother die, using his healing in vain on a woman chopped into pieces. I thought of the lord's disdain and lust for me in my version of the village, the twisted game he played with my comatose mother, his plotting and planning to match his power over mine, blow for blow. I knew what I had to do. I would not let him die this day. He had to suffer, to know firsthand what he inflicted upon those around him. I only hoped I could word it so that I would win in the end, so I could enjoy watching him vanish that day in what I now knew to be his future—with one direct look from my eyes.

Yes. It's clear now. Things have to be this way. I felt as if a force unseen took over me.

"Men of this village!" The words flowed so easily. The curse that had shaped my life tumbled out of me. "Love only one woman each and treat her as the goddess she is. Leave no woman without a man to worship her. Obey your goddess's commands, pine for her heart and body and suffer if she will not Return her love to you. Win her heart with obedience and affection to enjoy a small reprieve from your torment. Fail to feel the Returning of her affections, and rot away for the rest of your wretched existence."

There was a strange stirring throughout the room. The men cocked their heads, as if lost in a dream. The already lax grips on their swords grew even laxer.

The lord's face flew into a fury. His expression contorted with something I guessed to be pain, his eyes rolling backward in his head.

I smiled. "But I have a special command for the lord of this castle. Do not find your goddess for a lifetime after a lifetime and more. Until then, keep no living company in your castle, not even the company of living, breathing horses with which to ease your loneliness. Live the lives of many men, leaving a mere shadow of each life behind to keep you company and to remind you of how long you have suffered.

"And don't think that a pretty face will abet you, Your *Lordship*, in your quest to win your goddess's heart. All of you men, lord and guards, villagers and tormentors, cover your faces now, cover your faces always, or crumble under the eyes of the women around you and vanish forever as if you had never existed. Find sanctuary from this command only in the blood relations who know you are no more than breeding stock and among all women only once you have earned the love of your goddess, no sooner than when she ages from girl to woman."

The last words had not yet left my mouth when I saw the tip of the gouge jutting through the lord's chest. It dripped with blood, spilling drops on the stone floor. Lord Elric fell forward without a sound. Before he could hit the ground, he vanished, and it was the leather clothing, wide-brimmed hat, and golden bangle that broke the silence, clattering like the crash of thunder that would start an avalanche.

Avery stood behind where the lord had been, her mouth contorted into a look of primal lust. She licked her lips, raised both her ax and her bloody gouge, and shouted out a cry that reverberated across the castle walls. The other women joined in, running forward while shaking their axes, hoes, and pitchforks at the ceiling.

Lord Elric had been stabbed, perhaps dead before I gave my command to the lord of the castle. But I had spoken all of the command aloud before I could stop my wayward tongue.

But this wasn't what I'd meant to do.

The spell was cast.

The castle roared to life. A halo of violet light spread across the land and the ground shook.

As I fought to stand steady, my eyes darted about the entryway frantically, falling at last upon the small figure peeking through the crack in the door to the garden. The dark eye that locked on to mine was wide and frightened.

Ailill. Who I could see so clearly now would grow up to

be striking—perhaps more striking than his brother. Who was now the lord of the village and had been the moment Avery's gouge had struck the killing blow to their brother Elric. Who would now bear the brunt of my curse.

Who would one day love me.

No, he already loved me, in his childlike way. And that was all the more reason why my words would hold him prisoner, now and forever.

A flicker and then a flame burst to life in that small dark eye. I felt ill.

I sheathed Elgar, knowing I would never draw blood with the blade. It was no more meant for slaying monsters than the tree branch I had once called by the same name. Full of pride at myself and my power, like I had been as a child, I was just pretending at battle. I hadn't meant for this to happen. The cavern pool had called me to a dismal time, and I was just following the example of the first goddess.

No. The truth was too plain.

I was the first goddess.

I dashed across the short distance between myself and the garden doorway, shoving aside women, dodging spears, watching as the guards screamed and fell and vanished one after another. A man who didn't fall prey to an ax, a hoe, or a pitchfork melted into thin air with no injury, banished from existence simply by the look of a woman's eyes upon his face. Goncalo stumbled and turned around to avoid one woman's stab only to come face to face with my stare. His eyes widened, the newfound flame within snuffed out, and he was gone.

A sour taste rose high within my throat. I ran through where Goncalo had been and ripped the shawl off of my shoulders. *I have to cover him. I have to teach him to keep his face from women who don't love him.*

I almost stopped right there, realizing what I was thinking. But I knew I had to move on, that covering him was the right thing to do.

That he would be safe from my eyes, if not safe from the eyes of anyone else but his sisters'.

After a lifetime, I reached the door, my hands running wildly over the coarse wood until I gripped the iron handle. Pulling it open the smallest amount I could afford, I slipped inside and slammed the door shut behind me.

Ailill stepped back from me as I entered, tears flowing freely from his firelit eyes, his hands shoved forward weakly to block me. Ignoring his attempt to keep me from him, I flung the black shawl over his head and dragged him behind the nearest rose bush. Squeezed tightly between the wall and the blooms, we both got pricked and scratched and gouged by the roses' pointed thorns.

I crouched down to my knees to match Ailill's small height and shifted the shawl so that I could see his face, which I cupped in both hands with as much force and tenderness as I could inject. His chest expanded and contracted rapidly. The look of terror on his face felt worse than any blow that had been inflicted to my body.

I smiled, although it broke my heart to think of what my words had done. I formed the next few words carefully. "For you, Ailill, lord of the village, for you alone, I have another command."

Ailill's shallow breathing slowed somewhat, and his face grew less terrified. His eyes dared not blink and would not move from mine.

My words meant for Lord Elric, backed by the ferocity of the abused women among my ancestors, had been too powerful to undo. I couldn't speak a countermand directly, for I had passed my power to all of the village's women, and they knew nothing but contempt for their abusers. I had forbidden the lord company in his castle, I knew, but I wondered if Ailill would still get around my words by seeking company elsewhere. Avery, her hands now so soaked in blood, would be unlikely to put much thought into saving Ailill so fresh after her victory. If he ran to someone like Livia, to whom he was not blood related, Ailill could vanish from existence. Long before I could meet him.

But how could I save him? I felt the hot sting of my

foolishness, for even if I had intended the worst for Elric and the rest of the men, even those words rightfully placed would have harmed this poor, dear boy before me. I thought, too, of the men I knew from my time. I thought of Father and the shade he became following Mother's illness. I thought of Master Tailor and Jaron, stuck loving two women whose hearts would never Return to them—and also, by forcing them each to bear responsibility for a man's misery, what my words would do to rend Alvilda and Mistress Tailor unhappy. I thought of Mother and all of those who loved where love was not wanted. I thought of Nissa and Luuk and all the rest— children who grew up overnight because of the love I forced upon them. I thought of friends lost to love, and love lost to friends. I thought of Jurij, and all the lost hope of love I would come to know because I myself willed it.

There was no deep malice in my village's men. What disdain there was only existed because I had forced them to think of none other than their goddesses. Perhaps my words this day had made that happen, but they had doomed the men of my village, too. They had doomed us all.

"Ailill, though you may be bound by words already spoken, hide away and banish women and girls from your castle. Do not allow them even to look upon the castle, so that they may forget it and leave you alone. Treat the villagers well, but do not, if you can help it, walk among them—if you do, the earth will tremble, and the skies will rumble to scare the villagers away from you, to protect you from harm. The same will happen if a woman lays her eyes upon your abode. Await your goddess safely within your castle. She will find you."

The words came freely to me, but without the force I'd felt before. It was like these were my own words, and those others were someone else's.

The tears slowed their descent down Ailill's trembling cheeks. A snowflake appeared on his dark eyelashes, but the flame within his eyes couldn't melt it. Snow was falling, despite the previously temperate weather, threatening to blanket us in white.

"You will feel compelled to love your goddess, but do as your heart tells you. If you are ever to vanish at her direct gaze, you alone shall have the power to return."

I bent forward and kissed him atop the forehead. The frigid snow that peppered his scalp chilled my lips.

The roses beside us were blanketed in snow, hardly a trace of their red petals to be found. Letting go of Ailill's face, I yanked at a snow-covered blossom, not caring that a thorn poked my finger as I did. I tore out the thorn and placed the newly white rose in Ailill's open palm, giving his hand a tight squeeze with both of mine.

"Return back to life in your own time, if you alone will it. Return as if you had merely spent a time sleeping. And free yourself of woman's power upon your return." I bit my lip. "I command you to overcome the power of women at last upon your return."

I stood and pulled the shawl down over his face. A braver woman, a nobler woman, would stay and help the boy through the fate I had given him, but that woman was not me. There was no place for the kind of woman I was here, a pretender. The violet glow of the cavern was already calling for me.

Still, as I turned to go, I paused at the fountain, remembering the crying boy who would one day be entombed atop of its cascade of water. The more I thought about it, the more certain I was that the statue was of Ailill as a boy, now that I knew how he looked then. Had Ailill had that statue carved? Did it remind him of what I'd done to him, of what I'd done to all men, to women, too? What I wanted to do now was selfish, and I had been selfish enough to doom all of our kind. But still, my mouth opened.

"If, after your own Returning," I said, my back still to the shivering figure, "you can find it in your heart to forgive me, you, the last of the men whose blood runs with his own power, will free all men bound by my curse."

I clamped my mouth shut and marched forward. Through the door, past the torn and bloody piles of clothing, beyond the cheering women. I had played at leader, I had played at queen, and this is what my foolishness got me. I slipped away unnoticed into the secret cavern in the woods. I didn't look once behind me. My last act was to leave Elgar in the hollow of a tree I passed, waiting for Jaron to find it many, many lifetimes later.

Chapter Twenty-Six

Even without Elgar to guide me, the pool acted as before, but in reverse, its terrible purpose fulfilled. If the blade wasn't key to traveling, then I didn't know what was. I didn't know where the power came from, and it was just as much a mystery to me as the healing powers of the men. Had the suffering of women called me? Whatever the reason, I had answered pain with pain. I set in motion all of the misery that the men and women of my village suffered for generations. I had saved the women from torment, but the price was the free will of all men and the liar's choice of women.

All of that time I'd spent hating the laws of the first goddess—hating the very idea of goddesses—when I had made them all.

So lost was I in my thoughts that it took me a moment to realize the glowing cavern was lit up in red, not violet. I didn't test my theory, but I suspected it was a sign I was no longer welcome, that the past was forever closed to me. The beating orb at the bottom of the pool even seemed to cease, the silence seemingly pushing me away. So I left.

When I exited the woods, I expected to see the altered village on the horizon. I almost wanted to see it, to know that I couldn't go home, to have no choice but to devote myself to shielding the boy with a heart from the brunt of the pain I had caused him. It was a choice I wanted, a choice I should have had. But my feet carried me back to where I would live among those who suffered for my foolish tongue.

I headed toward my childhood home, not sure if my feet should instead take me straight back to the commune. But I was eager to at least see their faces. I didn't deserve comforting, and my heart hardened knowing that I would likely find little comfort awaiting me regardless. Little did they know, though, what real reason they had to hate me.

I halted a few steps from the front door. A chill brushed the back of my exposed neck and down throughout my soaked body.

The castle had returned.

My heart soared, my stomach hardened. But the ground didn't shake. They had worked, the words forming my final command. I'd given him permission to dispose of my power.

I pulled on the door in front of me.

"Noll?"

Jurij spoke my name. He stood next to the fireplace, his hand in Elfriede's, a stark scar across his cheek, his left eye wrapped in a bandage. Wounds from my kiss, as though the castle and the lord had never vanished.

Tears littered Elfriede's cheeks, her eyes neither on Jurij nor me but on the bed in the corner. Arrow sat alert by her side.

There sat my father, his arms thrown tightly across my mother.

My heart stopped. *Have I lost her a second—no, a third time?*

But her eyes were wide open, her pale oak face almost glowing.

"Noll?" she croaked hoarsely. "Come here, darling!"

I obeyed freely.

Tears shed down my cheeks, and I felt the moisture with

my fingertips like it was something entirely new. I'd forgotten the feeling. I hadn't cried fully since the day before my seventeenth birthday.

We hugged and laughed and cried, my family and I, long into the evening that was already half-gone.

***

"From what Gideon and Elfriede tell me, there's a strange gap in their memories that lasts about a month." Mother tilted her head to face me. "All they can agree upon is that there was suddenly a monstrous shake of the earth. Everything that happened since the wedding is in dispute. No one can remember clearly."

Including Elfriede's last words to me that day, I wonder?

Father slept soundly in the bed beside Mother. A few paces away, Elfriede and Jurij slept in the bed I once shared with my sister, Arrow comfortably nestled at their feet. Elfriede's breathing filled the air, as light and dainty as her speaking. The bed she shared with her husband, complete with a new headboard from Alvilda, no longer had room for me. There was no place for me in that house. But there I sat, at a chair pulled up next to the bed, my hand clutching Mother's.

"A strange thing." Mother picked up my hand and bounced it against her lap. "But there are stranger. Me sitting here, alive and well, for one. Aren't you tired?" she asked, her voice a whisper.

"I've spent enough time dreaming." I shifted a loose lock of Mother's golden and gray hair behind her smooth round ear. "I want to stay here and know that I'm finally truly awake."

In the last embers of firelight in the hearth, I could just make out Mother smiling, her head against the pillows stacked in a pile to support her back. "The past year. It all seems a dream to me."

You don't know the half of it.

Mother tapped the back of my hand with her free palm. "I wish you would tell me what's bothering you."

I did my best to smile and pulled my hand away so I could remove the rose from my hair. The petals crumbled nearly as soon as my fingers touched them. "I can't explain, not tonight. You're still weak, and it's been a long, long day."

"I'm feeling much better. Almost like I was never ill, just sleeping, and now I'm still getting used to the waking world." She stretched her arms above her head. Her face glowed in the dying firelight, and I knew she wasn't lying. "Do you know who healed me?"

I didn't dare to guess, not aloud.

Mother clasped her hands together over her lap. "It was your man. The lord."

I shook my head. "He's not my man."

Mother smiled. "So I hear. But he was unmasked. And quite handsome, I might say. Although rather strangely pale."

The corner of my mouth twitched. "Not as pale as his servants."

His "servants." The shades of all of his former lives. I shuddered to think just how many there were and how many years he had spent alone in his castle, only the shadows of his past selves to keep him company. I was surprised he wasn't driven completely mad. Or maybe he had been.

"No," Mother laughed, but then she bit her lip and looked pensive for a moment. "Noll, when I awoke, I found the lord sitting where you are now, his hands held over my head."

My instincts had been right; Ailill had finished healing my mother, even after all I'd done to him.

"There was a strange violet light shining everywhere. And then it was gone. I wasn't sure if I was still dreaming, so I tried to touch his arm, but he pulled away. I said, 'You're our lord, aren't you? You're Noll's man.'"

I leaned closer to my mother to hear his answer.

"But all he said was, 'Rest now. You're healed—I've given you all I had to heal you—but you still need rest.'"

I've given you all I had. His healing power was gone. He'd waited centuries for freedom, and his first act was to give up the last of his power. *For me?*

My mother continued. "I called after him as he headed for the door, two of those servants of his waiting to attend him. 'Wait! Let me thank you!'"

Don't go! Don't ...

"The servants and the lord stopped suddenly, but he wouldn't face me. 'No thanks are necessary,' he said. 'But I do have one request.'"

The lord's words thundered through my mother's mouth, his distaste as clear as if he were next to me: "'Leave me be,' he said. 'Instruct all the village to leave me be. Send no women, send no men. My servants will come to the village for what is needed.'"

Stay away. The little boy trembling in the garden, a black shawl around his head. The veil, the veil ... always the veil between us.

Mother shrugged. "And then he was gone. Gideon told me he and his servants jumped into the black carriage that brought them here and were gone into the woods before he could even ask how he had healed me."

I'd listened to Mother's story without comment, mashing my tongue into my teeth when I heard of the lord's break from me. Those final words were meant for me, I was certain. He said to stay away so I would leave him be. I'd have to. It was the least I could do, after what I put him through.

Mother wrung her hands in her lap. "What happened between you two?"

"I ... " I fumbled with the decaying rose petals in my hands. "I don't even know where to start." *Or if I could ever explain all that happened.*

"Well," said Mother, as she grabbed my hand in hers again. The petals fell to the ground, disappearing into the darkness at my feet. "May the first goddess watch over you and give you courage. You can tell me when you're ready."

I did my best to smile. "All right." I didn't think that day would ever come. Not if I had to rely on "the first goddess" to give me anything.

My eyes were just beginning to close when a pounding echoed across the house from the door, and I nearly fell out of my chair in fright. I jumped, my feet planted on the ground, my hands reaching desperately to pull it open. Who could it be at this time of night?

"Noll?" I heard Mother say. Father, Elfriede, Jurij, and Arrow stirred as the noise grew louder and louder, but I paid them all no mind. The door swung open, my hand clutching the handle, although I couldn't remember opening it so wide.

Before me stood a man and a boy unmasked, their grins truly as wide as their faces, one of the man's hands clutching a lantern above him, the other resting on the boy's shoulders. Beside them was Nissa, her face almost as happy, even though her eyes were puffy and tired.

"We don't need masks anymore!" screamed the boy. "The men in the commune started wandering around the village, telling people they didn't feel so sad anymore. That they didn't feel rejected by their goddesses. They didn't feel anything about their goddesses at all! They took off their masks, and no one vanished!"

"And the castle doesn't shake when we look at it!" added Nissa.

Of course. The rules of the village. Gone by the lord's remaining power.

The man lifted his hand from the boy's shoulder and extended it outward. I thought for a moment that he intended to hug me, but then Jurij brushed past me, and I spun to see Father and Elfriede behind me as well. Jurij and the man embraced, and the man sprinkled the top of Jurij's curls with his kisses while fingering the bandages on Jurij's face. A bit of the sparkle faded from his eyes. The eyes in which no flames were burning.

"Luuk!" Jurij picked the boy up and embraced him before setting him back on the ground. He mussed Nissa's hair. They were laughing, all four of them.

Elfriede pushed past me and hugged the man as well,

kissing both of his cheeks. "Goodfather, it's a pleasure to finally see you."

My heart had been so distracted; I'd taken too long to see what was right before me. I smiled, and the feeling was foreign to me, something from a dream I had long, long ago.

I stepped backward, wondering if I was still dreaming, if I could fall back asleep and pick a different dream, or if this was the one I'd always wanted. Father and Master Tailor shook hands. Elfriede scooped up the children in her arms and kissed both Luuk and Nissa on the cheek.

Jurij's eyes fluttered from one to the other, and at last they rested on me. Those eyes seemed to understand that I was the one responsible for what they'd seen.

Eyes without flames. Each man's eyes had lost the flames that bound them.

And I felt a strange stirring in my heart over the next few days as I walked the village and saw, one by one, the masked boys and men encounter the laughing, smiling faces of their peers. To see the others so free inspired them to grab a hold of their masks, throw down their coverings, and smash them.

***

"My father and mother are separating," said Jurij. We lay together among the violet lilies atop my favorite picnic hill.

We could just make out the cottage at the edge of the woods from where we were sitting. The door opened and Elfriede stepped outside, one hand clutching a bucket and the other tucking a strand of fallen curls into the kerchief she wore on her head. She looked no larger than a mouse from where we were seated. She stared up at us for a moment, and I wondered what she thought, seeing her hated sister sitting on the hill with her husband while she worked, knowing her man wasn't there to take the task from her. I wondered if he was really her man anymore, even if he still was her husband. Then she walked away, disappearing around the back of the home with her bucket to collect water.

Jurij didn't run to her. He barely looked at her. He didn't even mention her name.

I ran my fingers over the smooth and silky petals of a bloom. There were no thorns to cut me. "I'm sorry." For his parents, for his goddess—for everything.

Jurij shrugged. "I'm not. It's not as if they hate each other. In fact, I think a different bond has formed between them, now that they're not bound by a love neither truly wanted. And Mother will still help Father daily with the sewing."

I raised an eyebrow. "Mistress Tailor not one for woodcarving?" I asked, now knowing full well where Mistress Tailor intended to live.

Jurij laughed. "No. Auntie may love her, but she's not blind with her passion. She knows her craft would suffer if Mother encroached upon it. Auntie likes to put too many 'wild and useless' details into her carvings, after all."

I was not shaken when Alvilda made her confession; she was a woman in love with another woman, and Mistress Tailor had loved her all of this time, too. Women had always had a choice to love, after all—since I gave them that freedom. Still, even if a part of her always dreamed of the day in which Mistress Tailor would be hers to love freely, surely Alvilda regretted the loss of her lonely life just a little. Mistress Tailor seemed to irritate her almost as much as she made her happy. I was sure Mistress Tailor would also find a hardheaded partner just as vexing as the eager-to-please one she left behind.

"What about the kids?" I tried to imagine Alvilda as a mother, and I wasn't sure the role suited her. Still, she made a rather fun aunt, and I could see her discouraging the kids from working.

Jurij was oblivious to the mischievous slant of my inner thoughts. "They'll live with both of them, spending their nights at one's home and then the other's as they wish."

"And Jaron?" I asked, thinking of Mother.

Jurij stroked a blade of grass. "He's not a bad looker,

that Jaron, without his mask. I think he's having a hard time adjusting to a heart that's free." He leaned in to whisper. "They say he's been seen in the village with a *number* of women these past few nights already."

I grinned. Ah, well. Mother was married anyway.

Jurij hesitated. "He's not the only one having trouble adjusting to a heart that can now love freely."

Jurij's warm lips moved from my ear and to my brow, and he kissed me liberally.

I felt a strange sensation growing within me as Jurij pulled me tightly into his arms and moved his mouth from my brow to my cheeks and to my lips. I let my mind stop turning for just a moment, lost in crashes of pleasure I still felt in his embrace.

"Noll," whispered Jurij as he at last tore his lips from mine, "I love you."

For the second time in so many days, I cried. This time not from joy, but from the thought of how happy I would have been if Jurij had said that years ago. If he'd said that months ago. Weeks ago. Now I wasn't sure it was what I wanted.

I stared into his good eye for a moment, taking in the lack of flame within it. It was still so bright compared to the poor condition of his other eye, the eyelid drooping slightly, the scar down his cheek. I realized now all too well that the lord had had the power to heal—the deeper the malady, the longer it took. But he had Jurij in his castle a short while and had done nothing to heal his light injuries, other than to stop the bleeding. My chest hurt at what it might mean, but whatever my thoughts of Ailill's decision, I knew that all of the suffering could be traced back to me.

"I love you, too," I said, my hand running through his hair. "But I also love my sister. And so do you."

Jurij's grip on my back eased slightly.

"I'm torn," he spoke at last.

I felt a rush of relief. Even though he was no longer bound to love Elfriede, he loved her still. For I knew the heartbreak Elfriede would feel all too well if Jurij was torn from her side and thrust to her sister's.

I kissed Jurij's brow, and then I freed myself from his embrace. He went limp and let me tear away. My feet felt the call of the castle, the whispers of my true name on the chilling breeze that swept from the woods to the lily-covered hills surrounding my childhood home.

"Olivière ... "

And I would let my feet take me. I saw his face in the past, and he hadn't vanished. It was confirmation of what I couldn't believe to be true, no matter how strong I felt it. I loved him. For in my village, women and men are free to love whom they will. And that is their curse.

"Ailill ... "

Acknowledgements

Most authors will tell you it's a long road to publication. My road was little different, but knowing that these characters are in the hands of all of you kind enough to take a chance on a new author makes me remember the journey with nothing but fondness.

Thanks to Jason Yarn, the first in the business to show such enthusiasm for my work. Thank you for taking a chance on my sometimes off-the-beaten-path story, giving me detailed feedback so I could continually make it better, and sticking with me until we found *Nobody's Goddess* the home it was meant to have.

Thanks to Georgia McBride for providing that home at Month9Books. Your passion and vision for my story renewed my faith that this manuscript was one I had to get into readers' hands—which I couldn't have done without you and all of the hardworking Month9Books staff members. Thank you, Lindsay Leggett, for your editorial guidance and for suggesting my new title. Bethany Robison, your edits are so on point and your ideas so helpful; thank you for working hard to improve my book. Kerry Genova, my proofreader, thank you for your assistance and for paying close attention to details. My book has shaved off all of its rough edges and found an audience thanks to Month9Books's support.

Thank you to my beta readers, author Melissa Giorgio and my boyfriend Cameron Sherber, also known as my best friends, my most passionate fans, and my go-to people when I need support to keep moving forward. Melissa, we've known each other since we were teenagers and we both wanted to be published authors for as long as I can remember. I watched you shine with *The Silver Moon Saga* and I'm so glad that *The*

Never Veil Series will be out there in readers' hands, and on my bookshelf, alongside your books. Thank you for showing me around NYC, reading a number of drafts, providing the feedback I needed to hear, and letting your inbox get cluttered with countless emails from me throughout the day.

Cameron, thank you for supporting my dreams and reading my books. (I think they've helped turn you into a YA fan!) You're the best partner for bouncing ideas off of, and you make so many of my days much more fun and enriching. I love you.

Thank you, Mom, for encouraging me to pursue my passions and talents, and for first instilling in me the love of reading and writing. I wouldn't have had the opportunity to put so much into my fiction writing without your love and support. Thanks, too, to Sara for always getting excited over my writing news and sharing my love for YA fiction—I read, you "listen," but we both love the same stories. A little sister has a best friend from the day she's born when she has an awesome and supportive sister like you. Thank you, Anthony, for sharing Sara's enthusiasm for my writing news and for showing a lot of interest in the book. I hope you both enjoy it!

Thank you to the rest of my friends, my extended family, and Cameron's family and friends, who got so excited over all of my book news that I was reminded just what a big deal it is to have worked for so many years to get to this point. I'm so glad you can now finally all read it. A special thank you to long-time friends Dawn Huestis, Nancy Hunter, and Dr. Andrea Scherer and her husband Joseph SK Chang, my "gamma" readers who read a draft midway through the process to offer their insight; I really needed some fresh pairs of eyes at that point, and your suggestions helped me work out the kinks and decide what needed to be scrapped.

Thank you to all of my teachers and professors at Prairie and Carthage, particularly those who took a special interest in my writing and encouraged me to develop my writing skills and pursue the field as an adult. You made a difference in this student's life, and countless others'.

Thank you for reading!

AMY MCNULTY

Amy McNulty is a freelance writer and editor from Wisconsin with an honors degree in English. She was first published in a national scholarly journal (The Concord Review) while in high school and currently spends her days alternatively writing about anime and business topics and crafting stories with dastardly villains and antiheroes set in fantastical medieval settings.

OTHER MONTH9BOOKS TITLES YOU MIGHT LIKE

GODS OF CHAOS
WHERE THE STAIRCASE ENDS
VESSEL

GEORGIA MCBRIDE MEDIA GROUP
GEORGIAMCBRIDE.COM

Find more awesome Teen books at Month9Books.com

Connect with Month9Books online:

Facebook: www.Facebook.com/Month9Books
Twitter: https://twitter.com/month9books
You Tube: www.youtube.com/user/Month9Books
Blog : www.month9booksblog.com
Request review copies via publicity@month9books.com

JEN McCONNEL

Beware the witch who wields real magic.

GODS OF CHAOS

FROM THE AUTHOR OF DAUGHTER OF CHAOS